Reviewers Love Meli

"Melissa Brayden has become one of the most popular novelists of the genre, writing hit after hit of funny, relatable, and very sexy stories for women who love women."—*Afterellen.com*

Eyes Like Those

"Brayden's writing is just getting better and better. The story is well done, full of well-honed wit and humour, and the characters are complex and interesting."—*The Lesbian Reading Room*

"Melissa Brayden knocks it out of the park once again with this fantastic and beautifully written novel."—*Les Reveur*

"Pure Melissa Brayden at her best…Another great read that won't disappoint Brayden's fans. Can't wait for the rest of the series." —*Lez Review Books*

Strawberry Summer

"*Strawberry Summer* is a tribute to first love and soulmates and growing into the person you're meant to be. I feel like I say this each time I read a new Melissa Brayden offering, but I loved this book so much that I cannot wait to see what she delivers next." —*Smart Bitches, Trashy Books*

"*Strawberry Summer* will suck you in, rip out your heart, and put all the pieces back together by the end, maybe even a little better than they were before."—*The Lesbian Review*

"The characters were a joy to read and get to know. Maggie's family is loving, supportive, and charming. They're the family we all wish we had, through

"The tragedy is ver the top, and the characte characters and their friends

First Position

"Brayden aptly develops the growing relationship between Ana and Natalie, making the emotional payoff that much sweeter. This ably plotted, moving offering will earn its place deep in readers' hearts."—*Publishers Weekly*

"*First Position* is romance at its finest with an opposites attract theme that kept me engaged the whole way through."—*The Lesbian Review*

"This book is thoughtful and compassionate, serious yet entertaining, and altogether extremely well done. It takes a lot to stand out, but this is definitely one of the best Traditional Romances of the year." —*The Lesbian Reading Room*

"You go about your days reading books, thinking oh, yes this one is good, that one over there is so good, and then a Melissa Brayden comes along making everything else seem…well, just less than." —*The Romantic Reader*

How Sweet It Is

"'Sweet' is definitely the keyword for this well-written, character-driven lesbian romance novel. It is ultimately a love letter to small town America, and the lesson to remain open to whatever opportunities and happiness comes into your life."—Bob Lind, *Echo Magazine*

"Oh boy! The events were perfectly plausible, but the collection and the threading of all the stories, main and sub plots, were just fantastic. I completely and wholeheartedly recommend this book. So touching, so heartwarming and all-out beautiful." —*Rainbow Book Reviews*

Heart Block

"The story is enchanting with conflicts and issues to be overcome that will keep the reader turning the pages. The relationship between Sarah and Emory is achingly beautiful and skillfully portrayed. This second offering by Melissa Brayden is a perfect package of love—and life to be lived to the fullest. So grab a beverage and snuggle up with a comfy throw to read this classic story of overcoming obstacles and finding enduring love."—*Lambda Literary Review*

"Although this book doesn't beat you over the head with wit, the interactions are almost always humorous, making both characters really quite loveable. Overall a very enjoyable read." —*C-Spot Reviews*

Waiting in the Wings

"This was an engaging book with believable characters and story development. It's always a pleasure to read a book set in a world like theater/film that gets it right…a thoroughly enjoyable read." —*Lez Books*

"This is Brayden's first novel, but we wouldn't notice if she hadn't told us. The book is well put together and more complex than most authors' second or third books. The characters have chemistry; you want them to get together in the end. The book is light, frothy, and fun to read. And the sex is hot without being too explicit—not an easy trick to pull off."—*Liberty Press*

"Sexy, funny, and all-around enjoyable."—*Afterellen.com*

Praise for the Soho Loft Series

"The trilogy was enjoyable and definitely worth a read if you're looking for solid romance or interconnected stories about a group of friends."—*The Lesbrary*

Kiss the Girl

"There are romances and there are romances…Melissa Brayden can be relied on to write consistently very sweet, pure romances and delivers again with her newest book *Kiss the Girl*…There are scenes suffused with the sweetest love, some with great sadness or even anger—a whole gamut of emotions that take readers on a gentle roller coaster with a consistent upbeat tone. And at the heart of this book is a hymn to true friendship and human decency." —*C-Spot Reviews*

"An adorable romance in which two flawed but well-written characters defy the odds and fall into the arms of the other." —*She Read*

"Brayden does romance so very well. She provides us with engaging characters, a plausible set-up with understandable and realistic conflict, and ridiculously fantastic dialogue."—*Frivolous Views*

Just Three Words

"I can sum up my reading experience with Just Three Words in exactly that: I. LOVED. IT."—*Bookaholics-Not-So-Anonymous*

"A beautiful and downright hilarious tale about two very relatable women looking for love."—*Sharing Is Caring Book Reviews*

Ready or Not

"The third book was the best of the series. Melissa Brayden has some work cut out for her when writing a book after this one." —*Fantastic Book Reviews*

By the Author

Waiting in the Wings

Heart Block

How Sweet It Is

First Position

Strawberry Summer

Soho Loft Romances:

Kiss the Girl

Just Three Words

Ready or Not

Seven Shores:

Eyes Like Those

Hearts Like Hers

Hearts Like Hers

by

Melissa Brayden

2018

HEARTS LIKE HERS

ISBN 13: 978-1-63555-014-6

This Trade Paperback Original Is Published By
Bold Strokes Books, Inc.
P.O. Box 249
Valley Falls, NY 12185

First Edition: February 2018

Credits
Editor: Lynda Sandoval
Production Design: Stacia Seaman
Cover Design by Jeanine Henning

Acknowledgments

First, I should tell you that I drank more than my fair share of fantastic cups of coffee in the name of hard-core "research" for this project. Next, I should tell you that I have the best job ever! Book Two in the Seven Shores series came at just the right time in my life. I wasn't sure it was possible to learn something from the characters that you write, but I now know with certainty that it is. I've enjoyed my time with Autumn, Kate, and the Seven Shores friends a great deal, and look forward to more!

A high five and thank you go out to my editor, Lynda Sandoval, for her guidance, words of wisdom, and genius fixes.

A big debt of gratitude to Jeanine Henning, who did a fantastic job capturing the world of Seven Shores with her series of covers. I'm so proud they're mine.

Lastly, thank you to the readership, who have been so supportive and vocal and awesome about this new series. I'm thrilled it's found a comfy home with you all and hope you'll be on board for the stories yet to come.

For the Java Junkies

Chapter One

Autumn Primm's birthday arrived with a whimper that second Tuesday in February.

She hadn't mentioned it to anyone. In fact, she planned to ignore it altogether. That's right. Just any other day in the life of a newly thirty-four-year-old with very little to show for it. She wasn't rich, had no significant other, and lived a boring, predictable life. At least, those were the things she focused on recently.

But she did have her coffee shop, wonderful little highlight that it was, and a truly great group of friends that she refused to discount.

It was a few minutes before five a.m. when she pulled up to the standalone one-story building, home to her pride and joy, the Cat's Pajamas. The sign depicting a cat wearing loud pajamas and playing an electric guitar faced the street, dark and colorless, waiting for her to breathe life into its circuitry and kick off the morning officially. In just over an hour, she would flip the switch, igniting PJ the cat into vibrant color so he could beckon the world inside where she would welcome them with the aroma of freshly roasted coffee. Was there anything in life that compared to that first wonderful inhale? Shortly after six, the first customer of the day would slog their way through the glass door, bleary-eyed and in need of caffeinated assistance, and it wouldn't stop until she closed at nine that night.

But first, there was roasting to be done. Autumn's favorite time of the day, the thing that got her out of bed, jazzed, and ready to go.

The night before, she'd selected a new blend from Papua New Guinea, recommended heavily by her distributor. With her hands cradling the beans, she dropped her nose and took a deep inhale, soaking in their unique bouquet. After brewing herself a small cup from the raw green beans, she made her decisions and jotted down the specific roasting profile for the beans. She could always adjust it later, once the first batch revealed its flavors. The beans were on the sweeter side and came with prominent floral notes. A light roast would enhance the attributes that were already there and bring out the acidity and brightness of the coffee. Using the large metal scooper, she piled the hard, green coffee beans into the hopper and set the gauges. While the coffee roasted, she went to work getting the shop up and running for another day.

At a quarter to six, her assistant manager, Steve, arrived to work.

"Hey, Steve-O."

"Hey," her cheerful little nerd of an employee said. He was more than just an employee, however. Steve was her protégé. Her people. He understood the complexities of a coffee bean and how much you could do with it. "You start the roast?"

"Beat you to it."

He nodded acceptance. "Next batch is mine."

"Deal. Hey, how was the midterm?"

"Not fair at all. Half of the test had never been touched on in lecture."

"Bastards," Autumn said in solidarity, and made sure to look appropriately outraged. She was empathetic enough for it to be mostly genuine.

"Thanks, Autumn." He offered up a sweet smile, showcasing straight teeth with the exception of one crooked incisor. Gave him character. Steve wouldn't be Steve without it. The two of them got along fantastically. It was exciting to have someone to share her passion with, and Steve was someone she could count on. She'd taken him under her wing and schooled him regularly on flavors and roast profiles. He kept a pad in his back pocket full of notes from his various blends. Adjustments he wanted to make to times, intensity, and cooling tactics. The kid was getting good, and it was fun to watch his progress. Autumn trusted Steve. Liked him, too. She didn't know what she would do if she lost him once he completed his chemistry degree, though he claimed he had no plans to go anywhere. When he graduated, a healthy raise would certainly be in order.

That morning, they fell into their usual routine. Steve would handle the counter and she'd back him as needed, while also funneling in a myriad of other early morning tasks that came with running the business. Which reminded her, she'd not seen the billing on that new espresso machine she'd just incorporated to cut down on wait time. As she riffled through yesterday's untouched mail in search of it, she came to an abrupt halt at a large white envelope addressed to Ms. Autumn Primm in swoopy, swirly calligraphy. The envelope felt thick and heavy in her hand. The paper came with a rough texture that screamed of importance. She knew exactly what it was and dropped the offending envelope right there on the counter. She took a step back, her eyes trained on it.

Not today, on her birthday. It didn't seem fair.

She tried to go about her morning, chatting with her regulars, forcing herself to brighten into the perfect hostess each time a familiar face arrived. All the while, her stomach turned, and she stole glances at that white envelope, taunting her from where it sat on the counter, evil messenger that it was. Eventually, she'd flipped the damn thing over as she passed by, anything to hide the perfectly formed letters that spoke of elegance, and happiness, and joy to all…but her. Unfortunately, the regal seal on the back was almost as bad. Autumn swallowed back hot tears at the larger implication of the envelope's arrival and took a moment for herself in the prep room.

"Hey, Autumn," Steve called from up front. "Can you lend me a hand? We're backing up and I could use you."

"Yep," she called, already pep-talking herself into making it through this day if it killed her. She jogged in place for several seconds to shake herself out of the emotional fog that clung, heavy and imposing. Exercise had a way of focusing her. She returned to the front of the shop with her game face on, shocked to see her three closest friends standing there wearing pointy birthday hats.

When they saw her, the whole place went nuts, regulars and new customers alike.

No, no, no.

Following the cheers, they broke into the Happy Birthday song, and on the table closest to the counter sat a line of muffins blazing with birthday candles. She closed her eyes briefly and noted the awful timing. While she had every intention of sweeping her birthday under the rug of history, the most important people in her life had very different ideas. Her gaze moved over the faces of her closest friends, Gia, Hadley, and Isabel, who all lived in the Seven Shores apartment complex next door. They beamed as they sang, leading the customers in a loud, out-of-tune rendition.

"Happy birthday to youuuuuuuu."

As the room clung to the very last note of the song, Autumn burst unceremoniously into tears. *Bollocks*. "I ruined it," she said glumly from the chair they'd ushered her into. "You guys were so sweet, singing your song and smiling, and I ruined it. I'm so sorry."

"You didn't ruin anything," Hadley said, her bright blue eyes earnest and kind, her glamorous blond hair flowing free around her shoulders. Always at the ready, she handed Autumn a tissue.

"In fact, we could use some of those tears to put out a few of these things," Isabel said, gesturing to the still-burning muffins.

Hadley turned to her and offered one discreet shake of her head.

"No?" Isabel asked. "Not right now?"

"No," Hadley mouthed.

Gia took a seat across from Autumn. "What has you sad? Birthdays are supposed to be fun."

She glanced behind her to the counter to make sure Steve had the morning rush under control. Gemini, the new hire, had just clocked in, offering him some backup. If only she would refrain from asking each and every customer what their zodiac sign was before taking their order.

Autumn turned to her friends. "Well, first, there's the whole turning thirty-four thing I have happening today."

That simply opened her up to a series of rebukes from her friends, all on top of each other.

"That's young," Gia said.

"You're a spring chicken, Autumn," Hadley replied.

"And incredibly hot. I've always thought so." They all turned to Isabel, who shrugged. "She fucking is. Have you seen her hair? All red and curly and gorgeous. I hate you for your show-off hair," she said to Autumn with a glare, and sat back in her chair. "I'd also do you because of it. Boom. There. I just said it and I'm not taking it back."

Autumn laughed and that helped. "No one quite like you, Iz." There wasn't. Isabel Chase's medium-length dark hair, fair skin, and dry wit complimented each other to perfection. She didn't pull any punches.

"Thank God," Isabel said. "Can you imagine the shift in negative energy if there were two of us? The world can't handle more than one pessimistic woman with a heart of gold. No way." Soon, Isabel would head to work at Paramount Studios where she wrote for a new kick-ass TV show titled *Day Job* alongside her girlfriend, well-known producer Taylor Andrews. Hadley would get ready to open Silhouette, a clothing boutique on Rodeo Drive, and Gia, a professional surfer, would hit the waves for her daily practice session.

"And besides turning thirty-four?" Hadley asked, expertly moving them back on track. "What else has you so upset? Because I'm sensing there's more."

"I might as well just say it." Autumn exhaled. "Olivia's wedding invitation arrived."

Her friends nodded and exchanged looks. Through some sort of silent telepathy, Gia seemed to have been nominated to take this one. She dipped her head and caught Autumn's gaze from below. "We're here for you, you know that?" Autumn nodded. She did know. "But if it were me, I'd just toss that bad boy in the trash. Forget you ever saw it."

"Agreed," Isabel said, nodding. "I never knew Olivia, but her reputation is enough for me to know that you dodged a bullet with that woman."

Autumn smiled in gratitude, though her heart hung heavy. Her ex-girlfriend Olivia had been no walk in the park during their last few months as a couple. That recognition didn't assuage the gut-wrenching pain she experienced whenever she imagined Olivia, who had once been *her* Olivia, settling down and embarking upon a life with someone new. They'd probably head out on a series of tropical vacations. Jamaica maybe, or Cancun. And spoon. Autumn just knew they would spoon, something Olivia used to roll her eyes at.

"I think I have to open it," she said finally.

Hadley nodded. "Rip it off like a Band-Aid. I get that. Why don't we sit here with you while you do?" She reached discreetly for one of the fresh-baked croissants Autumn had delivered to the shop each morning. AKA: Had's kryptonite. "Oh, my dear goodness, these are so heavenly."

"No one but you says 'Oh, my dear goodness,'" Gia said, in mystification. "And then couples it with 'heavenly.'"

Hadley was too far gone on the croissant to care.

Next to Hadley, Isabel blew out the candles on the muffins. "Sorry. Couldn't take it anymore. Muffins needed saving. May I?" She held up a blueberry chocolate-chip and Autumn gestured to her to proceed.

"The invitation?" Gia prompted. "Where's the thing at?"

Autumn nodded and retrieved the envelope. With the invitation in front of her on the table, she looked up at her friends with a wobbly sense of determination. "Yeah, okay. Let's do this." Inside the envelope she found a black invitation wrapped in a large purple ribbon. In perfect purple script, she read that the honor of her presence was requested at the marriage ceremony of Olivia O'Dell and Betsy Rhoades. Betsy Rhoades: the opportunistic owner of the gym Olivia worked out at. Once Betsy started training her, it was all Olivia ever talked about. It wasn't long until they were burning calories together in other ways. Autumn set the card on top of the envelope. "I feel a little sick."

"The hard part is out of the way," Hadley said gently.

"Not if you actually go," Gia said, picking up the invitation. "It's in Tahoe. A destination wedding."

"There you go!" Isabel said, taking the invite from Gia. "You have a total out. That's what, like, seven hours from Los Angeles? You now have a pass to decline, and no one will even bat an eye."

"No." Autumn shook her head, a new form of courage surging in her chest as if necessary to combat the sadness. She took the invitation from Isabel and held it up in declaration. She wouldn't run from this. She couldn't. "I'll be there. I need to be." Three pairs of shocked eyes looked her way. She raised a calming hand. "I'll be fine. It's probably the closure I need. If it's okay with you guys, though, I think I'm gonna cut out of Breakfast Club a little early this morning. I think I need to work."

"Of course," Hadley said, but Autumn was already up and moving on shaky legs, knowing that tears were only moments away.

Damn birthdays and weddings and all occasions with cake.

Just damn them.

❖

"Oh, man. Is that Kate What's-Her-Name? I think it is," a male voice said, a few yards down the sidewalk on a sunny day in Slumberton, Oregon. "The one from the news? Remember?"

"Kate Carpenter. Yeah, I think so, too," a female voice answered. "Yeah, it definitely is. She still has a bandage on her arm."

Kate walked on, allowing the comments to roll off her, her eyes downcast to shield her face as much as possible.

"Hey, Kate, you're a hero!" the male voice called after her.

She didn't acknowledge him. Couldn't. It had been weeks since the night people started celebrating her, but it was like this town was too small to allow her to move on, and she desperately needed to. In a place where not much ever happened, something had, and the citizens clung to it, wringing free each and every awful detail of the fire with insatiable need.

She wasn't a hero. Wasn't even close.

It helped to get out of the house, where she'd been holed up for weeks now. The sunlight felt good on her face and the fresh air filled her lungs, making her remember its benefits. She also needed to be around people. If only they weren't *these* people, the ones who knew all about what happened. She'd made the mistake of trying to grab a beer a couple nights back. She sat on the far side of the bar and tried to keep to herself, which had proved to be an impossibility. People clapped her on the back. Offered to buy her drinks, dinner. Needed to know just how she was doing after it all. And how were those kids doing? Was the little girl in any better shape? When would she get out of the hospital? Were there any plans that she knew of for what would happen to them? She left feeling sick to her stomach, looking for respite, and like she'd taken ten steps back. She'd gone home and stayed there another three days until she was gasping for air again. Unsettled. Tormented. The people in town meant well. They thought they were saying nice things, and she didn't blame them. She was the one who was broken.

Kate made a sharp right into her brother's store on that sunny afternoon, grateful to leave the sidewalk that wound straight through the center of town. She loved the store and took a deep breath, enjoying the unmistakable smell: a mixture of coffee and books. Randy had opened the bookstore, The Plot Thickens, three years ago, and though each day was a struggle to stay afloat, the citizens of Slumberton worked to keep him in business, stopping in to buy the occasional book just to do their part. She'd say one thing for them: they looked after their own. Plus, everyone liked Randy. It was impossible not to, with his friendly disposition and vague resemblance to Where's Waldo.

"Whoa. Katie! Wasn't expecting to see you today," Randy said, beaming at the sight of her. "Coffee?"

"Sure. I'll take a cup." As he poured from the little stand set up in the corner, she thumbed through the new arrivals, grabbing up a handful of interesting-looking titles. She'd need them. He handed her the hot cardboard cup, the heat of which burned through to her skin with impressive speed. She glanced around for a sleeve, but then this was a bookstore.

"Want to grab some lunch?" Randy asked, with his usual affable smile. He was a year and a half older than Kate and had the uncanny ability to cheer her up when it seemed like the world crept in on her. Had been that way since they were kids. Same hazel eyes as hers, same dark hair and olive skin. In their younger years, people used to mistake them for twins. Kate never minded. She'd always looked up to Randy and appreciated his kind heart. In that way, he was different from other men she knew. Their dad, the guys at the station were all tougher, silent types. Randy was unique, a sensitive soul.

"Can't do lunch." She took a sip of coffee and let it burn its way down her throat, the discomfort somehow satisfying. It reminded her she still had a pulse, as gray as the world still seemed. "I'm headed out of town for a little while and wanted to say good-bye." She couldn't look at him when she said the words, the lump in her throat already forming. They hadn't spent much time apart, and saying good-bye to him would be the only difficult part of her leaving.

He came around the counter, concern causing his forehead to wrinkle like their dad's. "Whoa, whoa, whoa. I knew you were struggling. But this is not at all—is this really what you want?"

She nodded. "I think it will be good. Grab some breathing room for myself. Decompress. When I come back, I'll be patched up and ready to go again." She deflated some, knowing how unlikely that now seemed. She forced a ghost of a smile. "At least, that's the goal."

"For how long?" Randy asked.

"You know, I'm not sure. A month, maybe two. I have vacation time built up at work, and since they have me riding the desk anyway, this seems like a good time to put it to use." Kate had joined the Slumberton Fire Department at twenty-three years old, and after nine years of service, had taken exactly one sick day: the day of their father's funeral.

"So we're talking *months*? That's a long time." Randy sighed the way people do when they've been dealt a blow. She felt bad about that.

"I know."

He ran a hand through his fluffy hair. "Where you headed?"

"I'm thinking LA. Venice Beach maybe. I've got some prospects lined up on Airbnb that look halfway decent. I'll start driving and choose a place on the way."

"My sister's a nomad."

"I like the sound of that. I'll be home soon."

Randy nodded and smiled feebly. "Holding you to it. You'll call if you need anything?"

"Of course." She pulled him into a hug and held on, the contact the only place she'd found comfort in weeks.

"And, Katie?"

"Yeah?"

"I hope this helps. I just want you to be okay, you know? You're a good person. The best, really, and everyone here thinks so."

She loved this book loving, coffee swilling dork. "Thanks, Randy. I'll call when I'm settled."

"You better, or I'll be in California pounding on your door using Dad's scary voice."

She smiled. "And no one wants the scary voice. How much do I owe you for these?" she asked, gesturing to the books with her chin.

"Forget it. My going away gift."

"You're a good egg, Randy. Until another time," she said, in homage to their old childhood farewell.

"Don't commit a crime," he recited back.

God, they were really lame kids, weren't they?

With a final wave to Randy, Kate headed back into the world, chin down and thoughts dialed purposefully to dull. Her truck already carried her two suitcases, her laptop, a few choice novels to which she would add the new ones she'd just picked up. With a wounded heart and a dull ache in her throat, she left the only home she'd ever known. Not that there'd been a choice. She had to find a way to climb her way out. She had to find a way to breathe.

Kate flipped the radio to something loud and indecipherable

and made her way out of town, en route to the Oregon border. She couldn't help but wonder what California might have in store. If she had anything to say about it, nothing at all. Just a calm, quiet reprieve from the chatter of her recent existence.

All she asked for.

Chapter Two

The afternoon was bright and fantastic.

Bollocks. Autumn would expect nothing less. Why make this any easier on her whatsoever?

Apparently, the late-March weather knew Olivia O'Dell was getting married and made sure to get out of the way. Elegant white chairs with sculpted backs had been assembled into neat little rows overlooking the lake, which lapped in serenity. From behind the guests, a harp and flute combo played in beautiful tandem as the procession began. Olivia first.

"Oh my God, she's breathtaking," a woman said, from the row behind Autumn's. The music swelled, and from her spot next to Autumn, Hadley passed her a nervous glance. Autumn smiled back as if to say, "No big deal. I watch exes of mine get married every day." She had to admit, though, as Olivia floated down the aisle on her way to wedded matrimony (as if too perfect for her feet to meet the ground), she radiated. Her blond hair sat piled on top of her head, with little tendrils framing the side of her face like one of those women from the bridal magazines. The simple white dress seemed made to accentuate her now much-more-slender body. But it was the smile on her face that really sucker-punched Autumn. She'd seen that smile before, when it had been directed at her. It was Olivia's blissfully happy smile, only now it seemed to be her blissfully happy smile on steroids.

She was happier with Betsy.

Autumn had known that, hadn't she? But seeing it firsthand

cemented it in the worst way. Her stomach flooded with ice. Her eyes filled with tears and she dabbed at them. Everyone who wasn't Hadley would think she was moved by the emotion of the occasion and she could use that. She played it up, doing her best to look sentimental, touched, and joyful. Hadley, however, squeezed her hand in solidarity, and that helped. That grounded her. She didn't let go of Hadley's hand during the fifteen-minute ceremony, the longest fifteen minutes of her life. The fact of the matter was, she wasn't in love with Olivia anymore, and hadn't been in quite a while. So much had changed. She did, however, mourn for that time in her life when she'd felt like a part of something, instead of a ship adrift on the ocean of life, alone and anchorless. That was her. A lonely little ship, aging more and more as each day passed. The concept left a bitter taste on her tongue, difficult to swallow.

They let the other guests file out ahead of them. "There's a receiving line," Hadley told her quietly. "Want to skip it?"

Autumn nodded. "Definitely." She excused herself inside the nearby building to the restroom, passing the entrance to a beautiful ballroom with glass windows high enough to make the lake outside seem as if it stretched for miles, calm and smooth. The exact opposite of her own reality. Cascading centerpieces with gorgeous springtime flowers towered elegantly on each table as the staff set out carafes of Chablis. She blinked. It was so beautiful, and so *not* hers. She braced against the onslaught of regret.

When she emerged and rejoined the rest of the group outside, the cocktail party was in full swing. Hadley immediately handed her a bourbon and Coke. *Good wingman. Good wingman indeed.* While it would help, she was smart enough to sip the whiskey, refusing to be the drunk ex-girlfriend who made a fool of herself at the reception.

Oh, and there was Olivia's younger sister, Misty, headed straight for them. Luckily, she was a decent person.

"Autumn!" she exclaimed. "You came!" With her arms outstretched, Misty pulled her into a warm embrace. "Surreal, isn't it?" she said quietly in Autumn's ear. "I always thought it would be you two who..." She trailed off.

"Yeah, me too," Autumn said, and then moved them forward. "The ceremony was beautiful."

"It was." Misty nodded, placing a hand over her heart. "And is this your date?"

Autumn turned to Hadley. She could easily explain that Hadley was just her friend, but "date" made her feel like less of a loser. "Yes, this is Hadley. She's awesome."

Taking the cue without hesitation, Hadley stepped forward. "Pleasure to meet you."

Misty covered her mouth. "You two are adorable. And I mean that."

"Oh. Thank you," Autumn said, conservatively. Technically, she hadn't lied. She wouldn't go to hell for sidestepping a small correction, would she?

Once they were alone, Hadley turned to her, blinking innocently. "Does this gig come with benefits? I'd like to know in advance what I'm entitled to."

"Ha-ha," Autumn said, feeling lighter. "Not a chance."

Hadley shrugged, her turquoise eyes dancing. "Mayday," she said abruptly, changing gears. "Incoming at ten o'clock."

Autumn turned in time to see Misty heading their way with none other than the brides themselves. This was bad. This was more than bad. "Olivia!" she exclaimed happily. "Congratulations!"

Olivia beamed as she approached. "Autumn, you have no idea how glad I am that you came." They exchanged a weird cheek kiss that Olivia initiated. Not knowing quite what to do, she repeated the kiss when she got to Betsy.

"We weren't sure if you'd actually show," Betsy said, as if talking to a wounded child. "No one would have blamed you for skipping out."

"No one," Olivia said, mimicking her tone. Weren't they two peas in a pod? Both blond, tall, beautiful, and feeling sorry for Autumn.

"Oh, no. I wanted to be here. For both of you." God, that tasted awful coming out of her mouth.

Olivia glanced around. "Misty said you'd brought a girlfriend, which we're just thrilled about. At last you've found your footing. I'd love to say hello."

"Oh, no. Not—"

"You don't have to worry about it being weird," Misty said, stepping in. She turned to Olivia. "This is Hadley."

"Oh, I know Hadley," Olivia said as if Misty were an idiot. "Good to see you again."

Hadley nodded. "Congratulations to you both." She glanced with hesitation at Autumn, who smiled nervously back.

"So…where is she?" Olivia asked, wide-eyed and expectant. "This mystery woman. I need to meet her."

"She's right here," Misty said, again pointing at Hadley, this time with extra emphasis.

Autumn decided to help clear up the confusion. Confession time. "Hadley is my date for tonight."

"Your date?" Olivia glanced from Autumn to Hadley and back. "Oh, so you two are seeing each other? I didn't see that coming. At all. You always said Hadley was a Disney princess hopelessly lost in her own fairy tale."

"No," Autumn said, embarrassed now. "We're not seeing each other exactly. Had's just here to keep me company on the long drive. In a friend way." She turned to Hadley and dropped her voice. "The Disney character reference was a compliment, by the way."

Hadley nodded. "I embrace Disney. I can work with that."

"Oh, well then, where's the actual date you *mentioned*?" Betsy asked Autumn, smiling in satisfaction at what she probably already knew. Betsy had never been much of an Autumn fan and had worked meticulously to pull Olivia away from her. She was going to actually make Autumn say it out loud.

"I don't have a date-date," Autumn said, feeling about two feet tall. "Just me and my friend."

"Ohhh," Olivia said, making a sympathetic pouty face. "Well, that's okay." She touched Autumn's arm supportively. "You'll find somebody one day."

"Tell you what," Betsy said. "Come by my gym in a couple of weeks once we're back from Jamaica and we can get you on your way to a romance of your own." She made a circular gesture in Autumn's direction. "Turn that physique right around."

Autumn gulped and tried to recover from the bitch slap. "I think I'll just keep my less-than-desirable one."

"Autumn's got a *ton* of prospects," Hadley said, with maybe too much confidence to be believed. "Many admirers at the coffee shop. She fights 'em off. It's getting ridiculous."

"How quaint," Betsy said, which was clearly code for "boring."

"You should really take Betsy up on her offer to train you," Olivia said. "It will change your life. Changed mine."

Autumn got to watch the happily married couple exchange a lingering kiss right in front of her. Wasn't that just too cute for words? Her stomach turned and she sucked in air. Why was there less of it?

"We should greet our other guests. I hope you two have a nice time on our very special day." Olivia waved as if she were the Queen of England and turned to her larger grouping of subjects.

"That's the goal," Autumn called after their perfectly silhouetted forms.

"Sorry about that," Misty said, shaking her head sheepishly. "I guess I misunderstood."

Autumn forced a smile. She'd always liked Misty. "Not your fault. I should have been more clear." The end result had been no less mortifying, however.

Once they were alone, she turned to Hadley and blinked back the hot tears. The day had been hard enough, but now embarrassment overwhelmed her. The best part was that she didn't have to say anything to Hadley at all. She just knew.

"I'll drive."

Autumn nodded, grateful for Hadley, who was there to catch her on one of her more difficult days. While she might not have it all wrapped up when it came to life and love and her place in the grand scheme, Autumn was well aware of the fact that she'd hit it out of the park when it came to friendship. In the years since she'd opened the shop, those three women, first Hadley and Gia and more recently Isabel, had grown to mean more to her than she could possibly express.

"Hadley," she said, as they walked to the car.

"Yep?" Her blond hair bounced as she turned back expectantly.

"I don't really have the words. Just…thanks."

Hadley winked. "Hey. I've got you. You know that. And you don't need that stupid gym."

"Well, I'm not so sure."

"I am," Hadley said firmly. "I forbid you to go, to that one or any other. You're perfect, you hear me?"

Autumn smiled. "I do."

They decided not to stay overnight as originally planned. Instead, they hit the highway bound for LA, leaving the wedding and all its tailored perfection in Hadley's rearview mirror. For the first few hours of the trip, Hadley sang to the radio and Autumn let her mind wander, combing the expanse of her life thus far. Olivia had been her only relationship in the span of ten years. That accounted for a lot of alone time. Given, she'd devoted a good portion of her twenties to learning the coffee game. She'd put her heart and soul into the delivery business she'd started with two friends back when they were twenty-two and ready to take on the world. They'd roast coffee in a warehouse twenty-four hours before delivering it straight to their customers' doors in reusable wine bottles. It had been an exciting time in her life, in which she'd learned the ins and outs of coffee profiles and truly perfected her roasting technique. She'd killed herself, roasting, hustling, and delivering at all hours. Her friends eventually lost interest and moved on to nine-to-fives. She didn't blame them. That kind of grind, no pun intended, hadn't been easy. But Autumn had pressed on, working day and night to stash away the cash to open her own shop one day, building her name, her brand, until the time came to take the next big step.

"I've never really allowed myself the space to actually live," she said, breaking the silence in the car. Hadley turned the radio down and glanced over at her.

"What do you mean, actually live?"

"I've been so focused on my job, making my way, getting the storefront I'd always dreamed of. But even then, I didn't stop. Do you know how many hours I pull each week?"

Hadley cringed. "It's crazy. We've all talked about it."

"Exactly. It's over the top, because that's how important Pajamas is to me. It's everything I've worked for." She shook her head as reality rained down. "But somewhere along the way, I cared so much about the business that I stopped caring about myself. My life. I haven't lived, Had. I haven't carved out my little section of the world, and maybe instead of standing behind the counter and watching other people fall in love and take vacations and go on long walks, maybe I should leap over the counter and join in."

"I like this new philosophy," Hadley said, with a smile. "You deserve a chance to do *you* for a while. So you need a plan. What now? What's the first step?" It was like a lightbulb went off over that pretty blond head. "Ohh, we could look at dating sites! Or maybe join a wine club. They have fun events on the weekends with live music. I'm always so jealous of people who know about wine. That could be us."

Autumn smiled at her. "I want to have a baby."

"Wait. When exactly did you come to this monumental conclusion?" Isabel asked over breakfast the next morning. The look on her face was dialed to shock, but that was to be expected. They'd gathered around their usual table across from the counter for their own brand of Breakfast Club, which had slowly emerged as a morning tradition, offering them the chance to check in on each other before heading off into the world for their various jobs. Autumn found Breakfast Club entirely helpful to kick-starting her day and looked forward to that time with her friends. At Hadley's prompting, Autumn had shared her news with the group that morning.

Isabel grappled. "I'm just trying to gain a threshold for this whole thing."

"No, I get it," Autumn said, and sipped from her Pajamas mug.

In addition to her friends' regular coffee orders, all of which she had meticulously memorized as she did with all her customers, Autumn had put out some croissants and warm banana bread for them to snack on as they chatted.

"You have to admit, it's surprising. At least for us," Gia said, from her traditional spot at the table next to Isabel.

"I get that, but know it's something I've been thinking about for years now," Autumn told her, hoping to make them understand. "I've always wanted kids, I just imagined I'd have them with the love of my life. The picket fence. All of it. But you know what? There is no love of my life lingering on the horizon, and let's be honest, the clock isn't easing up."

"The clock's a bitch," Isabel said, and took a bite of banana bread. "So screw the fence."

Autumn nodded. "Sing it, sister. Not that you have to worry about that, Miss Deliriously in Love. In fact, you probably shouldn't even be a part of this discussion. You're one of them, the blissfully paired-up."

"I can't help it if my drop-dead-gorgeous boss, who I happen to adore and lust after, wants to have sex with me all the time. It's my lot in life." Three pairs of eyes shot daggers her way. Isabel lifted her arm in front of her face to block the death stares. "But it's only a matter of time before you each find your own versions of Taylor."

"Nice save," Hadley said, relaxing back into a smile. "You brought it right back around again with the glimpse of my future happiness."

Isabel raised her coffee cup in cheers.

Hadley stared dreamily into the distance. "As far as relationship goals go, yours is at the top of my list, Iz."

Autumn smiled just thinking about Taylor and Isabel and how well they complemented each other. They'd met when Isabel had been hired as a staff writer on a hit TV show Taylor executive produced. Since then, they'd moved onto a kick-ass new show about an ex-spy now living in suburbia that had everyone talking. Their love story was nothing short of amazing.

"Ditto," Autumn said. "And since my own Taylor is taking her sweet time showing her face, I can do this whole baby thing on my own. Lots of single moms out there, and they do just fine."

"You'll be a great mother," Hadley said, lifting her shoulders in excitement. "That's not even a question."

Gia raised her hand. "Are you sure this isn't a knee-jerk reaction to watching Olivia tie the knot? Just wondering."

Autumn thought on this. Gia, though she had a big heart, wasn't the type to hold back, and Autumn appreciated her candor. "I can't say it wasn't a wake-up call of sorts. It made me take a good, hard look at things. Call it a catalyst." She shook her head with confidence. "But no, this is not about Olivia. For the first time in forever, this is about *me* and what I want. I'm ready to take control of my life. Work less. Live more. Sit on the beach and write poems. Find a good ice cream shop."

"Well, yeah, about that ice cream," Hadley said. "Wait. You write poetry?"

"I don't. But I will try. It might rhyme at first, but I'll work on it. The whole point is to get me out of my rut."

Gia nodded. "Valid."

"Thank you," Autumn said. She addressed the group. "I want a family. Even if that family is just me and a little one, it would be more than enough. I'd be a part of something bigger than me and important and amazing. Raising a human being."

Isabel stood, looking mildly uncomfortable. "I may be the least sappy person in the room, but, damnit, now I have to hug you. There's an unseen force wielding its power and I must obey. This is out of my control."

Autumn laughed and accepted the embrace from her chair, an embrace that was promptly joined by Hadley and Gia, who piled on top of her. "Thank you, guys," she said, as her rebellious sentimentality bubbled to the surface again. There'd been a lot of the raw, nerves-exposed kind of emoting lately, and she'd like to move past it. This moment was significant, however, and she allowed the brunt of the emotion some leeway. "You guys could have made me feel stupid over this decision, or changed my mind altogether."

"We would never do that," Gia said. She really was a softy under all that hard athleticism.

"And I have very selfish reasons for my support," Hadley said. "I get to be the best aunt ever."

Autumn laughed. "Yes, you do. You all do." She slid the banana bread forward. "Now shovel some of this down your pie holes. I have a new roast to try out."

"Listen, you don't have to ask a girl twice," Isabel said, and grabbed three slices.

For the rest of the day, Autumn moved with an extra bounce in her step, noticing the nice weather through the window, the smiles on the faces of her customers. Everything seemed to have an extra shine with her new sense of direction.

She was going to be somebody's mom. How crazy and scary and blissful did that sound?

"You in there?" Steve asked, waving a hand in front of her face with a smile.

"Right here," she said, and handed him the carton of skim milk he pointed at.

"Must be some awesome daydream."

She grinned at him. "You have no idea."

CHAPTER THREE

The guy wasn't there.

Kate was supposed to meet her contact from Airbnb at 3:30. She'd showed. He hadn't. He also wasn't answering his phone. Damn.

Because she had absolutely nowhere else to be, she put down the tailgate of her truck and took a seat. The downtime allowed her the chance to take in the neighborhood. Even Venice, as laid back as it seemed, was faster paced than Slumberton. But, of course, it would be. Everything is when your town is literally named after sleep.

The best part about Venice? She didn't know these people. Not the ones who ambled past with surfboards or whizzed by on Rollerblades. A group of girls across the street held shopping bags from one of those tourist places that lined the beach. She didn't know them either, and that was exactly the point of her sojourn. The realization hit her, and a ghost of a smile touched her lips, the first real one in quite a while. As long as she didn't let her mind wander too far, she'd be fine. Escapism was what she needed.

"Did you know you're in a tow-away zone?"

Kate swiveled. Standing there on the sidewalk was a woman with curly red hair that fell partially across green eyes. Pretty ones. "What's that?"

"Your truck." The redhead pointed up at the sign indicating the times of day one could and could not park on that section of the street. Apparently, Kate was in violation. "It's before six."

"Oh. Gotcha. Thanks for the heads-up."

"No problem." But the redhead didn't leave. She stood there, watching. Kate knew because she could feel her stare against the side of her face. "But you're not moving. I only say anything because the cops around here are militant about illegal parking. Neighborly thing, you know."

"Cool. You're nice for telling me."

The woman nodded. "Sure." She walked on, turned back a moment, and then continued on her way. Kate watched her walk, enjoying the subtle sway of her hips. Feminine if not a touch sassy. She could never pull off sassy. Not that she wanted to.

"Hey! What's your name?" she called after the woman, shocked to hear the words leave her lips.

The redhead turned back, intrigue crisscrossing her features as if trying to work the puzzle that was Kate. "I'm Autumn. Who are you?"

"Kate Carpenter."

"Well, Kate Carpenter," she called, "I predict you have another ten minutes until that truck is snatched from beneath you by the po-po. Would be a shame, too. You guys look good together."

Kate placed a hand over her heart and grinned. "I'm touched by your depth of care."

"You're a cheeky one, aren't you?" Autumn said, pointing at her and walking backward. "Don't dawdle, now."

"Wouldn't want to dawdle," Kate murmured to herself with a smile. Venice wasn't so bad. She hopped off the tailgate, closed the back, and with a final wave to Autumn stepped into the cab. The short exchange felt like a badly needed exhale from the events of the past few months. Nowhere in the two-minute back and forth did someone look at her with pity, or hero worship, or ask with a heavy heart how she was doing. Yep. This was exactly what she needed. "Helloooo, Venice," she said quietly, and threw a final glance at Autumn's retreating form.

After finally getting in touch with her contact at Airbnb, he directed her to a small lot marked Seven Shores Residents Only where she could leave her truck. The unit she'd rented was described as relatively basic, but honestly that's all she required. True to the photos online, it was fully furnished and decorated in a navy and white nautical theme, complete with a life preserver hanging on the wall with the words "All Aboard" painted around its perimeter. "It's perfect," she said to the landlord, an intense guy by the name of Larry Herman. The series of pens sticking out of his shirt pocket were just heartbreaking for his dating prospects. She wanted to offer him a beer just to see if he'd ever relax.

"So, what do you want with it?" he asked Kate, staring her down.

"I'm sorry? I'm not following you."

"Why are you renting an apartment on Airbnb? Are you homeless? On vacation?" He paused as a new and alarming thought seemed to hover. "A criminal?" he asked, in a menacing tone.

"I'm a firefighter on leave, looking for some downtime. That's about it."

"Oh," he said, straightening like a flagpole. "Well, that's boring."

"Sorry to disappoint."

"Do you know what will disappoint me, Miss Carpenter? You not taking care of my unit. Or hosting any loud parties."

"Lay off, Larry. The routine is getting old."

He turned to reveal a brunette in her twenties sitting on a couch in the shared courtyard, a laptop on her knees. "This is none of your concern, Ms. Chase."

"It's Isabel, Larry. Call me Isabel. Same name as the last fifty times we've spoken."

"I'll stick with Ms. Chase, thank you."

She sighed. "You coming back to the complex later this week for Had's thing? You could do some sashaying and regale us with tales from your war reenactments. I never did hear if Washington made it out alive this time around."

"He always makes it out alive. It's a reenactment of actual events, which means it has the same outcome." He seemed a little worked up about the whole thing.

"Oh," Isabel said, smirking. "Fingers crossed for his chances next time." She was playing this guy like a fiddle and enjoying it. Kate was, too.

A pause. Larry took a step forward. "Did you say Hadley is having one of her gatherings?" Larry asked. The mention of this Hadley person seemed to perk him right up.

Isabel nodded. "One of her theme nights. I think this one is in dedication to Groundhog Day. She bought top hats for everyone to wear. Last I heard she was attempting to rent a groundhog."

He seemed perplexed and a little annoyed. "Groundhog Day was two months ago. It would be unorthodox to celebrate now."

"Yeah, she doesn't care. Have you met Hadley?" Isabel didn't wait for his answer. She looked around Larry and offered Kate a wave. "Hey, there. Don't worry about this guy. He's harmless. Aren't you, you weird and endearing little man?"

Larry scowled. "I'm not little. I'm over six feet tall."

She shook her head as if amazed. "I keep making that mistake, don't I?"

He glared. "I tend to make mistakes, too. Like forgetting to fill repairs on just one of my first-floor units, Ms. Chase."

"I enjoy your threats, Larry," Isabel said, smiling. "We should play *Ms. Pac-man* soon."

"I'll be by on Thursday."

"Done."

He turned back to Kate. "Sorry about that."

She shrugged. "I'm good. It's okay."

"Per our agreement, you have the unit for one month. Let me know if you wish to extend. It's been very popular." Without another word, the guy turned and left, walking as if on a mission, but then she had a feeling he always walked that way. She glanced at Isabel and inclined her head in the direction of Larry's retreating form. "Thanks. For the intervene."

"No problem. He can be a lot. Good rule of thumb is don't take the guy seriously, and bring up the name Hadley as much as possible." Isabel set her laptop on the coffee table and pointed at an upstairs apartment in the corner. "She lives there. He's madly in love with her but doesn't fully realize it."

"Hadley. Got it." She glanced behind her into the unit. "Should maybe be writing this down."

Isabel waved her off. "You'll be fine. This is an easy place to be. Everyone is super chatty, though, and I will admit that it caught me off guard at first. Consider yourself warned. In fact, I'm doing it now, which is kind of unlike me. I should shut the hell up."

Kate grinned. "I don't mind. It does seem like a nice place."

The outdoor courtyard was clean, well-kept, and surrounded by the white building trimmed with black shutters. In the center sat several wrought iron tables and chairs, next to a more comfortable area made up of outdoor couches with bright green cushions, the kind of place you'd want to spend time. Kate had lots of that.

"The quiet, scary guy who lived in your unit moved, so Larry had it furnished and is renting it out on Airbnb as a business experiment. We've seen a variety come through. I don't miss the bongo drums woman from three stays back."

"I can imagine. Kate, by the way."

"Isabel Chase. Nice to meet you." She picked up her laptop. "So, what brings you to Venice for the month? I mean besides all the naked people on the beach." She held up a hand. "Kidding. There are only like four naked people. The rest are half-naked."

Kate took a moment, unsure how to answer the original question. She needed to figure that out because it was likely one she would hear a lot. "Have you ever just needed space from…life?"

"Big time. Every day I was alive. I just never had the funds to do anything about it until recently."

Kate nodded, feeling a little uncomfortable. "I had some time off and some cash socked away. Literally in a sock."

Isabel seemed to enjoy that. "And here I thought that was just a cliché."

"I'm from a small town. Most clichés are based on our reality."

Without delay, Isabel set to typing. "I'm stealing that line. I hope you don't mind. In fact, I'm stealing it even if you do. It's that good." She pointed at her own face. "Writer. You?"

"Firefighter."

"Shut up."

"Sorry?"

Isabel held out her hand. "No. I didn't mean *actually* shut up—it's a phrase, a way of—you know what? Never mind."

Kate walked over to the couch. "Try me."

"Okay. But I don't want you to think I'm hitting on you, because I'm wildly in love with someone else, but I say *shut up* because you're very attractive and a firefighter, and now I'm the cliché myself, but"—she glanced around, leaned forward, and dropped her pitch—"that's a killer combo. You're going to do well here. It's just math."

Kate nodded. The job did tend to get her extra attention, a few extra phone numbers at the bar, but she wasn't looking to get involved. "I'm just trying to keep things simple. Sit in the sun. Read a book. Explore the neighborhood. That kinda thing."

Isabel nodded. "A standard vacation. You've come to the right place. Welcome to Seven Shores, Firewoman Kate. Or is it fireperson? I never know."

"Firefighter works for me."

"Do you play *Pac-Man*?"

Kate took a second with that one. "I could try."

"Bonus. I like you already."

It had been a nice welcome to what would be her home for the foreseeable weeks. The complex was perfect, she'd flirted with a woman on the street, and she'd even made friends with one of her neighbors. Bolstered by the relief that this had been the right move, Kate headed inside to unpack, pop a beer, and catch her breath for the first time in a long while.

Autumn had been sitting at La Palmita, the little Mexican restaurant she and her mother had been coming to for, well, her whole life, for just over forty-five minutes. Alone. She smiled at Esperanza, the owner, and did her best to project fine, happy, and not at all stood up by the very woman who gave birth to her.

"I'll bring more chips," Esperanza said, and took the bowl

Autumn had singlehandedly mainlined as she waited. And waited. And did some more waiting.

"I'm sure she'll be here soon," Autumn called after her to not seem like a total loser. "Probably just stuck in traffic. You know LA at this time of day."

Esperanza smiled but exchanged a disappointed look with the bartender. This woman knew her life too damn well. Autumn had always admired Esperanza, her restaurant and sense for business. In fact, she'd been a big part of Autumn's inspiration when she'd opened Pajamas. The customers at La Palmita looked up to Esperanza. Liked her, respected her, and she took time with each one of them. Autumn had wanted that for herself and hoped she'd achieved at least a little bit of what Esperanza had. Autumn smiled at her friend and mentor as she approached.

"Here you go," Esperanza said, and placed another bowl of freshly made chips on the table. She seemed to have personally taken over for the waiter Autumn began with.

"Thanks, Ez, but you don't have to wait on me."

"I do what I want," Esperanza said in a sassy, authoritative tone.

It made Autumn laugh despite the awkward wait.

This was to be her birthday dinner, which was already weeks late. Her mother, who had asked Autumn to call her Vicky when she'd entered the second grade, hadn't had time to get together with her before that night. Why? Autumn had no idea. Vicky didn't work and instead floated from one wealthy male companion to another, expecting them to support her financially, until the inevitable breakup when she came to Autumn for money. Though she couldn't count on Vicky herself, she could certainly depend upon her pattern. Suffice it to say, she and Vicky didn't share many of the same values, and definitely not the same work ethic. She tried Vicky's phone again.

"I'm here! I'm here!" Vicky yelled, upon answering. "Just slipping into some sassy heels in the parking lot, and then I will scoot my patootie inside to kiss my baby girl on her birthday."

"It's not actually my birthday," Autumn said. "That was a while ago."

"Close enough. See you in a sec!"

It wasn't that close at all, but Autumn let that fact slide.

Ten minutes later, Vicky walked into La Palmita as if she were the queen herself, waving and smiling at the patrons and kissing Esperanza on the cheek like they were long-lost best friends. Esperanza, to her credit, seemed to tolerate, if not return, the affection. Vicky sure knew how to draw attention to herself. That part wasn't new. It hadn't been easy being known as the one with the "sexy mom" when Autumn was in high school.

"There's my baby doll," Vicky said, and kissed Autumn on the cheek. She wore a brightly colored pink and yellow dress, as always showcasing enough cleavage to draw stares. Her bleached blond hair looked like it had been professionally blown out recently, as in an hour ago. "This girl needs a cocktail. You feeling like a cocktail?"

"Sure. Why not?" Autumn said, conservatively.

Vicky didn't happen to mention that she was close to an hour late. No apology. No explanation. That's just how Vicky rolled. Autumn knew better than to push the issue or she'd wind up apologizing herself when her mother flipped the whole thing and made herself the victim in the story. Their dysfunctional pattern wasn't hard to learn and sidestep. Life was too short to try and reason with her. She'd learned that lesson a long time ago. These days, Autumn strived for self-preservation.

Vicky tossed a glance behind her. "Esperanza, we're going to need some strong margaritas over here! We're celebrating tonight!"

Autumn winced at Vicky's loud mouth and privileged demeanor. "Hey, maybe don't yell. She'll get around to us soon. The place is busy tonight."

"Well, I'm thirsty. I don't know about you." And there it was. *I'm thirsty*. It was the perfect example of how Vicky approached any given situation. It was always what she needed, or wanted, or was deprived of that mattered most. Screw everyone else. The rest of the world was made up of merely supporting actors on Vicky's self-involved stage. In her mind, Autumn should be content waiting over an hour for Vicky as long as she arrived eventually. Esperanza should rush off and bring her drink immediately upon her arrival. It was simply how she approached life.

The rest of Autumn's "birthday dinner" went much the same way. Vicky talked all about her newest guy, Rocco, a financier from back east. By the time Autumn had polished off her plate of flautas, because honestly, she hadn't gotten a word in, she could have told you Rocco's favorite television show, his shoe size, and what kind of women he was drawn to.

When the bill arrived, Vicky finally shifted her focus. "So, tell me about you! What's new?"

Autumn opened her mouth to answer. She'd wanted to share her plans to become a mother, which was a huge step, but hadn't imagined she'd be cramming the information into their last few moments together. Still, this was the only real family she had in her life, and she wanted to share her news. Cue her nerves. "Well, there is something, actually."

"Oh, my God! Did you see Olivia's wedding photos?" Vicky exclaimed, and tossed her napkin onto the table. "I saw them on Facebook this week and just about died. She was absolutely the most beautiful bride! And those flowers!"

Autumn took a second to recover from the gut punch. "I did see them. Olivia had a wonderful wedding. What I was going to say a minute ago, though—"

"It makes me sad, though, too," Vicky said, plowing right ahead. "I want to be the mother of the bride at a wedding like that. I wonder if I'll ever have that chance. Are you dating at all?" Again, right back to her needs. "Rocco has some nice men that work for him. I could arrange an introduction."

"Men? Vicky, I haven't dated men since the Clinton administration. You know that. Why are we doing this again?"

"I just don't think you should close your mind to the idea. Double your options, you know? Lots of handsome boys out there who would kill for a crack at a date with you. After all, you are my daughter." Another thing: Vicky never understood or fully accepted

Autumn's sexuality. While she'd always been pleasant enough to the women Autumn dated, she seemed to hope Autumn was merely going through a phase. Vicky couldn't seem to wrap her mind around the idea that men wouldn't be everyone's focus in life.

"Not gonna happen," Autumn said, and sat back in her chair.

"Fine. A nice girl, then. You decide."

"Thank you." Autumn attempted to steer them back on course. "And speaking of my future—"

"Sweetie, can you get this one?" Vicky asked, sliding the check across the table. "It's been a tight month." *Not for getting your hair blown out, it hasn't.* Autumn swallowed the thought and laid down a credit card. Not a big deal in the scheme of life to pay for your own birthday dinner. Still, it left her feeling melancholy and small.

"It was great seeing you, sweetie." Vicky stood and kissed Autumn's cheek before they'd even had a chance to settle up and walk out together. "You can take care of the rest, can't you? I hate to cut out early, but I'm meeting Rocco across town, and traffic is awful. We're going dancing!" She twisted her wrists in the air and gave her hips a shake to demonstrate. The nearby table stared.

"Great seeing you, too," Autumn said quietly, and watched her mother sashay her way out of the restaurant for somewhere better.

"Happy birthday, Autumn," Esperanza said, and laid a hand on her shoulder. "Dinner is on the house tonight, and sopaipillas are on their way. My treat."

She looked up in surprise. "Oh, no. I couldn't let you do that. Please let me pay."

Esperanza's eyes carried warmth. "Your money is no good here. I'm just happy to see you in my restaurant."

"Thanks, Ez."

She turned to go and then hesitated. "She's a handful, your mother."

She tried for a smile and failed. "Don't I know it."

Another late-birthday dinner was in the books. She had survived it, and as far as Vicky went, Autumn would expect a call for cash in the next one to three weeks. In fact, she'd set her clocks by it.

"I'll say one thing for her, she raised an amazing daughter."

Autumn felt the smile blossom. "Thanks, Ez." She looked up at the woman who'd been more of a mother to her than her own mother would ever be, grateful as always that she'd been there to pick her up when she was low. They ate the sopaipillas together and caught up on all of the details of each other's lives. It was the kind of exchange she secretly longed for with Vicky, as unrealistic as that was. She used to fantasize as a kid that her mother would take her to the park to play, and afterward they'd go out for ice cream sundaes. Ludicrous, in the scheme of who Vicky really was. She was lucky if she'd remember to pick her up from school at a reasonable hour.

Autumn would be a better parent, she vowed then and there. She would be present, and kind, and interested, and active in the life of her child. She'd be like Esperanza.

It hadn't been the moment she'd planned on, or imagined, but she now knew who she wanted to share her big decision with.

She set down her fork. "Hey, Ez. I have something I want to tell you."

❖

"I miss Gia," Autumn said wistfully. It was close to closing at Pajamas, and Isabel and Hadley had dropped in to keep her company while she worked. She'd put on some Stevie Wonder, which seemed to send her to her happy place. Since the place was virtually empty, she'd sent her last employee home. "She's been gone so much lately. When is she back from the tour again?"

Isabel looked at Hadley from where she sat upon the counter. "I think she just said we're boring."

Hadley nodded. "She most certainly did, which can't be true. I'm interesting and a good listener."

"I'm sarcastic and witty."

"I throw fun parties and advise on fashion."

Autumn threw up a hand. "All right, all right. You're both pretty. You're both worthy. You can both go to the ball."

Isabel and Hadley clinked their mugs in solidarity. "But you're driving," Isabel said. "I plan to get wasted and lose the prince."

"Fine," Hadley sighed. "Let's drop him at the 7-Eleven." She turned to Autumn. "But to answer your question, the tournament wraps Friday night, so we should get G back on Sunday."

Autumn smiled. "Then all will be right with the world again. I don't like it when one of you is MIA. Feels like I left my house without my pants."

"That could bring in more business," Isabel said. "Just sayin' it's something to consider."

"You're such a mother hen," Hadley said, pointing at Autumn. "Which bodes well for your baby-making scheme."

"It's not a scheme, it's a life choice," Autumn corrected, pulling pastries from the display case for refrigeration. "But I'll take all the encouragement I can get."

"Your life choice is taking too long," Hadley lamented. "I'm ready to be Auntie Hadley already, kissing baby bellies and leading toddler parades through the courtyard."

"Really?" Isabel deadpanned. "You're going with Auntie?"

"I am." Hadley said brightly, and wandered behind the counter. She picked up a scoopful of roasted coffee beans and let them fall from the scoop to her hand, taking a deep inhale. "Speaking of arrivals, I finally met the dreamy firewoman. She's just like you said, Iz. I got swoony in my knees."

"Who's the dreamy firewoman?" Autumn asked, returning for another handful of pastries. "And why haven't I heard about her? Don't hoard all the gossip."

Isabel leapt off the counter and swiveled. "Stop. You haven't met her yet? She's been here almost a week. She's renting Larry's Airbnb unit. I'm not sure where she's from yet, but she's hot and broody. Dark hair. Kinda quiet. Very attractive."

"And a *firefighter*," Hadley emphasized, fanning herself.

"She fights fires. Actual ones, not just the TV kind," Isabel said, opening and closing her hands in a grabbing gesture.

"You two are in rare form. Hand me the nutmeg?" Autumn asked Isabel, who obliged.

"Oh, and she drives a blue pickup," Hadley said. "I saw her drive off in it the other day. Completes the package for me."

Autumn paused. "Nancy Drew, did you say a pickup truck?"

Hadley nodded. "I did. And I like being called Nancy Drew. Do it more."

Autumn kicked her hip against the counter. "Then I take it back. We have met. Kate is her name, if my memory serves."

Isabel shrugged. "Yes. If you want to call her Kate, sure, we can do that. I'm guessing you think hot-brooding-firefighter is too long. I'm open to criticism."

Autumn reflected on the woman she saw sitting on the tailgate of her pickup a week or so ago. "She doesn't look like a firewoman. She's too…beautiful."

Isabel inclined her head to the side. "I don't think they're rated on a scale of ugly to take-me-home-right-now. Could inspire a lawsuit."

Hadley nodded. "And no one wants a lawsuit. Can you imagine the—"

They turned at the sound of the door, and speak of the devil, there stood Kate herself. Just like that, three talkative women dropped into stark silence. Kate seemed to notice and glanced behind her in confusion and then back. "Oh. I'm sorry. If you're closed, I can go."

Hadley launched into an insta-smile, as if thrust into a surprise beauty pageant. "We were just talking about the injustice that is global warming. My friends and I were. Just now."

"Damn that La Niña!" Isabel said, not missing a beat. "Such a bitch."

"Isabel feels strongly on the issue," Hadley said, nodding matter-of-factly.

"I can tell. So, is this place still open?" Kate asked, hesitantly. Her hair was tucked behind one ear and fell past her shoulders. Her eyes were hazel, strikingly so, and they shone extra bright from all the way across the room. Her skin was olive, but not from a tan. No, that was natural.

"For ten more minutes," Autumn told her. "What can I get you?"

Kate glanced at the menu board. "Decaf coffee. House roast would be great."

Autumn easily scooped up a paper cup. "You're in luck. My custom blend." She glanced at Kate as she moved to pour the coffee and found Kate staring at her. In response, she smiled and stared back. And whoa. What was that passing between them? Out of the corner of her eye, she saw Hadley and Isabel exchange a glance, only she couldn't be bothered with why, because Kate's presence sent the warmest shiver right down her spine. She wiggled slightly against it, enjoying its dance.

"Hey, Autumn?" Hadley asked quietly.

"Yeah?"

"The coffee. For Kate."

"Right," she said, calmly. "On it."

Kate followed her down the counter where she poured the hot cup and fastened a to-go lid. She offered a lazy smile. "So, I had no idea that you worked here."

"She owns here," Isabel supplied.

Kate nodded. "Or that. Very cool." She accepted the coffee and handed over a credit card.

"Kate Carpenter," Autumn read off the card, reminding herself of Kate's last name. "Well, welcome to our little community, Kate Carpenter."

"Thanks. Are you here tomorrow?"

"We're here every day," Autumn said automatically, all the while noting that Kate came with a lot of presence. The room felt smaller with her in it. Autumn's senses shifted into overdrive, and every little detail of the shop seemed amplified. The smooth texture of the counter beneath her fingertips. The hum of the overhead lights. The whispering of her friends in the corner. Autumn found the whole experience rather astounding.

"No," Kate said. "I meant will *you* be here tomorrow."

"Oh," Autumn said, leaving her mouth in that shape for an extra beat.

"I stopped by two days ago and it was just a kid behind the counter. No you."

Isabel and Hadley slowly lowered themselves into chairs. The only thing that would have made the picture more complete would have been tubs of popcorn in their laps.

"I will be here tomorrow."

"Good. Then me too." Another two-way stare, a scorching one, ensued and the air around Autumn heated considerably. "'Night, everyone. Autumn." Kate made her way to the door and out into the night. Autumn and her friends turned to one another.

"I've never seen anything like it," Hadley said quietly.

"Have to agree." Isabel nodded. "That was noteworthy."

"So, not just me?" Autumn asked.

"Definitely not," Isabel said. "She wanted to put out your fire, Autumn. And I think you started one in her, too."

Hadley grinned and pointed at the door. "That woman right there is your walking alarm clock."

"My alarm clock?" Autumn asked.

Hadley walked to the counter and regarded Autumn. "What was your new goal? The one you described to me on the trip back from Tahoe."

Autumn met her gaze with a knowing smile. "It's time to start living."

Isabel folded her arms. "Let the living commence."

CHAPTER FOUR

Kate's lungs burned painfully and she couldn't see where she was going. Without her gear, she didn't have much time before the smoke would overwhelm her and take her down. The sound of hysterical screams persisted and kept her moving. No matter how heavy her limbs felt, no matter how hot the air was that sliced along her bare arms, she pressed on. Why hadn't she worn long sleeves today? As long as she could still hear the kids, there was no way she was turning back. But the hallway got longer. No matter how fast she moved, no matter how much ground she covered, the door drifted impossibly farther away.

She'd never get there. No matter what she did.

Kate sat up in bed, gasping frantically for air. The sound of her ragged inhales sent a bolt of terror as she clutched her chest and looked blindly around the darkened room for water. She didn't recognize her surroundings. Where the hell was she? Reality punctured her panicked brain.

The apartment in Venice.

Her heart rate slowed.

She was in bed, not back in that burning house. Not knowing what to do with herself, she threw the sheets off her body. Now covered in sweat, she walked the length of the apartment, not once or twice, but for the next hour. The movement had a way of calming her mind and anchoring her in the here and now.

She knew what had brought on the nightmare. Kate had promised herself that once she left Slumberton, she'd stop checking in on the kids, but that was asking the impossible. Ren had been released from the hospital after only a couple of days, but he was older, stronger. It had taken little Eva longer. She'd only been released earlier that day. Kate knew because the local news had covered her release and she'd pulled it up online. "Six-Year-Old Fire Victim Released from Hospital." Eva looked good in the one photo that had accompanied the article, if a little shy from the camera attention. She smiled meekly from the arms of the nurse who held her as she was transported from the hospital to a state home for kids. But what now? What would life look like for Ren and Eva when, in the course of one afternoon, their entire world changed forever?

Kate poured herself a shot of rum, an old trick that would slow her nervous system, bring down her adrenaline after a fire, and help her find a way to relax enough to sleep so she could get up and go back to work. As the alcohol burned a potent trail down her throat, she closed her eyes and waited for it to take hold.

Lighter thoughts would help. Anything she could come up with.

She visualized the ocean just blocks away. Her brother, and how he always left the bathroom such a mess when they were kids, as if a cyclone had blown through and knocked everything all over the counter. The really attractive woman from the coffee shop next door who made her palms sweat from the tiniest dip of cleavage visible beneath the blue apron. Autumn. She smiled. She liked this Autumn. She was funny, with a pretty smile. She also seemed like a genuinely nice person, which only pulled her more points in Kate's book. Autumn was fun to think about.

She drifted off to sleep easily, claiming the rest she needed and avoiding any and all mention of an awful afternoon just eight weeks earlier.

❖

"Yes, I'm calling for Autumn Primm," the female voice on the phone said.

Autumn tucked the phone between her ear and her shoulder. "You found her."

"Ms. Primm, this is Elise from Dr. Arocha's office."

"Oh, right!" Autumn said, straightening and excusing herself from the front of the shop to the storage room in the back. She'd been trying to get an appointment at the Holly Grove Reproductive Clinic for a week now. It was the best in the area, and she was prepared to be patient and wait for an appointment to open up if it meant her chances were greater for a positive outcome. "Thank you so much for calling."

"My pleasure," Elise said. "I wanted to let you know that we had a cancellation for Wednesday at three, and I thought I'd check and see if you had availability for an initial consultation."

"Oh, I'll make availability. Thank you! I'll be there," Autumn said, running an excited hand through her hair.

"I'm so happy we were able to accommodate you." The woman rattled off the details and Autumn took meticulous notes, excited for this first big step in starting her little family. She returned to the front of the store with a spring in her step and her heart set to vibrate as she prepared to start her afternoon roast, a South American blend that had become a house favorite.

"You seem happy."

Autumn glanced up to see Kate watching her from the other side of the counter. Her dark hair was in a ponytail today, and it swung slightly when she tilted her head. She wore cutoffs and a blue and green plaid shirt that she'd left open, revealing a black tank top beneath. Everything slowed down as Autumn drank her in for a few solid moments before breaking into a smile. Now, that was one way to kick-start your afternoon.

"That's because *I am* happy," she said. "Today is a good day. What can I get you to make your day even better?"

"Well, that's quite an offer." Kate shrugged and studied the board. "What do you recommend? I'm pretty easy."

Autumn let that one slide. "Well, I just got a new shipment of beans from Ethiopia. Just roasted this morning. They're glorious, but then I'm biased."

"I don't see how I can pass up glorious beans."

"Smart woman. For here or to go?" Autumn asked.

"Here."

"In that case, you get a mug." She held up an oversized blue mug with PJ playing a guitar on the front. "Coffee is always best consumed from a mug anyway. Feels heavy and warm in your hands and makes you want more and more. And, well, more coffee is always the goal."

"You know your stuff," Kate said.

"When it comes to coffee, I do. It's my thing. We all have them."

"Have a cup with me." Kate said it with that emboldened eye contact again. Not pushy or aggressive. Just…solid and friendly. She carried herself with a quiet confidence. Autumn hesitated, but Kate didn't move a muscle and simply waited patiently for her answer. Autumn glanced behind her in hesitation. Steve and her new employee, Rhonda, seemed to be in a groove, and the shop *was* in the midst of a lull. Then there was her new declaration to live more, get out there and experience life.

"I can probably snag a few minutes."

Kate smiled and inclined her head. "I'll hang out over there."

As she watched Kate walk away and select a table near the back, Autumn shook her head. She had no idea what it was she thought she was doing with Kate. Except she did. She was feeling alive for the first time in years, and that feeling had her craving more, like a dangerous drug you couldn't get enough of, because it made you feel so good. "Steve, I'm gonna take ten."

He nodded. "We got you."

"Thanks." She focused on Kate sitting at the table as she walked, slow and deliberate, swaying her hips because she was, okay, a little bit of a hussy.

Kate took a sip of the coffee as she watched Autumn, and smiled as she sat in the chair across from hers. "Autumn."

Oh, she liked the sound of her name on Kate's lips. "Yes?"

"This is the best coffee I've ever tasted."

"Thank you." She took a seat, basking in the compliment. It wasn't even close to the first time she'd heard that sentence, but hearing it from Kate, who she was blatantly lusting after, brought a bonus shiver. She took a sip of her own coffee, a cappuccino that would hopefully see her through the afternoon, and watched Kate, who didn't seem to mind. She stared back at Autumn as the air between them danced with a combination of electricity and anticipation. It only took a moment before she realized that studying Kate might be her new favorite pastime. Kate's full bottom lip and perfectly formed eyebrows—most likely God given—snagged her attention first, followed by the way her ponytail rested on her shoulder. She had a feeling Kate didn't have to do too much with her hair. She was just blessed with the kind of thick, dark, and beautiful tresses that probably tumbled into place when she stood up from bed each morning. The hazel eyes were guarded, though. That much was clear. Autumn wondered what was behind them, and what one would have to do to find out.

"So, what's your secret?" Kate said, gesturing to the coffee. "To the vibrant flavor. It comes right through."

"I can't tell you that. You might open up a coffee shop next door, call it the Dog's Business Suit, and I'd be out of luck."

Kate grinned. "I wasn't planning on it, but now I'll think it over."

Autumn smiled, trying to figure her out. "You're a mystery, Kate. But I'm immune to mysteries." They both knew she wasn't, that Kate had her attention. There was an underlying flirtation to the way they spoke to each other. Eye contact that went on far too long, banter that said they enjoyed the back and forth, and then there was that unspoken, unseen energy that radiates between people who are drawn to each other. They definitely had that last part.

"Don't take this the wrong way, but you're even prettier up close." Kate sat back in her chair.

"How could I take that the wrong way?"

Kate glanced at the ceiling and back. "I don't know. Might be crossing a line. We don't really know each other yet."

The *yet* was not lost on Autumn. The *yet* came with so many fun possibilities.

"It's not crossing a line," Autumn said, feeling daring for the first time in a while. "And thank you for what you said, but I'm not sure I can hold a candle to a mysterious out-of-town firefighter."

Kate offered a small smile, the kind that mattered. Most of Kate's smiles did—that much Autumn could already tell. She didn't throw away her smiles. While only occasional, they seemed sincere. "But here's the thing I don't get."

"And what is that?" Autumn asked.

"Why you agreed to have coffee with me. Unless…"

"What?" Autumn said, enjoying this.

"Unless we have a thing happening. We do, don't we?"

Autumn held her thumb and forefinger together. "Little bit. I think."

"Then I should come back tomorrow. Get more coffee." She took another sip, her eyes never leaving Autumn's. Her demeanor never far from calm, measured. "Ask you more questions."

"You haven't asked me any questions."

"That's next. Favorite hobby?" She ran her thumb across the handle of the mug.

Every little detail had Autumn captivated. That's how intrigued she was by Kate, how infatuated. "Knitting, but I never have time for it." She still owed her friends a variety of promised hats, scarves, and blankets. "As you can see, I'm utterly boring. I don't even participate in my own hobby."

Kate leaned in. "There is nothing about you that's boring, okay?"

Autumn nodded. Her heart was crazily pounding, having moved into her throat, and her stomach fluttered pleasantly. It's possible other parts of her…warmed. "Okay," she managed. "Not boring."

Kate shook her head. "Nope. I'll come back tomorrow," she said, and took another sip of her coffee. "We can talk more." Without another word, Kate stood and walked away. Stunned by the over-the-top sparks she'd just experienced, it took her a moment to wake the hell up so she could turn in time to watch Kate walk away, and God was she glad she didn't miss that very satisfying opportunity. If

Kate's thick hair, gorgeous lips, and hazel eyes weren't enough, her body was unreal.

"Help me, Father, for I have sinned," she mumbled and fanned herself. "And I'm pretty sure there'll be more sinning to come."

❖

John Grisham was a dick. Though Kate had never been a huge reader, her vacation to sunny LA had her wondering why she'd not devoted more time to books. Randy loved 'em. Started a whole business in their honor. Blew through them like candy when they were kids as Kate focused on girls, cross country, and…girls. But this Grisham guy had her eating out of the palm of his hand like a little bitch. It annoyed her how vulnerable she was to his plot twists.

"Something has you incredibly stressed out," Hadley said, as she approached with a friend.

Kate lifted the book and squinted against the sun that haloed the two. They wore shorts, T-shirts, and fashionable-looking sunglasses. Very LA. "Yeah. There's this law firm, and these funds in the Cayman Islands, and I don't know if they're gonna make it in time, right? I'm sweating it out. I've never been a book person, but because of Grisham I might be. I hate him for that."

Hadley laughed. "Preaching to the choir as far as books are concerned. They're my drug of choice. Need a break? I hear espionage can be taxing. Oh, and this is Gia. She lives next door to me. We're headed to the beach."

She nodded. "Hey. I'm Kate."

Gia grinned. "Your reputation precedes you."

Kate didn't know what to say to that.

"You coming with us?"

"To the beach?" Kate asked.

Gia looked around. "On a day like today, it's the only place to be."

Kate hesitated. "Ah, you know, I haven't gotten around to buying a suit."

"Follow me," Hadley said, without missing a beat. "Bring Grisham."

Kate did as she was told and followed Gia and Hadley to the second floor and Hadley's apartment, which, she had to say, was way nicer than the one she'd rented. Except maybe it was just everything Hadley had done to it. Beautiful drapes, matching furniture, and soft, serene colors. She had a knack.

Hadley studied her. "You don't strike me as a woman who would wear any sort of pattern."

"No to the pattern," Kate said confidently. "Basic is best for me."

"I'm thinking two pieces, all black. Done." Hadley didn't wait for a response and hurried off to a bureau in the corner of her bedroom on a very serious mission, returning just moments later with the suit she'd described.

Kate hesitated at the two-piece component. She opened her mouth to say so, but Hadley held up a finger. "No. I'm good at fashion. You're gonna have to trust me on this."

Gia sat on the arm of the couch with a grin on her face. Out of the sun, Kate could see that her long dark hair and brown eyes were accentuated by a deep, and flattering, tan. "I find it's best just to listen to her. She's rarely wrong about these kinds of things."

Kate, knowing full well this was not her area, nodded. "Black two-piece it is."

"You can change down the hall and to the left," Hadley said, pointing down a short hallway.

So, she was heading to Venice Beach with two people she barely knew, wearing a bathing suit that she never would have picked out for herself, in the middle of what would normally have been a workday. Life felt foreign, but for whatever reason, Kate wasn't the least bit fazed. What was even crazier? She didn't look half bad in the suit. She made it a point to stay in shape for work but never really wore anything that required it. Apparently, Hadley was the real deal. She put her jeans on over the suit bottoms for the walk to the beach and exited Hadley's bedroom.

Hadley's eyes went wide when Kate returned to the living

room, and she turned to Gia. "Am I good at my job or am I good at my job?"

Gia nodded and raised her eyebrows in appreciation. "After this, you need a promotion."

❖

The Eagles, bless them, serenaded Autumn as she took one order after another, pleased with the groove she'd established for her afternoon.

"Hey, Kev. Medium iced Americano for you?"

"You got it," Kevin said, and forked over the cash, sliding down the counter to wait for Steve to prepare his drink.

"Stacy Q from Best Buy!" Autumn said happily. "What'll it be?"

"My usual, but I need to add a couple of razzmatazz iced teas for my coworkers."

"On it," Autumn said, and charged her card. "How's Jack?"

"Away on business. I'm single for the week."

"Live it up, girl."

"Wine and poker in his absence."

"Nice!"

The afternoon rush at Pajamas had arrived in full force, but she and Steve were ready. Well, she and Steve, and Rhonda from the community college up the street. She'd hired Rhonda the week prior before finding out that Rhonda felt cotton was somehow from the devil, but had a definite affinity for all things sweet. In fact, baked goods mysteriously disappeared from the display case at a remarkable pace while Rhonda lectured them all on how every other textile known to man was superior to her sworn enemy, cotton. Outside of Steve, Autumn had a difficult time finding good, reliable help. The revolving door at least added a bit of afternoon entertainment, as she never knew what she was in for with these kids.

As she rang up Jake-the-crossword-puzzle-guy's house roast, Autumn felt a text vibrate in her front pocket. She glanced at it ninja style so as not to look unprofessional in front of a customer, even if it was just Crossword Puzzle Guy. *Emergency. We need a delivery*, the text from Hadley read.

"Rhonda? Can you tag in for me?"

With a heavy sigh, Rhonda set down her chocolate chip cookie and took Autumn's spot at the cash register. She silently prayed the customers weren't chastised for any basic cotton blends. She would need to speak with Rhonda sometime soon about her fabric beliefs and when and when not to express them.

Kind of in the middle of my shift, she typed back. *But an emergency sounds important. What gives?* She smiled at the woman perusing the menu board and glanced beneath the counter at the readout on her phone.

Gonna want to make an exception.

Why is that? she asked Hadley, her interest snagged.

Firefighter has killer abs and she's wearing my two-piece.

Will that be three iced coffees, then? she typed back automatically. Some things took precedence, and Kate's abs on display might be one of them. She was not above objectification.

You won't regret this. Hadley added a winky face to the end of the text for good measure.

When Autumn arrived at their typical spot on the strip of Venice Beach far from the throngs of tourists, she found Hadley alone on her towel wearing her vintage 1950s white and blue striped bathing suit, stealing some rays. In an attempt to blend in with her surroundings, Autumn rolled up the bottoms of her jeans and lost her shoes. She'd ditched her apron back at the shop, leaving her in a plain white T-shirt, which would have to do. The warm weather was a tad early for April, but Autumn wasn't complaining. With the tide rolling in, she soaked in the sound of the beach all around her like food to the starving: waves crashing, seagulls chirping, and the tunes from Hadley's radio. She never got tired of this place. Wasn't possible.

"You came!" Hadley said, sitting up and popping her sunglasses on top of her head. "A smart decision."

"You know, I forget all of this is still going on in the midst of the workday. I take it you're off?"

"Close," Hadley said. "I'm meeting with a new designer later this afternoon. Trudy, who's the new store manager, by the way, wants a revamp. Hipper, modern, more accessible, and it's apparently up to me to make that happen."

"I like that. If I could afford it, I might actually want to shop there now."

"Never say never." Hadley accepted her iced coffee and pointed down the beach. "They're throwing a Frisbee. Get down there. It's awesome."

Autumn blew Hadley a thank-you kiss and headed down the beach where Gia threw an easy glide to Kate who—holy hell, looked like *that* under her clothes. Autumn sucked in a breath and her body went numb. But not for long. It woke back up again quickly and with a vengeance. And now her body wanted things. Wanton things. Demanded them.

"Those for us?" Gia asked, trotting over to her with a grateful grin.

Autumn glanced down at the tray in her hands, forgetting what the hell she was doing with it. "Oh. Right. Yeah. For you guys."

"You're the best," Gia said and snagged her drink.

Kate joined them and Autumn's gaze moved across the smooth olive skin, trim waist that flared to the subtle curve of her hips. The abs on Kate were insane, but she didn't dwell there for long. The bathing suit top dipped in the front, showcasing just a glimpse of her breasts that seemed not full, but not small either. She had perfect breasts. Autumn sighed as the physical longing persisted. She shifted against it, her new lot in life where Kate was concerned. Autumn shook her head. Of course she had perfect breasts. It would be too easy if she didn't. When Autumn remembered that there was a larger world around her and raised her gaze to a more appropriate eye level, she came face-to-face with Kate, who had missed none of it.

Damnit.

Caught in broad daylight!

The blush slammed her cheeks and they heated uncomfortably. She had two choices here: shrink like a wussy little violet, or own the fact that she was a grown woman with desires, and wants, and… okay, very potent needs. She brightened and handed Kate an iced coffee. "Looking good out there, Carpenter," she said, with a wink.

Kate bit her bottom lip through her smile. Biting her lip? Was she trying to kill Autumn there on the beach? Kate was a diabolical sex genius intent on taking down the women of Venice, and Autumn seemed to be target number one.

"Thank you," Kate said. "For this as well." She held up the plastic cup and took a pull from the straw. Autumn flashed to a rather juvenile fantasy of Kate rubbing the sweating cup across her body, but stopped herself because it was hot enough out here and coffee was serious business.

"She's never played Frisbee before," Gia said, hooking a thumb at Kate. "Can you believe that? She's a prodigy."

Kate glanced at the ground and then back up. "Just trying to keep up with you." As confident as Kate seemed in her interactions with Autumn, there was this whole other side to her that edged closer to vulnerable when the spotlight hit. She wasn't comfortable with too much attention.

"Would never have guessed it was her first time," Autumn said casually, careful not to gush. Or stare. That is, until Kate's gaze flicked to hers and held. Their connection sizzled.

Gia looked from one of them to the other. "Oh. I have to head to a sponsorship meeting in an hour and should probably freshen up. Autumn, sub in for me?"

"No, you don't have to do that," Kate said, waving off the idea. "We can stop."

"Maybe I want to play." Autumn stood taller, making the challenge clear.

Gia laughed and ran backward a few feet. "You two don't go having too much fun together. It's only Wednesday."

"No promises," Autumn called back. "Shall we?" she asked Kate once they were alone.

Kate extended her hand in an after-you gesture. Honestly, Autumn hadn't thrown a Frisbee since she was maybe thirteen, and even then, she wasn't very good. But it's not like she would pass up this opportunity. Not to mention, Kate was new to the game, too. They'd be perfectly compatible.

"Hit me," Autumn yelled, arms out.

"I don't think that's the goal of the game," Kate called back calmly.

"Stop stalling, there's a game happening here."

Kate smiled and gently sailed the Frisbee her way, and wouldn't you know it? She caught the damn thing. Unable to hold back, she held it up in the air and leapt for joy several times. And then a couple more for good measure. "Did you see that? I'm a natural."

Kate regarded her with a hand on her hip and a shake of her head. "Are you going for cute? It's working."

Autumn laughed. "I'll take cute and raise you masterfully skillful." She repeated the same sliding motion she'd just seen Kate demonstrate and sat back and watched as her Frisbee fell like a pound of flour just six feet in front of her.

"Uh-oh," Kate said, looking serious. "Have I been doing it wrong?"

Autumn retrieved the Frisbee and held up a finger. "Very funny. Just wait. I got this."

"Waiting!" Kate called. She held up both hands. "Right here. Nice and easy."

She *could* do this. Winding her arm around her body, Autumn released the Frisbee with a little more oomph this time, only to watch it sail violently to the right of Kate and straight into the encroaching tide. *Bollocks.* But Kate didn't hesitate and took off after the wayward Frisbee, and caught the very edge. Speaking of masterfully skilled.

"I am *so* sorry!" Autumn called to her. "Did you get wet?"

Kate glanced down at the spray across her suit. "It's a bathing suit. I'll live." She shook the water off her feet and ran back into the sand. "Again?"

"Why not! I can't get any worse, right?" Autumn yelled.

Honestly, she had nothing to lose anymore. The jig was up: she wasn't an athlete and she wouldn't be impressing anyone on this beach today.

"Don't take your eye off it," Kate called encouragingly. She ably sent the Frisbee in Autumn's direction. At the last second, a gust of wind lifted it up and to the left, forcing Autumn to back up and then move forward and dive left only to end in a crumpled heap in the sand. Triple failure. And, ow! Oh, okay, something had just given way painfully. She attempted to stand, but the blast of pain sat her right back down. All right, maybe she'd just hang out in the sand for a little while. Wasn't awful here.

Her dismay was short lived, however, because Kate was kneeling by her side almost instantly with concerned eyes. "Hey, you okay? You went down a little hard."

That's when Autumn realized that her own hand was holding tightly to her ankle, which throbbed a bit. "I think I just turned it the wrong way. No biggie."

"I'm so sorry about that," Kate said. "I guess the Frisbee caught a weird pocket of air."

Autumn smiled. "You have nothing to apologize for. I can be a klutz sometimes. And the wind was being a bitch."

"Still." Kate stared at her ankle in disappointment, as if the sight of Autumn on the ground crushed her. It was sweet. "Let me take a look."

"Okay."

Kate gently moved Autumn's hand and lifted her foot, pulling it into her lap as the sun shone brightly overhead. The world seemed to slow down a little.

"Are you a doctor now, too?" Autumn asked quietly.

Kate tossed her a glance and smiled. "I'm trained as an EMT. For work."

"Right," Autumn said, bracing against a flutter as Kate's fingers pressed softly into her skin. "This hurt?"

Autumn shook her head.

"What about this?"

"Nope."

Kate set about examining each inch of Autumn's ankle for acute pain, checking in with her as she went. "I think you're in the clear as far as any broken bones go. Do you think you can stand?"

"I can definitely stand," Autumn said, and did so. She took a couple of wobbly steps.

"Careful. You okay?"

"I am. Just putting weight on it hurts a tad." And she was limping slightly. They both saw it.

"Tell you what," Kate said, and scooped Autumn into her arms. "I can help with this." She then proceeded to carry Autumn across the beach to Hadley.

"Whoa!" Autumn laughed. "You should warn a girl before you…" But the words died on her lips when she realized her proximity to Kate. She smelled like the beach and oranges. The perfect combo. Those full lips were inches from hers as they walked, her own arms around Kate's neck, holding on. She fixated on those lips and wondered how they'd feel beneath her fingertips or, better yet, how they'd taste. Sweet like oranges?

"Autumn?"

"Yep?" she said, snapping out of it.

It was Hadley's voice that had burst the bubble of her quick little daydream. She sat on her towel looking up at them with a knowing twinkle in her eye. "You okay?"

"More than okay," Autumn heard herself say through the fog.

Hadley laughed. "You can drop her here, Lieutenant."

Kate gently set her on the towel next to Hadley and ran back for the drinks and Frisbee.

"You're bad," Hadley said.

Autumn laughed. "Lately I seem to be. It does hurt, though. I'm not making that part up."

"Of course it does," Hadley said with a grin. "But I don't think the ache has anything to do with that foot."

Autumn answered with a flip of her sunglasses onto her face and big smile. "Just having a little fun is all."

"Like I said, the new you is bad. And I love it."

Chapter Five

When Kate met Eva for the first time, she was counting the ants on the sidewalk. She'd seen the dark-haired little girl out in front of the dilapidated house on the end of her street multiple times, and wondered, with concern, if she was too young to be so close to the street on her own, no adult in sight.

"Hi," Eva had said, as Kate approached. She had her hair in a messy braid she'd likely assembled herself and looked up at Kate with bright eyes and a friendly smile—as if her day had just been made by Kate's presence on her sidewalk.

Kate was on her way to meet friends at Ricardo's Cantina for a birthday celebration for her pal Keri, who she'd known since grade school. She'd opted to walk instead of drive in case she decided to have more than one drink. The work week had been killer, with several assists to neighboring towns, but this little girl seemed like a bright spot.

"Hi back," Kate said in return. She'd never really spent much time around kids, but she liked them well enough. "What are you up to out here?" She glanced around for an adult, but saw no one.

"Counting the bugs," Eva had said, pointing at the line of ants marching dutifully into the storm drain beneath the curb. "There are a lot. See?"

Kate knelt to survey the ants. "There are. How many do you think?"

"Probably more than a hundred." The little girl looked up in awe. "Tons!"

Kate nodded. "I think you're right."

"What's your name?" Eva had asked, straightening.

Kate did the same. "Kate."

"Oh, I'm Eva. My brother's Ren. We live there." She pointed behind her to the house. The screen door had been removed and sat propped up against the garage. A car sat in the driveway on cinder blocks. It hadn't moved in months.

"Who lives with you?" Kate asked.

"My dad and my brother."

"Anyone else?"

"Nope. Just me and two boys." She said it like it was a hefty burden.

Kate smiled at that one. "Well, that's nice. I have a brother, too. Is your dad home?"

"Not right now. He had to leave when it was still dark this morning."

So the kids had been alone all day with evening approaching. "Do you know where he went?"

Eva set to walking the seam of the sidewalk as if it were a tightrope. She flung her braid from her shoulder onto her back. "No."

Kate nodded and kicked the rocks on the sidewalk next to Eva. "So, who is taking care of you?"

"Ren."

She glanced around, but saw no sign of him either and hoped, at the very least, he was a teenager. "Is he older than you are?"

"He's nine. I'm six. He's on the next street at his friend William's house, but they didn't want a girl to come. I didn't want to anyway." She rolled her eyes, but Kate didn't quite buy it. She'd been left behind.

"Well, of course not."

Kate sighed, now aware of the fact that there would be no birthday celebration after all. She took a seat on the curb, and for the next two hours, she and Eva got to know each other while the sun set. She told Eva about being a firefighter and getting to ride on the truck. Eva told her about the sheets on her bed that had little hearts on them and how one day she would have a brown pet rabbit with floppy ears named Woody.

"Can I braid your hair?" Eva asked. "It looks soft."

"Why not?" Kate said, and allowed Eva to move behind her.

They passed the time until Eva's father returned home just as darkness descended, presumably from some sort of job, though he looked a little scruffy and unkempt. Even from a distance, his eyes cut dull and bored. The man nodded once at Kate stoically but made no move in her direction to inquire about who she was or why she was sitting on the curb with his lonely child.

"See you later!" Eva said to Kate, and ran to her father, who took her hand. The two headed inside the house together without exchanging so much as a word. Eva hadn't seemed afraid of him, though, which was something Kate had been watching for. That was something, at the very least.

They became friends after that, she and Eva. Chatting on the sidewalk every few days or taking walks together whenever Kate came across the little girl all alone. It made Kate feel better whenever she spent time with Eva, to know that she was doing okay. She finally met Ren, too. A tussle of dark hair and green eyes. Less talkative, but every bit as sweet with a dust of freckles across his face.

She'd asked some of her colleagues at the station about the father, and when she came up with very little, she moved on to her friend Eddie, a beat cop at the police department.

"The house at the end of Claymore?" he'd asked. She nodded. "Jay Higgins. Yeah, he's a bad dude, Carpenter. Steer clear. In and out of jail on possession charges, solicitation, small-time burglary, you name it. He can't live clean."

"What about his kids?"

"From what I heard they go back and forth from him to a loser buddy of his when he's otherwise engaged." Code for incarcerated. This wasn't sounding good at all, but it's what she'd suspected.

"Listen, Eddie. We need to get someone to check on the two kids. They're left on their own way too much, and if he's dealing out of that house, it's not the place for them."

He nodded. "Then let's do it."

They met and filed a report with a woman from DHS, but then there hadn't been time for an investigation before the lives of those kids changed forever.

Kate pushed herself up from the couch in Venice where she had been stretched out flat on her back. Her chest compressed tight and hard, the air in the room scarce. She was doing it again, allowing her mind to wander back in time and play the same "what if" game that always trapped her in a haze of self-hatred. No more. She needed to get up and out of the apartment, distract herself, which had been the whole point of the trip.

Thank heavens for small miracles. Autumn was behind the counter at the Cat's Pajamas when Kate pushed through the door. Her gaze settled on Autumn's features as she chatted animatedly with a customer. Smiling, laughing, being Autumn in the middle of any normal day. No heaviness, no regret, just…Autumn. She exhaled and the world felt lighter.

"Well, look what the cat dragged in," Autumn said, as she watched Kate approach.

Kate caught the joke. "You must say that to everyone who walks in here at some point."

"First time, actually." Autumn offered a wink along with that lie.

"How's the foot?" Kate asked.

"Good as new."

Kate sent her a skeptical look, and Autumn softened. "Okay, it hurts a little when I walk with any real purpose, but it gets better by the hour. A minor sprain."

"Pay close attention to it. If you notice the pain spike, let me know. After that, call for a doctor's appointment."

"I will do that." Autumn stared at her. "I think I just got lectured."

Kate nodded. "It's rare, but it happens. Sorry about that."

Autumn shook her head. "You have nothing to apologize for. It's nice that you care. Let me guess," she said, scooping up a mug, "whatever is fresh?"

"You're good at your job."

"And you're charming."

She watched Autumn make her coffee with precise turns and fluid flicks of her wrist. It was the perfect coffee ballet that left her feeling homey, and impressed, and infatuated. A combo she'd never quite experienced.

"Joining me today?" Kate asked, inclining her head to the table they'd shared a few days back.

Autumn offered a sly smile. "I would love to, but I had to let one of my employees go this morning, and I'm down a worker this shift."

"Sounds dire."

"If you have any affinity for cotton whatsoever, it certainly was." Autumn began wiping down the counters. She worked hard to keep the shop in tip-top shape, that much Kate had picked up on. Autumn took a lot of pride in Pajamas, and it made sense. The coffee was outstanding. The atmosphere was unique. The vibe was friendly. She'd created something pretty awesome.

"Then tonight." She didn't phrase it as a question. The day had been rough for her so far, but Autumn was like a drug. She made things better.

"I'm sorry?"

"Let's get out of here. Together. Show me somewhere unique to LA. You choose."

Autumn tossed the towel onto her shoulder and her eyes sparkled. "Done."

"That was easy." Kate leaned up on her toes and then back. Nerves swirled fast and furious as she second-guessed the impulsive invitation. Maybe it was best to just keep to herself while she was here. Because Autumn was a thread that, if she pulled on hard enough, could unravel into something she wasn't in any position to handle. She'd come here to simplify things, not add to what was already on her plate. "I'll swing by here at seven," she heard herself say, in betrayal of rational thinking.

"Seven thirty, and I'll pick *you* up. I happen to know where you live." She pointed at her own face after hearing the words out loud. "Not a stalker."

Kate raised an eyebrow. "If you say so." She handed Autumn a five. "Keep the change, and pay attention to that foot today."

"Yes, Lieutenant."

It was a title she'd heard a million times, but it sounded different coming from Autumn's lips and sent her a surge of energy followed by a noticeable shiver. She didn't mind the shiver.

As she walked the short distance home, an alarm bell sounded. Wait. What the hell did she just do? Yes, Autumn was beautiful and had a firm grasp on her attention, but she should swallow the overt chemistry and save herself the inevitable headache. She should. Shouldn't she?

Kate was unavailable, plain and simple. Even to herself.

Yet she'd lost her head and gone and asked someone on a date? What was wrong with her? She closed her eyes and refocused on how to take back control.

Okay, okay. She could do this. So she was flying without a net and would need to resolve that quickly. Easy enough. She'd level with Autumn. Put it all out there and apologize if she'd been unclear. Didn't mean they couldn't spend a nice evening together and give her the distraction she sought. She needed to get out, and Autumn was about the only person who could capture her attention and distract her from the train wreck of memories holding her captive.

She needed tonight. She needed Autumn.

But in fairness, it was time to be honest about what she could, and could not, offer.

❖

Autumn knocked three times on the door of the downstairs unit Kate had rented but didn't have to wait long. Kate opened the door in low-slung dark jeans and a red sleeveless top that was form fitting and sleek and showcased a more dressed-up version of Kate that Autumn had yet to encounter. Wow. She took note of the small four-leaf clover on a silver chain around her neck. She'd seen it on Kate before. The necklace was simple, and beautiful.

"You look great," she said, trying for casual as she breezed past Kate into the apartment. It wasn't her first time inside the unit she and her friends had nicknamed the Love Boat, but it was the first time she'd been inside since Kate had taken residence. Those were Kate's books on the coffee table and her groceries in the fridge. Behind that bedroom door was where Kate slept. It was as if her presence had overtaken the place for Autumn, making her see it anew. "I see you've settled in."

Kate glanced around. "I have. Yeah. It's a nice apartment. Lucky to have found it." Autumn was acutely aware of Kate's gaze as it swept over her form, making her unusually self-conscious.

"What?"

Kate shook her head. "You're out of your work clothes." In fact, she was. She'd dashed from the shop early and had taken the round trip to her house in West Hollywood just so she could look nice for tonight. She'd selected a forest green sundress and paired it with a pair of flat, yet overly strappy, brown sandals. She loved the overly strappy part and the way the leather wound around her ankles.

"I can't show up in my apron. I have to keep you on your toes."

Kate smiled. "You don't have to work too hard for that. I promise." There was a shyness in the way she said it, which only perpetuated the intrigue. Kate was steady and sure when it came to her own flirtations with Autumn but seemed on her heels and, dare she say, nervous when it came to the effect Autumn might have on *her*. It was an unusual combination, but one Autumn didn't mind a bit. The give and take of the playing field felt wonderfully balanced, not to mention charged to the hilt.

"Where to tonight?" Kate asked, dipping her head and flashing those hazel eyes.

"Well, I was thinking. How do you feel about stars?" Autumn placed a hand on her hip.

Kate paused. "Celebrities? I'm not sure I know that many by name, but I hear LA is full of them."

"That part is true. But I'm talking about the celestial kind."

"Oh. Those I know a lot more about." Kate seemed to relax at the clarification.

"Perfect, then I know just the place you need to see. Follow me, Lieutenant Carpenter. I'll drive."

Half an hour later, they pulled into the parking lot of Griffith Observatory just as the sun snuck from the sky, leaving the horizon heathered in fading pinks and purples. The property was perched high on a slope of Mount Hollywood in the midst of scenic Griffith Park. The vantage point offered not only a striking glimpse of the sunset but breathtaking views of all of Los Angeles below. It really was an excellent spot to introduce Kate to her city and all its too-often-unrealized beauty.

"Oh, wow," Kate said, staring in awe at the surrounding landscape. From the perimeter of the property, LA twinkled below in preparation for the impending nightfall. They approached the railing and looked down, taking a moment to just absorb the vast landscape, the lush hillside, and the City of Angels below. "I don't know that I've ever seen a view like this one."

"Because there's nothing else like it." Autumn pointed across the mountain at the pièce de résistance. The air was hazy, but you could still make it out. "Look right through there. See it?"

Kate attempted to follow her gaze. "Not sure. What am I looking for?"

Autumn moved closer, placing her almost cheek to cheek with Kate as she directed her focus. "Right across the top of my hand, in the distance. Do you see it?"

Kate took a quick inhale. "Would you look at that? It's the Hollywood sign. In person!"

Autumn laughed quietly, their proximity unbroken. She enjoyed every minute of their crisp crackle of chemistry and the heat that moved from Kate's body to hers. "It's saying 'Hey, welcome to La-La Land.' "

Kate laughed and straightened, turning her body toward Autumn but not moving from her space. "That's amazing. I wondered if I'd catch a glimpse of it before my stay here ended."

"No choice. It's on the mandatory LA visitor list." Autumn drank in the gorgeous views all around her, the horizon, the art deco building capped off with stunning domes behind her, and her even more beautiful companion right next to her. She decided she liked her evening very much. She rested her forearms on the railing and looked out. "I used to come up here when I was a teenager and think about all of the amazing things I was going to do with my life regardless of what my mother said. Somewhere along the way, I stopped coming. Now I'm wondering why."

"Your mother was difficult?"

"Big-time. Still is. She qualifies life based on the two M's: men and money. Neither of which I found much interest in, leaving her horrified and letting me know it every day."

"That's awful."

Autumn shrugged. "There are worse things in the world than horrified mothers."

"I guess so. What about the rest? The hopes and dreams. How did they work out?" Kate asked. "Did you do all the things you planned for yourself?"

Autumn took a moment with the question as regret snaked up her spine. "I didn't, actually. I got caught up in the day-to-day grind, no pun intended, and a lot of those dreams fell by the wayside. It's depressing, honestly." She looked out over the expanse of her city and wondered about the future. Her future.

Kate nodded. "Yet."

She turned. "What do you mean?"

"Well." Kate leaned her back against the railing. "You didn't do all the things you planned *yet*. You're young, and your whole life is still ahead of you."

Autumn smiled at the lifeline. Kate, she was finding, had a kind heart. "Yet. I can get behind yet. Shall we go inside before you give me a heart attack with that railing?"

Kate glanced behind her. "Makes you nervous?"

Autumn sighed. "A lot of things about you make me nervous. But yes, the idea of you tumbling away from me to a dramatic death in the valley below? That would be one of them."

"And here you struck me as a risk taker," Kate said, straightening.

"Risk taker, thrill seeker, adrenaline junkie are all things I aspire to and sometimes claim to be. But if we're being honest, I play it pretty safe."

Kate met her gaze and held on. "Nothing wrong with that."

"Yeah, well, sometimes it's in one's best interest to cut loose. Walk on the wild side."

"Is that what we're doing tonight?" The overt hazel of Kate's eyes had Autumn warm. *Very* warm.

Autumn bit the inside of her cheek, enjoying the give and take. "I think that's a very good characterization."

"Me too."

"Shall we head in?" Autumn asked, already backing in the direction of the observatory.

Kate passed her a lazy grin that moved all the way through her. "Right behind you."

They roamed the interior of the observatory, and Autumn watched in captivation as Kate took in each of the exhibits with kid eyes. "This place is so cool," she whispered as they moved from room to room. Autumn was pretty sure the whisper indicated the reverence Kate felt for the space. She felt it, too. For the most part, the observatory was deserted, giving them space to explore all on their own. It also allowed Autumn to watch this new version of Kate: wide-eyed and happy, as she moved with interest from one exhibit to the next, pointing out interesting details to Autumn along the way.

"You're really into astronomy," Autumn said, after Kate detailed her infatuation with the Big Bang.

"I guess. It's been a thing since I was young. Not a lot of people know this, so keep it on the DL, but I won second place in the third-grade science fair with my Styrofoam model of the solar system."

"Wow. And you still agreed to come out with me tonight?"

"I would have won first, but I made Pluto way too big."

"And why wouldn't you? Pluto is a fan favorite."

Kate nodded and flipped her palms up in agreement. "It has the best name and the best vantage point to keep an eye on all the other planets. The others always felt untrustworthy to me."

"Without question. I've never trusted Mars. I mean, do you have rings, or don't you? Make up your mind."

Kate chuckled and they continued their perusal through the cavernous building, reading, investigating, stealing glimpses of each other while not being secretive about it in the slightest. It was a sexy game, and Autumn was finding she wasn't half bad at it.

They spent the most time in front of the large Foucault Pendulum, watching its continuous sway back and forth, always a constant. As the day progressed, the pendulum would take down pegs signaling the progress of the Earth's rotation beneath it. Kate shook her head. "No matter what we're doing, whatever thing is going on in our lives, this pendulum continues to swing."

"It's humbling when you think about it," Autumn said, her eyes glued to the pendulum. "A reminder that the world is so much bigger than what's right in front of us. Makes all of life's daily troubles seem a little less consuming."

Kate nodded, the glimmer in her eyes dimming. "Some of them."

Okay, Autumn had clearly touched on something there. As they walked to the Hall of Sky exhibit, she couldn't help herself. "Is that what brought you to LA? You needed to get away from some sort of problem? And if I'm overstepping, you can just tell me to shut the hell up. You wouldn't be the first person."

Kate slid her hands into the pockets of her jeans. "I would never tell you to shut up. But yeah, I guess you could say I hit a rough patch." Kate passed her a glance and then turned her attention to a replica of Saturn as she spoke, never meeting Autumn's eyes. For someone so astute at eye contact, it was telling. "There was a fire I worked not too long ago. Back home. It was pretty bad."

"I'm sorry," Autumn said, leaving it there. She understood that whatever Kate was going through might be beyond her ability to offer advice. She could be a friend, though. She was good at that. "It must be hard, having such a high-stakes job. The worst thing that could happen to me in a given day at work is I run out of milk. The horror."

Kate shook her head, turning to Autumn finally. "What you do matters, Autumn. Don't go selling yourself short."

The comment took root and spread comfortably. Kate seeing value in her job somehow counted for more than she would have predicted, and since when did she care so much about what people thought of her? Kate felt different, a fact that Autumn didn't seem to mind at all. "Thank you for saying that, but I'm not sure it really compares to saving lives. I mean, let's be forthright."

"It does compare. Don't say that. You make people's day better. I've experienced it."

Autumn studied Kate, who had that faraway look in her eye again. "So, this particular fire was a doozy, I'm guessing."

Kate nodded solemnly and swallowed. "Have you ever wished more than anything for a do-over? A day or an afternoon or even an instant that you could go back and handle differently?"

"I have a smart mouth, so yes, most definitely. Is that what you wish for with that fire?"

She nodded but said nothing. The haunted look of regret that slashed across Kate's features was entirely new, and it gut-punched Autumn. She wanted more than anything to pull Kate close and take away that look forever. It didn't quite seem appropriate, though. They barely knew each other, which was odd, because somehow it felt like they did.

"Hey," she said quietly and took a step in. "While I don't know the details, I'm confident that you did everything in your power that day. We can't control the awful things that happen in the world, Kate. We can try, but we'll never succeed. You're a hero for what you do."

Kate's gaze hardened, flicked to the wall, and held. "No. Don't say that. I'm not. I know you mean well, but you're going to have to trust me on this." Something rigid and unforgiving had overtaken Kate at the mention of the word "hero." Autumn took a metaphorical step back. This was sacred ground and she wasn't about to trudge her way across it, not when Kate was this raw.

"I'm sorry. I didn't mean to—"

"No, I am," Kate said. "We were having a great time and I got all serious on you."

"Hey, it's okay. I'm all ears if you ever want to talk about it. Doesn't have to be tonight."

Kate nodded and stared at the wall of stars. When she looked back again, the warmth had returned to her features. "Thank you. I'll remember that. For now, I think we should head to the planetarium."

"Oh, yeah? And why is that?"

Kate pointed at a rectangular sign on the wall. "Because there's a show starting in five minutes."

"Take me there," Autumn said, without hesitation.

Ten minutes later, nestled in their ultra-soft recliners, Autumn found herself quite literally starstruck as she gazed up at the darkened ceiling of the planetarium as stars and celestial bodies sparkled brightly, all underscored by a soothing female voice that helped them ponder their place in the vast, unseen universe. The story transported them from the Big Bang, to the Library of Alexandria, to Galileo's Courtyard, and beyond. The journey was bold, educational, and thought inspiring. Centering around humanity's place in the larger world, the presentation brought into sharp focus for Autumn that everything had its place and reason for being.

Even her.

She thought about her year, her sense that life was leaving her behind, and her impending plans to take control at last. She thought of the new little being she could potentially bring into the world, and her heart stuttered and filled. The two of them would be part of all of this, of the vast and mysterious universe. The understanding gave her goose bumps as she snuggled deeper into the recliner.

She turned her face against the leather and watched Kate, who stared up at the domed ceiling, captivated. Her eyelashes, Autumn noted, were exceptionally long and full. You didn't see eyelashes like those too often. Her mouth naturally turned down ever so slightly, almost as if it were upside down. Then there were her large, luminous hazel eyes that came with the power to undo a person when they focused on you for very long. Autumn was learning she very much enjoyed being undone by Kate.

They'd left the armrest between them in the upright position, which allowed the sides of their thighs to touch. Autumn blinked against the feeling of Kate's jeans pressed against the fabric of her dress. As she returned her attention to the stars, she caught Kate turning in her peripheral vision. Moments later, she still felt the stare as it caressed the side of her face. So, she wasn't the only one preoccupied by their proximity. She glanced down in time to see Kate's hand slide into hers where it rested on her leg. The purposeful gesture stirred something low in her stomach and she gave Kate's hand a squeeze, reassured by its grip. As the journey through space continued, the tips of Kate's fingertips inched inward, lightly brushing the inside of Autumn's thigh. The touch was so minor, it was hard to say whether Kate intended the potent effect it had on Autumn. But, oh, potent it certainly was. Her eyes fluttered. Her breathing shifted to shallow and her stomach knotted. Autumn ached for just a little bit more from that touch, and almost as if Kate could read her mind, she gave it to her, sliding her hand out of Autumn's altogether and resting it fully on the inside of her thigh, just beneath the hem of her dress. Autumn turned her head and met Kate's gaze, and saw her own desire mirrored right there in the dark depths.

"We should go soon," Autumn whispered purposefully, shifting into the touch.

Kate nodded, a small smile playing on her lips.

It was a fun dance, whatever was happening between them, and Autumn was determined to drink in every minute of it. She'd sat on the sidelines for far too long. To be in the thick of it now, making eyes at someone like Kate under a galaxy of stars, was perhaps the most excitement she'd had in years.

The drive down from Griffith Park was gorgeous. She took the winding path slowly so they could enjoy the night around them. The skies were clear and the temperature perfect—not too cold and not too warm. California had delivered big. They'd rolled the windows down and the soft breeze licked through the car as they drove. Autumn had never been more aware of the stars in her entire life than she was tonight. They seemed like friends now, and she smiled up at them with affection, anticipating just what might happen next.

Chapter Six

The night was young, and they both knew it.

Expectation hung in the air around them, though what exactly that meant, Autumn wasn't sure. Kate was exciting, and new, and kind, and sexy as hell—but she hadn't really thought past all that. In fact, that was half the fun, living by the seat of her pants, in the now.

Kate studied her as they approached the Seven Shores courtyard—empty, due to the late hour on a weekday. "We could head to my place, have a drink to close out the night." God, that was a good suggestion.

Autumn hesitated. "I will be happy to take you up on that offer, but do you mind if we make a quick stop at the coffee shop?"

Kate studied her curiously. Yes, it was odd to interrupt their date for work, but in the midst of the hustle to make it home and back to Kate's in time, she hadn't put in her grocery order, which, if she did not remedy soon, would leave her with no morning delivery.

"Lead the way."

"Perfect. I can be really fast. I never forget to do these kinds of things. It's just been an unexpected week."

"In more ways than one," Kate said, in agreement.

When they arrived at Pajamas, the shop was dark and still, having closed an hour and a half earlier. The aroma of coffee still lingered, however, which for Autumn was like a welcome hug.

"It's strange being here after hours," Kate said quietly, following Autumn inside. "It's like everything's asleep for the night."

"You're not afraid of the dark, are you?" Autumn walked backward toward the prep room.

"I'm definitely not afraid of the dark," she said, with very attractive confidence. The moonlight slanted across the glint in her eye.

"What are you afraid of?" Autumn asked quietly. "Anything?"

"I live in fear of losing at *Jeopardy*." It was a deadpan, and a good one.

"You're lying," Autumn said, not buying for a minute that Kate Carpenter spent any amount of quality time with Alex Trebek.

"I never lie, and I happen to be really great at *Jeopardy*. Try me sometime."

Autumn laughed at how serious Kate became at the challenge. Well, okay. *Jeopardy* was clearly important to her, which was endearing in its unexpectedness. "You're on. You're also unpredictable. I'm calling it now."

"You're calling it? Well, all right. Good." In one move, she grabbed Autumn by the wrist and pulled her in, right there in the center of her darkened shop.

Autumn let out a little gasp before finding Kate's darkened eyes. A moment later, she was kissed into next Tuesday. Scratch that. Wednesday. Sweet Lord, she'd needed this. Someone had just hit the switch that snoozed her brain and woke up her body, and they weren't messing around. Kate's arm slid around her waist, holding her close. The security of that touch was almost as decadent as the kiss itself. Not to undersell the hot-damn-inducing kiss. Kate's lips pressed to hers firmly at first before relaxing and exploring. Her mouth moved slowly over Autumn's, who pushed herself onto her tippy-toes to even out their height difference. She slid her hands up Kate's chest, enjoying that little journey, and wrapped them around her neck, bringing them chest to chest. The vantage point also allowed her to sink further into the depth of that kiss.

Kate ran her tongue along Autumn's lower lip, and she was a goner. She kissed Kate back with an urgency she'd not experienced in quite a while. A lie. Ever. She'd never been this turned on by or attracted to another person. She'd never kissed anyone blindly, passionately, in the middle of her darkened coffee shop. She loved who Kate turned her into, allowed her to be. Because this, right here, was like iced water to the thirsty.

She'd fantasized for a while now about sliding her hands into that thick hair, and the reality of that experience surpassed her every expectation. She eased her fingers through the soft strands, reveling in the payoff. She gripped and held on for dear life as Kate's tongue pushed into her mouth, sending her to Desire City on the express train. It took everything she had to keep her clothes on—and Kate's, for that matter. The only thing stopping her was the room, outfitted with so many uncovered windows and facing a popular public street. *Bollocks.*

She nodded against Kate's mouth. This was exactly the kind of escapade Autumn had been looking for. She moaned quietly, and the sound trickled through the dreamy haze to her brain like a flare. This was just a hookup, right? Her body lit up hot with arousal. Every part of it. But were they both on the same page?

They were, she assured herself, as her fingers delicately stroked the bare skin between Kate's shirt and jeans. They definitely were. She was so soft right here. This little patch of skin was everything. She wondered about the rest of Kate.

Alert!

But what if they *weren't* on the same page?

Damnit.

Her inner Jiminy Cricket wouldn't leave her the hell alone. She didn't want to lead Kate on, but she very much wanted what was happening between them to continue—and preferably as soon as possible.

"I should see about that grocery order," Autumn said, and took an abrupt step back like a record player scratching to a clumsy halt. What in the hell? She internally berated herself for ending the best few minutes of her past year as she led the way to the prep room through the double doors behind the counter. "Want to come?" she tossed out behind her, in attempt to salvage…well, anything.

"Right behind you," Kate said, with a soft, reassuring smile.

God, the things that smile could make her do. She was a saucy minx, if she did say so herself.

When they arrived in the prep room, Autumn turned the overhead lights on at half. Kate leaned casually against the stainless steel table on the wall across from her computer workstation. "You look really good leaning against a table," Autumn said. Hearing the words out loud had her cringing and wondering how she could suck them back in. "That was an awful line," she said, feeling the heat blossom on her cheeks. "Should not have said that out loud. I realize that now." Clearly, not the saucy minx she thought she was.

Kate, to her credit, was nice enough to look amused. "It wasn't awful at all. You're a forthright person. You say what you think." She glanced at the ground and back up, finding the word. "It's refreshing."

Autumn decided it was now or never. "I should maybe explain—"

"Before we get caught up—"

They laughed at the overlap. Autumn held up her palm, giving Kate the floor. "You first."

"I'm into you," Kate said simply. "But I'm only here for a short time. My life is back in Slumberton."

Autumn nodded, the words ushering in a sense of relief.

"Your turn."

"I'm trying to have a baby."

Kate's eyebrows leapt to her forehead. "Did not see that coming."

"Right? Maybe should have warmed up to that sentence, but it doesn't make it any less the case. This is probably not the best time to get involved with someone."

"No, I would imagine not." Kate took a minute, her gaze never leaving Autumn's. "So what I'm hearing is that we're two highly unavailable people, standing in a"—she glanced around—"a kitchen?"

"A kind of kitchen." Autumn smiled. "Close enough."

"Standing in a kind-of-kitchen, very much enjoying—"

"The hot-damn kissing." Autumn didn't even care how that one sounded. It was the only way to classify what they'd done.

"Yes. That." Kate exhaled slowly, her eyes roaming Autumn's body like some kind of sexy-stealthy panther.

The look that came over Kate in that moment curled Autumn's toes. Her heated stare licked its way from Autumn's eyes to the dip of cleavage in her dress and there was no denying her intentions.

"Kate."

"Yeah?"

"I think you should come back over here."

"And that grocery order you need to put in?"

"Right." Autumn all but smacked herself in her stupid head. Damn the groceries for killing the moment. "Right. No. Let me send that off real quick."

She turned to the PC mounted on the wall. She'd had it installed at height level, so she could quickly access orders and get back up front to her customers without a lag. "Just take me a second," she said, pulling up the site. "Oh," she said, closing her eyes at the feel of Kate's body, lightly pressing against hers from behind. Kate's hands on her waist. Kate's mouth on her neck. Suddenly, her knees didn't feel so strong and she gripped the counter for support. What were groceries again? Surely, no one needed them. Not badly enough. Kate slid down the strap of Autumn's sundress, revealing her bare shoulder. Her lips trailed down Autumn's neck, kissing her way to that shoulder and back again. "What are you doing to me?" Autumn breathed, her head a hazy fog, her body a tinderbox. Her grocery order abandoned for all time.

"Is this okay?" Kate asked between kisses. "I can stop if—"

"More," was all Autumn managed with an emphatic nod, still gripping the countertop. Was that clear enough? She could send a telegram. A skywriter, anything. She felt Kate's hands ease down her back to the hem of her dress. She slipped both hands under and skimmed upward. Autumn swallowed against the feel of those hands against her bare stomach. Every nerve ending shifted to high alert in the most wonderful way. Kate didn't mess around. These weren't light touches, but firm and confident. "Yes," she whispered, nodding against the fantastic sensations that thundered her way. "More." Those warm hands inched upward, drawing up the fabric of her dress with them. They met the undersides of her breasts and she exhaled.

"What do you put in your hair," Kate said, burying her face in Autumn's curls and inhaling. "Is that hibiscus?"

Autumn nodded as Kate's hands inched upward with agonizing slowness to her breasts. "Sure, hibiscus. Let's go with that." It wasn't as if her brain worked with Kate's fingertips now circling the outsides of her breasts, taking her time. She sucked in air as Kate cradled them fully. When she set to kneading them, Autumn whimpered as the little pinpricks of sensation darted across her skin and straight to her center. She leaned back against Kate, who easily supported her.

"You're so soft," Kate said in her ear, kissing the lobe. Autumn wasn't sure what it implied about her, that she felt powerless in this moment and liked it so damn much. She liked surrendering to Kate. This was her inner bad girl making an appearance, and why the hell not? She'd been good for far too long.

Kate's fingertips moved to Autumn's nipples and swirled around them before taking hold of them, turning, massaging. Autumn's hips moved of their own accord, pressing backward into Kate, needing that contact.

"Yeah?" Kate asked, pushing back. She was asking permission. Autumn could feel the warmth of her exhale across her temple. Autumn nodded, the unvoiced answer hopefully clear. If she had the words, she'd beg Kate to take her. Plead with her.

With one hand still cupping her breast, Kate's other snaked lower, dipping into the top of Autumn's underwear. Thank God she'd worn the sexy ones with the high-cut thigh line—just in case. She sucked in a breath and waited. Kate wasn't in any hurry, and that made this whole encounter, in the back of her store no less, all the more thrilling. She relished the languid throbbing of anticipation. "Kate," she said slowly, liking the way that name felt coming off her lips.

"Hold on," Kate said, by way of instruction. And she did,

looping an arm behind her, around Kate's neck for support. Moonlight slanted in from the window above the refrigerator as Kate touched her for the first time, causing her thighs to quiver and a moan to escape her lips. Her body liquefied and rocked against Kate's fingers that stroked her evenly. Methodic heaven. Her own heartbeat thundered in her ears and her eyes fluttered closed as she enjoyed the climb. Her grip tightened in the hair at the back of Kate's neck, and the moan it pulled from Kate threw gasoline on her already blazing four-alarm.

That long-forgotten excitement of feeling desirable and wanted was back like a lost friend. Kate pushed inside her and Autumn lost her breath. Her hips bucked back and their erotic dance found a speed much more satisfying to her end goal. The pressure built and built in intoxicating torture until she crashed magnificently into a blinding abyss of white-hot wonder, of pleasure, of inarguable ecstasy. Thank you, universe! She was on overload. The generous payout was just that good. When the wonderful sensations ebbed, receding bit by bit, Autumn fell slack against Kate, who held her tight and close. Relearning where her knees were, Autumn pushed herself into a wobbly but upright position, straightened her dress, turned, and lifted her gaze to Kate expectantly.

Only the look on Kate's face wasn't smug, or arrogant, or proud—all things she had the right to be—but gentle and kind as her gaze settled on Autumn's still-flushed face. The surprise had Autumn's unsuspecting heart squeezing in a manner she wasn't prepared for. That *kindness*.

"You're good at that," she heard herself say. It wasn't the most thoughtful sentence she'd ever uttered, but with her brain only recently restarted, it was all she had.

Kate's smile bloomed and she tucked a strand of hair behind Autumn's ear. "Yeah, well, you make it easy."

Autumn quirked a smile. "Did you just call me easy? I think I heard easy."

The soft grin slid from Kate's face. "No. I wouldn't ever—"

Autumn placed a finger on her lips. "I was kidding. You might have to get used to that if we're going to be friends."

"Oh. Okay then," Kate said, relaxing. "I can work on that."

Autumn took a long and very necessary breath, as she attempted to remember her original trajectory. Groceries. On the computer. For this week. Before her world had been rocked by a woman she didn't know a month ago. "I need to hit send on this grocery order, and then you're taking me to your place, because we're not done."

"I am?" Kate asked, but didn't wait for an answer. "I'm in favor."

"Oh, there will be favors," she said, quite seriously.

Kate shook her head. "You're good with words. And plays on words. I'm not."

"No. You're more of a quiet type." She took both of Kate's hands in hers and squeezed them. "Trust me when I say that you shine in a multitude of other ways that don't require words at all."

She watched as Kate, the firefighter who ran into burning buildings, blushed. The world was perpetually interesting.

Ten minutes later, and post grocery order, Kate let them into her apartment. The space was quiet and still, and Kate set to flipping on lights. The crackle of energy between them had yet to settle, and Autumn wondered if it ever would.

"All aboard," Autumn murmured, as she took in the overly embraced nautical theme that Larry was so insistent would appeal to vacationers.

Kate moved behind the kitchen counter and placed both hands flat on the surface. "What can I get you?"

"Are you playing bartender? I like it."

Kate shrugged. "You always get my drinks for me. Probably my turn."

"Well, yeah, but you pay me to do that."

"Good point. What can I get you for some hard cash?"

Autumn laughed. "Do you have wine?"

Kate disappeared to a lower level cabinet and appeared with a bottle. "The red kind."

"The red kind? You're not a wine drinker, are you?" Autumn proclaimed and accepted the bottle handed across the counter.

"No, but I'm trying a few new things while I'm here. Thought I'd give wine a shot."

Autumn nodded sagely. "Ah, testing the grape-infused waters." She turned the bottle around so it faced Kate. "This is a Malbec from Argentina. A bigger red, which I happen to love."

"Then I'll pour us each a glass."

"Thank you, bartender." Autumn smiled and realized that her legs still wobbled wonderfully. A hearty endorsement.

As the deep red liquid cascaded into the glass in front of her, she saw this as an opportunity to learn more about Kate. In fact, she was overcome with the urge to know everything about this mysterious woman who had waltzed in and brought Autumn's mundane existence to a whole new level of stimulating, and not just metaphorically.

She raised her glass. "Thank you for this. Now tell me about your family."

Kate seemed surprised by the question. "Really? Okay, let's see…" She came around the counter with her glass of wine and took a seat in the armchair, tossing the pillow with the embroidered seagull onto the floor. She stared up at Autumn, who leaned against the counter. "My parents married really young. Eighteen. Had my brother, Randy, a year later and me two years after that."

"Wow, sounds like they were a couple of kids in love."

Kate smiled. "Big-time. They worked incredibly hard for what we had, which was never that much. My mom was a fantastic chef at the retirement home in town, cooking for the seniors, who adored her. Called her 'Sweet 'Ums' as a nickname because she was exactly that."

"What was your favorite dish of hers?"

Kate got a faraway look in her eye, as if she'd been transported to a happier time. "Without a doubt, her spaghetti and meatballs. She always winked and gave me an extra meatball. I didn't tell Randy."

Autumn smiled. "I like her already. And they still live in Slumberton?"

"She died when I was seventeen, of ovarian cancer."

Autumn's lips parted in surprise, but Kate didn't slow down.

"My father owned his own locksmith company and was everyone's best pal. It probably helped that he practically gave his services away. He was loud and fun, the life of most parties. The best storyteller you'll ever meet, hands down. He was killed when he ran his truck into a tree coming home late one night from the bar. He was never really the same after we lost my mom. Drank a lot to mask the pain he was too tough to acknowledge."

Autumn struggled to come up with the right words, when in fact, there were none. "I'm so sorry, Kate. You lost them both. Doesn't seem fair."

"It's okay. You rebound over time. Feels strange talking about them, though. I haven't in…years."

"Then I consider it an honor. And Randy?"

"Still lives in Slumberton with his wife, Tessa. He's a good guy. We look out for each other, check in every couple of days. He owns a bookstore. Was always the academic in the family."

Autumn headed to the couch, where she'd be closer to Kate. "Is it odd that I haven't heard of your town?"

"Nope." Kate shook her head. "Would be odd if you had. About eleven hours north of here, just across the Oregon border. Unsuspecting, quiet little place."

"Which explains why you don't talk a whole lot."

"True." Kate smiled at the thought. "I talk to you. That's rare for me. Not sure you realize."

"You do. I'm lucky. And if you think about it, that's twice for me tonight." She pointed at Kate and grinned, proud of her own cheeky reference.

Kate studied her. "You're a firecracker, you know that? That's the word that comes to mind when I think about you."

"A firecracker, huh? Explain."

Kate shook her head as if not sure quite how, until the explanation seemed to occur to her. "Well, you're always full of energy, fire. Plus, there's the hair."

"The hair?" Autumn smiled. "Aha, a redhead reference. Okay. All right. I'll take firecracker and raise you a brooding hottie."

Kate pulled her chin back. "I can't believe you just called me a hottie. You can't do that."

"Well, I did."

She raised a finger and sat forward in her chair. "And I do not brood."

"But you do."

Kate's eyebrows scrunched. "Well, then I need to stop that immediately."

"Oh, please, don't," Autumn said, dipping her head and catching Kate's gaze. "The brooding is good. *Really* good."

Kate held Autumn's gaze and nodded, her eyes darkening. "Do you know what else was good?"

"Tell me."

"The shop earlier."

Autumn felt her temperature climb at just the vague mention of what they'd done in her storage room. "The night is young, you know. I could leave if that's what you prefer, or…"

Kate's cheeks dusted with a formidable blush and it was enough of an invitation for Autumn, who was aiming to even out the score. She placed her glass on the coffee table and crossed the short distance to Kate, where she climbed easily onto her lap. "Hi," she said quietly, looking down at her. She traced the line of Kate's collarbone as Kate watched with rapt interest.

"Hey."

With a hand behind Kate's head, Autumn sank into a heady kiss that left her out of breath and making plans. Kate's hands slid up the fabric of Autumn's sundress to her thighs, which had her arching her back and pushing against Kate. But this was so not about her right now…

"You know," she said in exaggerated enthusiasm as she stood, "I've not seen your room yet, and I'm known for being a curious person. Show me?"

Kate took a final sip of her wine, and her eyes noticeably danced. "Through here," she said, and led the way to the bedroom down a short, darkened hallway. She flipped on the light when they entered, and Autumn took in the medium-sized bedroom. There was a queen-sized bed jutting out from the wall with a painting of an exotic-looking mermaid hanging above.

"Friend of yours?" Autumn asked, as she placed her arms around Kate's waist from behind. Kate turned in them.

"We've only just recently met."

"Good. Then you won't mind if I..." She hit the lights, leaving them in darkness with only the sound of their quiet breathing. With a gentle hand to the front of Kate's shoulder, she walked her backward toward the bed. "There are things. That I want to do to you."

With the back of Kate's knee against the bed frame, Autumn had her where she wanted her. "You think we can take this off?" she asked, giving Kate's shirt a tug. Kate obliged, unbuttoning her shirt as Autumn watched. The bra underneath was black, illuminated faintly by the light from the hallway, and held back the breasts Autumn had only glimpsed the tops of on the beach the day she'd turned her ankle. She swallowed. Good things came to those who waited.

"What about these?" Autumn asked, unbuttoning Kate's jeans and taking the zipper down slowly. She watched as Kate took them off the rest of the way, revealing black hip-huggers beneath. "You like black." Autumn slipped her arms around Kate's waist and felt her way down her bare back until she cupped her ass, which was, quite frankly, the best ass she'd ever had her hands on. Toned. Athletic. Awesome.

"I like black," Kate repeated, seemingly in a haze. She captured Autumn's lips in an open-mouthed kiss. While Autumn had imminent plans, she could also kiss Kate all night long. Resisting that temptation, she pulled her mouth away and pushed Kate softly on the bed. With measured speed, she pulled her dress over her head, discarding it on the floor.

Kate's eyes were on her, and the least she could do was put on a show. She took her time unclasping her bra. When she finally let it fall, Kate's lips parted. The cool air danced across Autumn's skin, her stomach, her breasts, and she enjoyed it, knowing that in moments, there would be nothing cool about her temperature. She slid her thigh-high bikinis down her legs with measured ease and watched as Kate blinked and sucked in air. That stare made her wet. She climbed onto the bed and straddled Kate, sitting atop her naked and rocking ever so slowly. Kate's hands were on her, moving up her thighs, her back, down to her breasts. She closed her eyes and murmured, "Wow."

"No, no," Autumn said quietly. "I need to see you if you're going to touch me." Kate's hand slid between Autumn's legs, but her eyes obeyed, opening and meeting Autumn's gaze. She'd never seen such intensity behind Kate's eyes, and her arousal skyrocketed all over again. Refusing to forget the mission, she dipped her head and kissed the tops of those breasts, until she couldn't wait any longer and freed them entirely, making quick work of Kate's bra and tossing it onto the floor.

"Fuck," Kate breathed, as Autumn licked and sucked each nipple. Through Kate's little gasps, Autumn found great motivation, though she remained keenly aware of Kate's hand between her legs and what it was doing to her as she worked. Her eyes fluttered at the ever-increasing buildup and she wondered if she'd beat Kate to the finish line.

No way in hell.

She upped her game and concentrated solely on the beautiful woman beneath her. Kate's breasts fit perfectly in her hands, and Autumn closed her eyes at the rush that came from touching her this way. She wanted to touch more of her and dropped her hand down Kate's stomach, beneath the waistband of her hip-huggers into fantastic warmth. It wasn't enough. She eased herself down the bed, forcing Kate to release her, and removed the last stitch of clothing from Kate's body. She parted her legs and happily went to work with her mouth until Kate squirmed quietly beneath her detailed attention. She gave and gave, taking Kate to the brink with her tongue and then pulling back, enjoying the give and take, the sounds she elicited. It felt good to take control. In desperation, Kate clung to the headboard and circled her hips against Autumn's mouth in search of release. Autumn was ready to give it to her. She pushed inside and pulled Kate into her mouth all at once, holding nothing back. When Kate's body bucked and shuddered, Autumn raised her gaze to enjoy the beautiful show. Kate's brows were creased and she turned her cheek against the pillow one way and then the other, with a few quiet cries escaping her lips. Autumn crawled up the bed beside Kate, trading her hand for her mouth and easing Kate back from the heights she'd just taken her to with soft, intimate touches.

"I'm wrecked," Kate managed, grasping Autumn's wrist, yet still moving beneath her touch.

"Really? Because I could keep going. I have nowhere to be."

Kate smiled and shook her head. "Can't take any more."

"Well, okay," Autumn said, withdrawing the attention. She tucked a strand of hair behind Kate's ear, loving that she had the power to take Kate to those heights. She didn't have long to pride herself, however, as with one unexpected stroke from Kate, her body, primed and ready, sent her over the edge into her own blissful oblivion.

Autumn wasn't as quiet as she clutched Kate and held on for the ride.

Distantly, she heard Kate chuckle and murmur one word: firecracker. She couldn't help but smile at its use herself. With Kate, everything felt fun, easy, and unencumbered. While there might not be nights like this for them in the future, she would hold on to the heated memory of the things they'd done to each other, and how much she'd enjoyed it.

"You don't have to go," Kate said, fifteen minutes later when Autumn began gathering her clothing from various spots on the floor. She was being nice again.

"I think it's probably for the best, don't you?" Autumn asked.

Kate paused, biting her lower lip. Not helping. "Yeah, I guess you're right."

Once she'd put herself back together again, Autumn returned to Kate's bed and sat on the edge. Kate turned on the bedside lamp and sat up with the sheet wrapped around her from the chest down. For the first time since they'd met, she looked surprisingly youthful with her features relaxed. Her eyes were bright, and her smile came with a whole new quality, one Autumn could only describe as genuine. Kate seemed *happy*, and it made Autumn's heart flex.

"Thank you for tonight," Autumn said and touched her cheek. "I had a lot of fun at the observatory…and after. After probably wins, though."

"Me too," Kate said. "I saw stars during both."

She laughed. "Just so you know, any other time in my life, you would be in some trouble."

"And so would you."

Autumn smiled, and a sadness moved to the center of her chest. "You're a good one, Kate Carpenter." She gave Kate's chin a little shake in place of anything more intimate. The window to their stolen evening was closing, and Autumn took a proverbial step back. "Come by the shop tomorrow."

"No choice. You've got me hooked on that Americano thing."

"Then victory is mine." She pointed at Kate and stood. "Do me a favor and stay here so I can remember you just like this. I'll let myself out."

Kate nodded. "Good night, Autumn. You're a good one, too."

Autumn looked back at her, naked beneath that sheet, and memorized the image, forever and always.

When she arrived home in the wee hours of the morning, she didn't go right to bed. She took a seat at the kitchen table and sorted her mail, too aflutter from that night to settle in. Yes, she had to be up in three and a half hours, and for convenience, maybe should have just stayed with Kate, mere feet from her store. But in doing so, she might have confused the message, the one they'd decided on together. Kate would head back to Oregon at some point soon. Plus, Autumn had a lot on her plate already, and for the first time in a long while, she was happy with her plate. Excited to embark on this journey to parenthood and the whole new life ahead of her. The most logical course of action would be to make whatever existed between her and Kate as simple as possible.

They'd had their fun, and now they'd wisely shelve it.

As a bonus, she'd still get to see Kate's beautiful face in her shop for a little while longer. Maybe they'd even flirt here and there. She smiled. Tonight had been just what she'd needed. As she sat at her kitchen table, she felt confident and in control of her own life for the first time in far too long.

And maybe a little naughty, too. She gave her shoulders a tiny shake and touched the grin on her lips. A little late night sexcapade never hurt anyone. This night was most definitely going in the books.

Chapter Seven

"Hi, Jennifer. It's Lieutenant Carpenter again. I was just calling to, uh, check on the Higgins kids. See if there was any update to their status." She'd called the Human Services case worker at least twice a week, and the woman, barely twenty-three and green as hell, had been good about keeping her in the loop, probably bending the rules because of Kate's connection to the accident and job affiliation.

"Good news!" Jennifer said. She heard the shuffling of papers through the call. "We have a lead on a temporary placement for Ren, and we're working to see if they'll take Eva, too."

"Wait. You wouldn't separate them, though, right? If the people say no to Eva? After all they've been through, those guys need each other." There was a pause on the line, and Kate paced the length of her living room as her blood pressure rose. These kids needed a break. Separating them now would be the worst thing possible. She pinched the bridge of her nose and waited for a response.

"That would be ideal, of course," Jennifer said. "But the system isn't always that easy. Through my sessions with Ren, I've learned that the kids haven't seen their mother in three years, but that means she's out there somewhere. We're doing what we can to track her down and see what her status is."

"Well, that's something. Maybe she doesn't know about any of this, and who knows how that man treated her when she was around?" She ran her fingers through her hair. "We need to find her."

"We're working on that."

Kate nodded. "And Eva, how is her recovery progressing?"

Another pause. "Well, she's made progress but still has moments of setback. The burns to her lower leg have been slower to heal, which has made her uncomfortable." Kate closed her eyes, knowing the caliber of pain that accompanied those kinds of burns. The fire hadn't disfigured Eva outright, but she would carry scars on her left side extremities.

"Will you tell her I'm thinking about her. Ren, too. And, Jennifer?"

"Lieutenant?"

"Do everything you can to keep those kids together in the meantime."

"Working on that, too," she said.

After hanging up, Kate felt the ever-present cloud overhead and knew that it would stay there the rest of the day unless she got herself up and out of the apartment and not thinking about the Higgins family. She'd slept in after the amazing night with Autumn, woken up alone, and wandered about the apartment for hours until she'd gathered the resolve to call Jennifer and find out what she needed to know.

Forcing herself into self-preservation mode, she hopped in the shower and let the hot water detangle the stress from her limbs. She smiled. This wasn't the first time that day she'd been aware of her body. Waking up after the things Autumn had done to her, she'd stretched languidly and smiled at her mildly sore limbs and sated libido. Everything still tingled nicely. She hadn't had sex in, God, six months now, and Autumn had offered much more than a welcome back. In fact, she was so many things, that Kate didn't know where to begin. Funny, quick, and kind, and pretty. So pretty. Maybe the prettiest woman she'd ever seen, like some sort of movie star without the star part. She was just Autumn, which was the highest form of compliment Kate could come up with.

It was early evening by the time Kate finally emerged from the apartment.

"*Ms. Pac-Man* tournament," Gia said, as she jogged across the courtyard to Isabel's door.

Kate passed her a questioning look, because what?

"Don't just stand there. Follow me."

Perhaps it was the urgent tone in Gia's voice or the inarguable order she'd dealt, but Kate found herself trotting behind Gia like a soldier into battle, a battle she was wildly unprepared for but curious about all the same.

"Take that, you little ghost bastards," Isabel said, from her spot on the floor of her apartment. Her Ms. Pac-Man flew around the screen gobbling pellets like a piglet in a feed yard. Ms. Pac-Man, Kate noticed, changed direction frequently, and part of Isabel's process seemed to be flailing herself around on the floor right along with her. She leaned drastically when Ms. Pac-Man turned in one direction and then leaned drastically the other when Ms. Pac-Man reversed, all the while hurling filthy insults at the ghost-looking-things that chased her. Kate took a seat on the couch, captivated by it all. She'd never seen anything like it.

To Isabel's credit, it seemed to be working.

"Fuckers better get out of the way," Isabel bit out, dodging a blue ghost. "I will fuck you up, and everyone you've ever met."

Kate shook her head and looked over at Gia. "She takes this seriously."

"Well, yeah," Gia said, as if it were the most vital of missions. She pointed at what seemed to be a score sheet displayed on the refrigerator. "Iz holds the Seven Shores record as of now, but trust me, it's temporary."

"Is not, Malone," Isabel said, her eyes not leaving the screen.

Gia nodded. "It ends today."

"As in, you probably stayed up all night dreaming it would."

"As in, I was dreaming of your mom," Gia said easily and smiled.

Isabel gasped. "My mother is dead."

Kate's eyes widened until she realized that no offense had been taken. This is what these two did. "Okay, so what I'm picking up is that you two move that retro little Pac-Man with a bow around the screen and trash-talk each other."

Isabel paused the game. She turned slowly to Kate, just as Gia did the same. They stared at her solemnly as if that comment, over all the others uttered in the past few minutes, was the one that had gone too far. "There's so much more to it than that, Kate," Isabel said, with focused intensity. "It's a good thing you're here."

Gia nodded seriously. "We'll help you."

The door to the apartment opened and Autumn entered, still wearing her apron. She looked tired in the cutest sense, and Kate enjoyed the fact that she alone knew the intimate reason why. Her gaze landed quickly on Kate, who she offered a small smile, before taking in the larger room.

"You called me over for this?" she asked, incredulous, and pointed at the screen. "This *Pac-Man* woman again? I thought something important was going on."

"I called you over because you needed a break," Gia told her. "And something important *is* going on. Kate is going to learn the glory of the game."

"Oh, well, why didn't you say so?" She took a seat down the couch across from Kate. "I did need a break. And can I say that people are grouchier than normal today? Not a lot of pleases or thank-yous happening. One guy knocked over his large latte, hurling coffee all over three different tables and the clothing of two customers, and didn't say so much as an I'm sorry before walking out of the shop. Who does that? Can we call his parents?"

"Did you have to clean it all up?" Kate asked.

"I put my new hire, Simon, on it."

"You have a new hire?" Isabel sounded so excited by the prospect you'd think Autumn had announced she would be hosting a million-dollar *Ms. Pac-Man* tournament. "I adore your new hires. What's this one like?" she asked, and leaned as close as one could get to the ground without actually touching it. Curious, Kate tilted her head sideways to try and experience it.

"He doesn't really speak. He will, to customers, but not to me or any of my other employees. It's a quirk, and I'm trying not to take it personally."

Gia studied her. "A selectively mute employee could make for good stories."

"Well, gear up then, because Simon-the-Nodder is now a part of our lives," Autumn deadpanned.

"How's he feel about cotton, though? That's the real question."

"You know, he doesn't say." They stared at each other before busting up, fist bump required.

"Son of a bitch on a Triscuit!" Isabel shouted.

"That's not a phrase," Autumn said.

"Nope," Gia replied. "But I see your Ms. Pac-Man just died like a little bitch. Kate's up, and then I take you to school."

"Oh. I don't know that I'm up for it," Kate said. "Zero experience with video games."

"Then this will be all the more fun for us," Isabel said, with a twinkle in her eye. She handed Kate the controller, and Kate reluctantly took Isabel's spot on the floor.

"I'm not doing those crazy moves," Kate forewarned them. In her peripheral vision, she saw Autumn smother a smile with her hand.

"No moves required," Gia said. "Everyone has their own form. Do you."

And then the game was on. She moved the little Ms. Pac-thing around with the controller, doing her best to dodge the ghosts who swarmed her like kids on Santa Claus. "Back the fuck off," she heard herself say under her breath, followed by chuckles from the peanut gallery behind her. "What is this red one's problem, anyway?" she asked, as she reversed directions, stealing a few of Isabel's dramatic moves without even meaning to. The tension crept up her neck and her face felt hot. She had no idea why she was so quickly competitive, but she so was. She needed to evade those ghosts and badly.

"You're good at this," she heard Autumn say in wonder.

Kate threw her body to the right. "Are you kidding? I am not. They're all over me."

Gia pointed at the screen. "Yeah, but you're almost done with the first level and still have all your lives."

"She's a prodigy," Isabel whispered reverently.

Kate continued playing, losing her lives slowly but surely,

ending up nearly completing level three. Apparently, she'd done well for her first time, and she hated to say it, but the game was *fun*. "I see why you guys enjoy this. It's…freeing."

"That's exactly what it is," Gia said, and took the controller. As she flew through one level after another, they all watched in awe.

"Why are you off so early today?" Autumn asked Isabel. "How are we supposed to watch fantastic television if you're not there to write it?"

"You're in luck because I happened to have stayed up all night finishing the first draft of a big episode. Turned it in this morning just after three a.m. and knocked off early since my brain was beyond fried."

"I can only imagine," Autumn said and winced. "Hope you had coffee."

"Yes, Caffeine-Yoda, I did. You've trained me well." Isabel paused. "Interesting occurrence, though. In the wee hours of the morning, when I was tucking my draft in for the night, I heard footsteps walking through the courtyard. So *odd*," Isabel said, her expression dialed to concern, "that someone—who looked so much like you, by the way—passed below my window and headed to the parking lot." Isabel's knowing gaze moved from Autumn to Kate and back again.

"I have a twin? Get outta town!" Autumn exclaimed.

Kate rolled her lips so the smile didn't show.

"This is fantastic news. I'll call my mom and notify her."

"Mm-hmm," Isabel said suspiciously. "I have your number, Primm."

"And I have yours. I'll call you after my parents." With that, Autumn stood. "Break is over. Must make sure Simon-the-Nodder hasn't nodded the business straight into the rack and ruin."

"I'll walk you out." Kate stood.

"Shocking," Isabel said, good-naturedly. "Isn't that shocking, G?"

"What's that?" Gia asked, lost in a haze of *Ms. Pac-Man*.

"I'll tell you later as you self-destruct."

Kate laughed and pulled the front door closed behind them,

leaving Isabel and Gia to their trash-talking tournament. She and Autumn walked a few steps in silence, before Autumn turned to her, shielding the sun from her eyes. "You didn't stop by the shop this morning. Is it because it's weird now? Please feel free to say so if it is."

"No. It's not weird now." Kate dipped her head. "It's the opposite of weird with you, which is nice."

Autumn smiled. "I can accept the opposite of weird. Isabel would say it can go on my business card next to 'Coffee Bitch.'"

"Killer combo." Kate lost herself for a moment in the little flecks of gold the sunlight accented in Autumn's green eyes. The same eyes that had darkened in the most memorable way when she touched Kate the night before. She rolled her shoulders to move herself beyond the shiver-inspiring flashback. If Autumn's eyes were amazing, her hands and mouth were heaven-sent.

"Where did you go just now?" Autumn asked, her voice soft.

"I was thinking about last night."

Autumn shook her head. "You're dangerous, Kate Carpenter." She headed off across the courtyard, then turned back moments later, as if she just had to say more. "Most people would have made up a lie right then, you know. Said they forgot to buy milk or something."

"I told you. I always tell the truth, and you asked me a question."

Autumn paused. "That I did." Her eyes danced. "What am I gonna do with you?"

"Free coffee for a year?"

Autumn raised an eyebrow. "You're getting quicker with the comebacks. This place is rubbing off on you."

"Foot soldier in training."

"A sexy foot soldier. See ya later, Lieutenant. Avoid those daydreams. I'm off the market."

Kate smiled and watched her go. The dark cloud had been lifted, at least temporarily, and she knew exactly who was responsible.

❖

Three days later, the waiting room of Dr. Arocha's office was outfitted with precisely four straight couples and one lesbian couple, all perfectly paired and waiting to see the doctor…together. As happy little units. Autumn had known from moment one that if she were going to have this baby, she would be doing it on her own. While it wasn't what she'd imagined for herself growing up, it was her reality, and she was okay with it. Still, she noticed when the woman across from her squeezed the hand of the man she was with, and when the lesbian couple exchanged the sweetest of smiles. "It's going to be fine," another man said quietly to his nervous wife. She smiled at them all. They seemed like nice people. They just made her wildly aware of her "party of one" status.

"So, I've made a decision," she told Dr. Arocha, once she'd been called back to his office. As lead doctor at the Holly Grove Reproductive Clinic, he had a massive office, complete with very expensive-looking furniture, which they now sat on together, as if old friends on a pair of couches catching up.

"Tell me where you're at," he said warmly. They'd met briefly a week prior, and he'd sent her home with some information to peruse about the process and encouraged her to examine every step to be sure she was ready.

"I did what you said after our first consultation, and I want to move forward. Alone."

He clapped his hands once, thrilled with the answer. "Excellent. Then let's get started right away. We'll put together a calendar and get you started on medication to prep your body."

"That quickly. We can just…"

"We can," he said with a smile.

"Oh. Okay. Then yes, let's get started right away. Did you hear the part where I said I was doing this alone? With no one else? Because I am."

"Wouldn't be the first," he said, as if it were the most casual thing in the world.

"No, I mean, I know that. But in the waiting room, all the couples. Happy. Smiling. I just wanted to make sure you know that it's just going to be me, and only me, at these appointments, and that

I am okay with that. Totally fine." She beamed at him for credibility. He would surely see how happy she was! Just look! Autumn wasn't sure why she needed her doctor to understand, but maybe she didn't want him feeling sorry for her at any point, or thinking that she wasn't as thrilled to be embarking upon this journey as those couples out in the waiting room, because, God, she wanted this baby more than anything, and her doctor should know that.

"If anything," he said gently, "you should be proud of your decision. You know what you want for yourself and you're taking action."

"Right. That's true," she said, soaking up the encouraging words and their salving effect on her psyche. "I think I needed to hear that, because I will be alone. Just so you know."

"I think you mentioned that once or twice." He smiled and moved to his desk, where he brought up her file on his computer. Impressively, the large screen on the wall lit up, mirroring his monitor and allowing her to follow along. "You're thirty-four, so it's good that we're doing this now."

She nodded, understanding that was code for "decrepit." Right on cue, a graph of a woman's declining fertility came on the screen, and she watched the bar chart dwindle with each age notation. "Okay, that's depressing," she said, studying the chart and realizing that in just a year, she'd fall off the medium-sized bar to the short one.

"Don't think of it that way," Dr. Arocha said. "It's science, and we're ahead of it."

She shook it off. "Okay, so what's next?"

"We drew blood today, and as soon as those results are back, we'll have a better idea of your egg reserve. Next, we'll schedule an ultrasound to make sure everything looks okay. Have you looked at donors?"

Oh, God. No, she hadn't. How surreal was it that she'd be picking a guy off a website to father a child? And what if she picked the wrong one? Behind door number one was a happy, well-adjusted child, and behind door number two could be a miniature Jeffrey

Dahmer. How was she supposed to differentiate? Gah! "Not yet. No."

"Take your time, and let Steph, our coordinator, know if you have questions about that part of the process."

She smiled and sighed. The donor search was on. It was now or never.

At work that afternoon, Autumn's mind had apparently taken a leave of absence without notifying her. She'd forgotten the regular order of one of her newer customers, an order she'd committed to memory and nailed the last two times the woman had come in. Today, she had to ask, which was cringe-worthy for the pride she took in offering a personal touch. Later, she'd forgotten to start the afternoon roast and had trouble making correct change from the register. When the perfect foam flower she'd nailed hundreds of times wouldn't materialize in the way she wanted it to, she just about quit life. While she wanted to ask herself what the hell was going on, she knew exactly what it was. The doctor's visit had her preoccupied and nervous.

"Something's on your mind," Kate said, an hour later as she paid for her Americano.

"Is it that obvious?" Autumn tossed in a biscotti, simply because it was nice to see Kate's face. It centered her, brought her back down from the crazy clouds of worry. Kate had her hair down today, parted on the side. She looked pretty. Autumn wanted to tell her so but held back.

"Maybe not obvious to the larger world. Is to me. I'm happy to listen if it would help. I'm good at it."

Autumn chewed the inside of her cheek. "I don't know that you want to hear all about it."

Kate seemed to backpedal. "No pressure. If you change your mind, you can find me over there." She held up her copy of *The Rainmaker* by John Grisham and headed off to what Autumn was beginning to think of as Kate's table. A few more customers came through, and Autumn struggled to focus on their orders, asking one man to repeat his again…twice. Embarrassing and well below her standard of doing business. She shook her head in exasperation and decided to throw in the proverbial towel.

"Steve, I'm gonna take ten for everyone's benefit."

"We got it," he said, and indicated Simon, who nodded his agreement. The concerned look Steve passed her meant he knew she was off her game.

"I went to the doctor earlier," Autumn said to Kate, without so much as warm-up conversation. Nope. Autumn jumped right in, flopping into the chair next to Kate. "It messed with my head, and I can't get back on track no matter how hard I try."

Kate closed the book. "How come?"

"This might be too much information."

"Try me." Kate leaned forward and offered a soft smile. When Autumn concentrated on that smile, everything else fell away, and seemed easier. Why was that?

"I'm supposed to pick a donor. A sperm donor." She lowered her voice for that second part.

"And you don't want to?" Kate asked, her eyebrows drawn up into a knitted bow as she clearly tried to piece together what the hell Autumn's problem was.

"I don't know how. This is a big deal."

"It is."

"This decision will determine the rest of my life, and I don't know what to look for, how to organize my thoughts on the subject, the criteria for…genetic selection. It's all beyond me."

"Oh." Kate sat back in her chair as if it were no big deal. "First of all, I think you cut yourself some slack, because this is not something most people go through. You're allowed to be off-kilter about this."

"You think so? Good, that's a valid point." She ran her hand through her curls and absently hoped she didn't have crazy hair to match her frazzled disposition. "Do I have crazy hair?"

Kate laughed through the sip of coffee she took. "No idea what that means. No?"

"Sorry. I got distracted." She made a gesture as if to wave

it away. "Back to donors, which I shouldn't beat myself up for stressing over."

Kate tilted her head in thought. "I think if it were me, I would look for someone I'd want to be friends with."

"Huh," Autumn said, sitting back in her chair and letting that comment wash over her. "Friends."

"Ignore me if I'm wrong on this, but seems like so many people get caught up in good looks when, at the end of the day, no one wants to hang out with a fantastic-looking asshole."

"Good point." Autumn nodded. "Fantastic-looking assholes are awful. So maybe I'm looking for someone I really seem to like and should worry less about the genetic matchup."

Kate smiled and held Autumn's gaze. "I think it's a great starting point."

Autumn pulled in a breath and let it out slowly, feeling infinitely lighter now that she had a direction to move in. Coming over to talk to Kate had been a great idea, and now she could breathe again. "You're good at this. Unsuspectingly so."

Kate took a sip of coffee. "Nah. I just wing it."

"Show-off." She winked at Kate and went back to work feeling more like herself, and this time, easily found her groove. Didn't mean she didn't steal little glimpses of Kate reading her book. Autumn loved the look she got on her face when she was lost in concentration, far away with a touch of concern tossed in—which said she cared about the journey. Sometimes she bit her lower lip when she turned the page or shook her head, almost imperceptibly, as if she just couldn't believe what she was reading. Honestly, she could watch Kate read a book for hours. It was a shame she actually had a job to do. When Kate waved to her on the way out, she felt the loss immediately. The day shifted to boring, drained of excitement and color. A shame.

"So, I have to pick a donor," Autumn said. She'd strolled into the courtyard shortly after closing the next day to find Hadley on the outdoor couch, lying flat on her back, still in her upscale work clothes. She looked impeccable and exhausted.

Hadley's head popped up like a dog at the word "treat." Her blond hair was pulled into a loose twist, and her eyes went wide. "A donor? Does that mean what I think it means?"

Autumn pulled the laptop from behind her back. "It does. I'm nervous about this part, but I feel like it's a now-or-never scenario, so I should shut up and put out. Not like sex, though."

"Are you asking me for help?" Hadley asked, pushing herself into a sitting position, her hand over her heart as if touched beyond measure of God.

"I think we can both admit that I've never been good at doing that."

"Nope. You suck at it, so let's skip right over that part. I'm declaring myself officially a helper." She nodded toward the laptop. "Open that thing and let's look around. Hurry!"

"Okay. Take it easy," Autumn said, feeling bolstered by the support. She took a seat next to Hadley on the couch, and with Had peering eagerly over her shoulder, she opened the website she'd avoided for weeks. Faces of the donors, all handsome-looking men—okay, some not so handsome—dotted her screen. "Where does one even start?" she asked, already feeling overwhelmed by the breadth.

"With that one," Hadley said. "He looks like Leonardo DiCaprio, and you know how I feel about *Titanic*. I will sing Celine Dion right now if you do not stop me."

"No Celine. You can Celine later. Focus."

"Trying."

"All right, let's take a closer look at the Leo look-alike," Autumn said, clicking on his face as Hadley began to quietly hum the theme from *Titanic*. "No humming either."

Hadley balked. "Do you know what you're asking?"

Bachelor number one was definitely good looking. Sandy blond hair, bright blue eyes, and a smile showcasing shiny, straight teeth. She sat taller. Maybe this whole exercise would turn out to be fun after all. What was there to be afraid of? That's when she saw it. "He's a mortician," she announced, pointing at the screen of doom. "No, no, no. What if my child is fascinated with dead things?

I don't do well with bodies. I don't even go to scary movies. I'd live in fear."

"You're being ridiculous," Hadley said. "My dad loves golf and horse shows. Your mom is shallow and opportunistic. Neither of us inherited those traits."

"Yeah, well, that's not a risk I'm willing to take."

"Okay, fine. I'm with ya," Hadley said, as Autumn took them back to the general pool. "Oh, okay. Look. This one looks like Superman. He even has the smart little curl in front. Click him. Click him!"

"I do like superheroes." Autumn clicked his face and scanned his profile. Tall, athletic. He'd been on his high school rowing team. She didn't know much about rowing, but that seemed impressive. You had to be strong to row, and practice religiously, so dedication went along with it.

"And he's an artist, too. Sensitive *and* athletic," Hadley pointed out.

Okay, Autumn liked those qualities. A lot. Kate's words echoed in her head. But would she want to be friends with this guy? She kept reading to find out.

"He's also arrogant," Autumn supplied in dismay. "Listen to his paragraph where he explains his motivation to donate. 'I've accomplished more in the past ten years than most people do in their entire lives.' Who says that about themselves?" she asked. "No one should. I don't care if you're an astronaut sitting on the moon. He's eliminated simply for bragging."

"Just like that, huh?"

"Just like that." Autumn turned to Hadley. "This is too important to mess around with, you know?"

Hadley nodded. "Vanquish his ass." She whispered the last word of the sentence.

"Still haven't mastered the swearing, huh?"

"Not yet," Hadley said, and stared quietly at the ground in shame.

They sat together on that couch for the next hour and a half. Hadley seemed to find her groove, knowing when to encourage

Autumn and when to back off. And just when Autumn was ready to close the laptop, call it a night, and steal a few hours before returning to Venice, she saw the profile. An eighth-grade English teacher who'd visited twenty-eight countries and was taking night courses in the pursuit of his master's. He was decent enough looking, wore glasses, but wasn't perfectly chiseled like some of the other prospects. Somehow that made him friendlier to her, more accessible.

"I like him," she said to Hadley, after scanning the ins and outs of the profile. "He seems like a real person, someone you could grab a beer with and talk about world issues."

Hadley squinted. "You never talk about world issues."

"Well, maybe I aspire to. If he were my friend, I just might do it."

Hadley smiled. "Valid point. I like him, too."

After they scanned his family history and found no major issues, conflicts, or skeletons in the proverbial genetics closet, Hadley turned to her. "What's the verdict?"

"I'm going to sleep on it, but I think maybe I've found him." She shot a glance to the stars. After her and Kate's trip to the observatory, she'd become increasingly aware of their presence, always watching over her. Did they just witness a major moment in her life? She smiled at the likelihood.

Hadley squeezed Autumn's hand. "Your face lit up when you read his profile. This could likely be the guy."

Autumn opened both palms. "He likes art and football. Both."

"Can't go wrong playing fantasy football in an art gallery."

"Right? And, Had"—she gestured to the now-closed laptop—"he even mentioned that a good cup of coffee is how he likes to start his day. That's good people right there."

Hadley smiled warmly at her. "I'm really happy for you. It's like everything is coming together for you. And now, with Kate, it seems like you're even getting your groove back."

Autumn reflected on Kate, how it was her words that had steered Autumn through this process, set her on a path. She was grateful, and thought the world of Kate, but she was also a realist. "She's great, but we're both pretty unavailable right now."

"Oh, see, there you go ruining all of my romantic happily-ever-after fantasies. Tell me there's hope there for you two."

"I can't do that. I'm trying to have a baby. Not exactly the best pickup line, and Kate has things of her own going on back home. She's here for a limited amount of time and is trying to simplify her life, not add to it."

"I hate it when you go and make sense. I prefer to dream."

"I wouldn't ever want you to stop. It's the very best thing about you." She gathered her belongings and stood. "Get some sleep. You've earned your friendship badge tonight."

Hadley clapped happily under her chin. "Consolation prize. I'm feeling better already. And, Autumn?"

"Yeah?"

"I'm really proud of you. Genuinely."

Autumn wasn't an emotional person, but there was something about the way Hadley said those words that had her misting up. "Thank you. For the first time in a long time, it feels like I'm working toward something for me, you know? Carving out my own destiny."

Hadley nodded with confidence. "And you're going to knock it out of the park."

Chapter Eight

The day of the fire had started off like any other day in Slumberton. Kate was off for three days after pulling a long week at the firehouse, sleeping over, and waiting for something to happen. Not much did in Slumberton. A few vehicle fires, an occasional rescue, but that particular week had been noticeably slow. She'd been waiting, just waiting, for something they could respond to. A life to save, a difference to make.

She'd give anything to take all that back now.

You wouldn't have known it would be an important day in Kate's life given the way it started out. She'd washed her truck that morning, stopped by The Plot Thickens to say hey to Randy before picking up a few groceries at the Stop and Shop. Instead of mowing the back lawn as she'd planned, she'd goofed off that afternoon and lost herself in a movie on television, the name of which she couldn't have told you, even at the time. The bright spot would be happy hour with a few of her friends and coworkers at Mitchy's, the most popular of the three bars in town. As usual, she and her pals from the station would drink and joke and argue good-naturedly before the party would inevitably break up around ten p.m. They'd all disperse by foot or cab to their various houses and do it all again the next week. It's what you did in a small town.

Only happy hour that day never happened.

She'd been on her way to Mitchy's when she heard the screams. It had taken her a minute to understand that they were not sounds from a raucous barbecue, or teenagers goofing off with nothing else to do in the small community. No, these were inarguable screams of panic, raw and shrill, and awful. A shiver moved up Kate's back when she heard them. Instinctively, she followed the sound, doubling back from her route to the bar, stopping only to grab a blanket from the backseat of her truck. Once she changed direction, it wasn't the screams that led her to the house, it was the billowing smoke, beckoning her like the most garish of genies. She called it in on her phone as she ran, only discovering once she got closer that it was the Higgins home on fire.

Eva's and Ren's.

Her heart stopped and adrenaline surged.

"We got a house fire," she told dispatch, doing everything she could to remain in control, to honor her training. "Twenty-four ten Claymore. House at the end of the street. Possible three people inside. Smoke billowing and flames visible."

The screams she'd heard had come from a gathering of neighbors, who stood along the curb looking on, horrified. When she arrived on the scene, Kate quickly assessed the situation and asked if anyone knew the cause or if anyone was inside. No one did. One of her older neighbors, a man, moved toward the house and back again. He wanted to do something but wasn't sure what.

"Sir, I need you to move back. Can you do me a favor and move everyone across the street?"

Grateful for a task, he nodded emphatically and did as Kate asked.

Flames were already visible on the exterior of the home, licking their way up the B side of the house, which was bad news because she didn't have her gear. Protocol would keep her outside the building until backup arrived and she was properly outfitted in her turnout gear and radio, but protocol could go to fucking hell, there could be kids in that house. *Her* kids, the ones she looked out for. How could this have happened? She shouldn't have let it. It was a ridiculous notion, but it was what fled through her mind that evening.

"Stay here and let rescue know I'm inside," she told the man before running up the sidewalk to the home. She didn't think, she acted. There was nothing to think about. She stopped at the outdoor faucet next to the garage and doused the blanket with water. The front door was unlocked and not overly hot, which allowed her to take a step inside and assess the situation. From outside, it looked like the blaze was centered on the B side of the house, and what she saw inside confirmed that. She made an initial sweep of the small downstairs living area and kitchen. It was clear. The smoke came from the stairs off the living room, which set her on a path to the second story, and the likely source of the fire. The lungful of smoke that hit her as she ascended the stairs stalled her progress, leaving her coughing to clear her airway. Amateur move. She pulled her shirt over the bottom portion of her face and moved slowly, taking in what she could. She listened and heard the quiet sound of a child yelling the word "help" over the low roar of flames not far away. Her throat tightened and burned as she moved toward the sound, staying low, the blanket under her arm, willing her heart to slow its incessant thumping. She was in control. This was no different from any other scene.

Only it was.

"Eva, Ren, stay where you are!" she called out. "It's Kate. I'm on my way to you. Don't worry." Flames traveled the seam of the wall where it met the ceiling, slithering rapidly and crackling in her ears. She took note of how fast they spread. Her calculations left her just a minute or two to evacuate the inhabitants before the fire took hold and raged beyond control. The door to her left at the top of the stairs stood closed. She squinted through the thick smoke to another door open at the end of the hallway. Unsure which room to try first, she listened. Another cry pulled her to her left and she had her answer. She placed a hand on the door and pulled it back from the heat.

"Hurry," she heard Ren yell from inside.

It was all the prompting she needed.

She pushed the door open to see Eva and Ren sitting together on a bed, a cartoon bedspread pulled all around them, insulating them from the smoke. Ren sat in front of Eva protectively, as tears streamed down both faces. The room hung thick with smoke, and flames licked into the room from the closet. Kate quickly realized that the fire had most likely originated from the room at the end of the hallway and was burning its way right. No time to think. She extended a hand to the kids, who refused to move from where they sat. She didn't blame them. The fire was hot and sweat trickled down the sides of her face.

"It's okay," she told them. "Walk straight toward me. Don't look over there, only at me. See my eyes? Look right here."

Ren, though tentative, stood and pulled Eva along with him, staying close to the side of the room free of flames. All the while, Kate heard a clock ticking in the recesses of her mind. They didn't have long. When he was close enough, Kate took hold of his hand tightly. Eva automatically reached for Kate's shoulders and she scooped her up with her other arm.

She had them.

Moving quickly now, Kate turned back the way she came only to find that the hallway had been overtaken by flames. She didn't hesitate. She set Eva down temporarily, pulled the blanket from under her other arm, and turned to them.

"I'm going to wrap this around us. It's like a shield and it will protect us."

"Like on *Wonder Woman*?" Eva asked, tears still streaming. She reached for Kate, who scooped her up once again, holding her tight.

"Exactly like Wonder Woman. We're going to go fast, okay?" In the distance, she heard the wail of sirens approaching and knew the cavalry was close. Police, fire, ambulance, and volunteers. The town would rally. The only question was would there be enough time? "When I say go, we're going to duck our heads and run, staying under the blanket. Just like Wonder Woman. Ready?"

Two terrified and hesitant faces nodded, surrendering to her leadership.

She forced a smile and nodded back. "One, two, three, go!"

They moved quickly, the fire now devouring the walls of the hallway, the smoke making it almost impossible to see. This was their only shot. Eva clung to her, squeezing her arms around Kate's neck, burying her face. Ren held tightly to her hand, the blanket pulled around them all for protection. The heat slammed them as they walked, hot, oppressive, and overpowering. The sound of the fire's roar assaulted Kate's ears but she pushed on, tasting the acrid smoke along the way. It felt like a million years before they neared the top of the stairs, but there they were, just a few feet away.

They were going to make it. They were not going to die in this house. At the very least, she was getting these kids out of there if it was the last thing she did with her life.

Six steps away. Now five.

She felt the fire nip at her heels, and the pain flared bright and sharp on her ankles. She shook her pant leg and kicked at it with her other foot to smother the flames.

Four steps. Three.

She coughed, struggling for air. Her lungs rejected the smoke and seized.

Two steps. One more.

That's when the world shifted on it axis. The floor beneath them buckled with a loud, startling crack. They were falling, the three of them, to the story below amidst burning beams and splintered wood. She clutched Eva to her chest, angling as best she could to land on her back, to insulate the little girl from the impact of the fall. But Kate didn't remember landing or the impact. Just the image of a large beam crushing the coffee table next to them on the floor, sending sparks flying into the air. The couch caught fire and went up like a tinderbox, sending a wash of heat to her face. She slammed her eyes shut instinctively and braced against the scorching flash. Kate could make out the clamor of voices as they entered the home. She turned and blinked, doing her best to see what she could in the smoky, fire-laced chaos. Guys in turnout gear. Her guys. They were here. They would help. She tried to move and winced at the pain that sliced through her back. Eva was gone from her arms. Damnit, no. What had happened to Eva? Ren was next to Kate, moaning quietly. "Help them," she said, again and again, but her voice was hoarse, barely a whisper. "Please. Help them."

The next time Kate opened her eyes, she was in an ambulance

in front of the house. Evening had crept steadily to night, and the sky had lost the sun entirely. Rescue workers streaked past. Someone had transported her there, but she must have passed out from the smoke inhalation and had no memory of those details. Attempting to speak, she erupted into a coughing spell, her lungs rebelling against the ash and the soot. Through it all, she studied her surroundings and attempted to push herself into a seated position, ignoring the searing pain. Her skin had been burned, her arm and her side and the backs of her ankles, that much she could tell. Not badly though, nothing she couldn't push through. She ached from the fall, but she could push through that, too. The doors to the ambulance stood open and she could hear the spray from the fire hose from nearby.

"The kids!" she heard herself call out, only her voice was raspy and sounded nothing like hers. They had her masked up and sucking on oxygen. She pushed the mask aside. "Are they out? We need to get them out."

"They're with Rescue Five. The medics are treating them now," said Luella, a private company paramedic Kate had come to know and respect from the field. She repositioned the oxygen mask over Kate's mouth and nose. "Thanks to you. Now you need to lie back and let me do my damn job."

"I don't know if the house was clear. Did anyone clear the house?" She sat up, wanting more than anything to go back in there but knowing that her injuries could put herself and everyone else at greater risk. It was a helpless feeling.

"Lie back down," her captain said from outside the ambulance. "The whole place fell in on itself and the rest is about to go. It's unstable and I've already given the abandon structure call. We'll talk about why you busted in on your own later. For now, sit there and rest, and don't fucking move."

Kate swore quietly, feeling helpless and frustrated. "How are they?" she asked Luella.

She met Kate's eyes. "From what I can tell, the little girl got the worst of it, but they're both holding their own."

"I should have been faster. Fuck." Kate shook her head, reliving each moment, critically reviewing what she could have done better, more efficiently. It wasn't until hours later at the hospital when she heard the news. One deceased in the master bedroom, a male in his thirties. No, no, no. She blinked at the wall as the full meaning of that information settled. Eva and Ren had lost their father. It wasn't her fault. She knew that underneath the giant weight that sat on her chest, but that didn't lessen the dread that descended. She swallowed back the bile that rose in her throat and gripped the metal bars along her hospital bed, looking around for something, anything she could do to take it back.

This had happened on her watch.

A single firefighter on the scene without turnout gear could only do so much with a burn already in progress. Still, she felt lost in that bed, knowing the most important person in those kids' lives was gone. Whether or not he'd been a great father didn't matter, he'd been *their* father.

"You're a fucking hero, Carpenter," one of the guys said, from the side of her hospital bed an hour later. His hair was sweaty, and he still had soot on his face from working the scene. It turned her stomach. She'd sustained minor burns, sprained her ankle in the fall, and scored some pretty awful bruising to her lower back. A day or so at most and she'd be released. Didn't matter.

"No. Don't say that," she'd told him adamantly, rejecting the hero notion outright. In fact, it made her sick. "I should have cleared the house." The thought consumed her, making it difficult to concentrate on anything else. She combed through every detail of those critical moments, as if they were on fast-forward in her brain, looking for some small thing that she could have done differently. She found several, and they would haunt her forever.

"You are, though," Charlie said, from the back of the group of guys.

He'd started with her in the department all those years ago when they'd been probies together. Why didn't he get it?

"It's a miracle you got any of 'em out, Carpenter. Focus on that. That fire was a beast. I've never seen anything burn so fast. Fucking balloon construction," he muttered.

Kate wasn't buying it. But that word, "hero," continued to pop up over the next few weeks, in cruel misnomer. She couldn't seem to shake it, no matter how hard she tried. The local news was no help, running a feature piece on the rescue with her as their centerpiece, regardless of the fact that she'd refused to participate or give them so much as a quote.

In the days after her release, investigators ruled that the fire had originated in the master bedroom and was likely the result of an abandoned lit cigarette. Drug paraphernalia had also been found in a cluster nearby, and the tox screen on Higgins had him more than a little high. Didn't mean he deserved to die. She'd spent hours in front of her laptop, Googling the guy, combing through his social media pages to learn more about him. He'd been a sprinter in high school, winning the district meet. He posted occasional photos of the kids online and apparently made a mean pot of chili. She couldn't decide whether humanizing him made it easier or harder to live with. Not that she could have pulled herself away.

Once she'd been discharged, she visited Ren and Eva, taking them stuffed animals and ice cream. Eva had smiled up at Kate from her hospital bed, her brown eyes sparkling even in the midst of all that had happened to her. How was that possible? She'd shed some tears, sure, but overall, the kid was hanging in there. "Are you really Wonder Woman?" Eva asked one day as Kate sat alongside her hospital bed.

"Nope. I'm just Kate, your friend." She handed Eva a napkin to catch the dot of ice cream threatening to dribble down her chin.

"You look like her, and Wonder Woman saves people. You do, too."

"I don't know about that."

"I do," Eva said, with confidence. The words tore through Kate's heart, causing her chest to ache. She didn't remind Eva that she'd been unable to save their father. Thus far, Eva hadn't mentioned his loss more than a handful of times, but perhaps the reality hadn't had a chance to sink in. Eva seemed to be working through it, still taking in the information. Kate knew better than to push, choosing to keep her fingers off that bruise. "You're going to be okay, you know that? Both you and Ren."

Eva had nodded, considering the words. The corners of her mouth turned down with worry. "Maybe." The little girl stared hard at the bedsheet she clutched tightly in her free hand. "But Dad's not coming back."

And there it was.

Eva didn't cry as she said the words but seemed tired, melancholy. It was in that moment that Kate realized Eva's unexpected strength. She was a fighter, but she didn't deserve this. No kid did.

Kate had never thought of herself as an emotional person and was usually adept at swallowing her own feelings for the sake of keeping a level head and dealing with whatever situation she faced. That quality had always served her well. Emotions just got in the way. But this moment was different, and the tears entered her damn eyes whether she wanted them there or not.

"No, Eva, he's not. I'm really sorry about that. He loved you very much, though. Always remember that."

Eva nodded solemnly and handed Kate her ice cream. "I don't think I want any more."

"That's okay," Kate told her, and set the dish to the side. Eva snuggled into her blanket and faced the wall, done with talking.

Thinking back on that moment now gutted Kate as she remembered the sad resignation on Eva's face. She pulled out her phone, prepared to call and check on the kids, see what kind of progress Jennifer over at DHS had been able to make, when a knock on her door interrupted her progress. Expecting Gia or Isabel or another one of her neighbors, Kate was shocked to see her brother standing outside her apartment. She glanced around behind him trying to assemble the pieces that had brought Randy to her door so many hours from Slumberton. Happiness to see him trumped all investigation, however.

"Randy?" she asked quietly, and allowed him to pull her into a tight hug while she rode out the surprise. He wore a red baseball cap that hid his fluffy curls and made him look so much cooler than she was used to. They'd never in their lives gone so long without seeing each other, and damn, he was a sight for sore eyes. "What the hell? How did you get here?"

"Drove. Same as you." He beamed at her and she remembered the power of his smile. He was the kind of person whose smile was genuine, honest. She loved that about him. "Wanted to see where you shacked up."

She squinted in amusement. "I think that means something different than you think it means."

Randy shrugged good-naturedly. "Are you going to invite me in? I drove a hell of a long way."

"Yeah, yeah. Of course," she said, stepping out of the way, unable to wipe the smile off her face. After a brief tour of the space, they settled into the living room, and he got to the real reason for his visit.

"So, you were just out for a spin across state lines?" Kate asked with a quirked eyebrow.

"I guess I was just worried about you," Randy said quietly. "You're not the type to just run off for weeks at a time, you know? I wouldn't be doing my job as big brother if I didn't make sure you were okay."

She nodded, knowing she'd have chased after him, too. "I know. Just needed to catch my breath, regroup from—"

"All the attention?" he finished for her.

"Yeah. Too much going on back home, and I couldn't breathe." She gestured behind her. "I was actually just about to call and check on the kids."

"They're doing better, from what I hear." He sat forward on the couch. "They found the mom, who seems to be stable enough with a house and a job, about two hours from here in Santa Barbara. She's not been entirely helpful."

It didn't surprise her that Randy would know the details. She was confident all of Slumberton had passed the information around three times over.

"But she's going to take them, right?"

Randy inclined his head from side to side. "It sounds like she's hesitant. I wish I could say it was looking better."

She stood, anger bubbling to the surface. "That's bullshit. These are *her* kids. She needs to step up for them."

"Yeah, well, not everyone looks at family the way we do, Katie."

"I'll go visit her then. See if I can reason with her somehow. If she's a decent person, like you seem to think she might be, she'll come around."

"Not a good idea." He crossed to her, shoving his hands into his pockets. "Let the professionals handle it. You're dealing with enough. It's not up to you to sort out those kids' lives." He poked her shoulder lightly. "You take care of you."

She nodded, knowing that the further in she got, the harder it was to come back out. She sighed. Randy was right, and she hated that. "Right. Yeah. I know."

"Speaking of taking care of you"—he turned around and picked up the bag he'd come in with—"half a dozen fresh glazed from Dawn of the Doughnuts. Made this morning. Picked 'em up before I hit the road. You're welcome."

Kate grabbed the bag and inhaled the sweet smell through the grease-soaked paper from her favorite donut shop in Slumberton. "Oh, wow. Man, I missed these." She hugged the bag to her chest like a long-lost teddy bear.

"Thought you might have felt that way. But don't get caught up with those. You're taking me for an early dinner, and then I'm hitting the road."

"You're not staying?"

"Can't. The book club is meeting at the store tomorrow, and it always brings me some much-needed revenue. But take me for a steak and a beer, and I'll tell you all the town gossip you missed."

"Done." She grabbed her keys, glanced at him, and smiled. "It's good to see your face." Not wanting to dwell in the land of sentimentality, a place she'd never been very comfortable, she thumped him once on the shoulder and headed for the door. "What's with the cap?"

"I'm trying something new."

She slipped into a playful announcer voice. "Randy Carpenter leaps into the land of fashion."

"I'm too nerdy for fashion. Stop it."

"Can't. I'm your sister."

Dinner was much of the same, and it felt good to fall into a familiar groove, especially with someone she felt as comfortable with as Randy. She could be herself, but at the same time not worry that someone would be whispering about her at the next table over, for the good or bad. It was the best of both worlds.

"So, what do you do here anyway?" he asked, pushing his plate away. For a slight guy, he'd polished off a twelve-ounce ribeye in remarkable time.

She raised a shoulder. "I read a lot. I've hit up the beach a few times. Seen some of LA, and have become surprisingly awesome at *Ms. Pac-Man*."

"*Ms. Pac-Man*? That's random. Since when do you play video games?"

She laughed. "No idea. Very unlike me."

"So, that means you've made friends here?"

"I tend to be quiet and stick to myself, as you know, but yeah." She nodded. "A handful. It's been an unexpected perk. I think it's the complex I'm staying in. Social place."

"And women?" Randy had always pushed her on that front, wanting her to date and eventually settle down the way he had. A total broken record on the topic.

She hesitated for too long and felt it. "Nope, nothing like that."

"I don't believe you. Your cheeks are red like that time when you cut the hair off all your dolls and blamed it on the dog."

"How do you know he wasn't guilty?"

He stared at her, unwavering.

"Fine." She set down her silverware. "There's a woman who I've spent time with, but it doesn't have relationship potential. We're friends who…appreciate each other."

He took a satisfied pull from his beer. He'd cracked her as always. "Why no potential?"

"She lives here, for one. Plus, I'm a mess, and she's trying to have a baby."

"Whoa."

"Yeah, now you get it."

He chuckled. "You sure know how to pick 'em, Katie. Remember that time you dated that mime?"

She gestured with her beer. "I didn't know she was a mime when I asked her out."

"I wish you'd asked her out of that damn invisible box she put herself in at the bar that night."

Kate squinted at the uncomfortable memory. "If you'll remember, I did. Mortifying. The guys at the station never let me live it down."

"What was her name?"

"Sparkles, if memory serves."

He chuckled. "No, the pregnant, pretty girl. At least, I imagine she's pretty. Your women usually are."

"My women? Wow." Kate took a swallow of her beer. "I didn't know I had *women*. But yeah, she's attractive. Not pregnant, though. Not yet, anyway. I guess that's still coming."

"Name?"

"Autumn." She suppressed a smile at the sound of the name leaving her lips. She savored the feeling, tasted the word. She liked saying it.

"That's a nice name," Randy said. "Autumn. Shame about the screwed-up timing."

"Yeah." Kate's thoughts drifted pleasantly to their date, followed by their night together. She felt heat prickle on the back of her neck and spread. She took a deep breath. "A definite shame."

"That's new. You really like her." Randy leaned in as if he'd just discovered the killer in a game of Clue. "You never blush. What the hell, Kate?"

"Knock it off. So what if I do like her? You can truly like spending time with another person without having to, I don't know, declare undying love for them. We don't have to ride off into the sunset to appreciate hanging out with each other." Kate had no idea why she was defensive.

"That's true, I suppose. Is that what you're doing? Just hanging out? Because it sounds like you're hooking up."

She struggled to come up with the perfect answer. Honestly, she wasn't sure herself. "It's been both."

Randy sat back in his chair and stared at her with a grin that made her want to tackle him right there on the floor of the restaurant.

"It's not going anywhere though, okay? You're gonna have to trust me on this one and get that smirk off your dumb face." She flashed to the eleven-year-old version of herself yelling at him in the kitchen over cereal.

"Understood," he said, like a little know-it-all. "You got this. Let it be known that I will welcome her into the family with open arms."

"Let it be known? I'm going to pummel you. You will fly across this restaurant." She couldn't pull back the smile.

"Sure you are. Come at me, bruh." Randy's eyes danced and he tapped his chest.

She covered her eyes. "You have to stop watching so much television. It's embarrassing."

He pulled his face back. "You love it."

Underneath it all, Randy made her laugh. He also calmed her the hell down in a way no one else could. She took his words to heart, too, even when she gave the goofus such a hard time for butting in. It was good to see his face.

She hadn't moved past the information he'd brought with him from home either. Once they'd said their good-byes after dinner, she pulled up a map on her phone and traced the thin line of the highway from Venice to Santa Barbara.

Would you look at that?

As it turned out, the two cities were not that far away.

Not that far away at all.

Chapter Nine

It was ten past two in the afternoon, and Autumn was late for her doctor's appointment. It was possible she'd been putting off leaving Pajamas until the last possible second, not exactly looking forward to the experience. The idea of sitting alone in that waiting room again had her psyched out. But if she was actually going through with this thing, and she most definitely was, she needed to pull herself up by the bootstraps and get it the hell together. She was a strong, successful, independent woman and always had been.

Today was no different, damnit.

She pushed open the door to the shop, ready to take on the world, just as Kate pulled the handle to enter.

"Whoa," Autumn said, meeting Kate's eyes and smiling in reflex. "Sorry 'bout that. I guess I was in my own world."

"That's okay," Kate said. "You're leaving?"

The disappointment gave Autumn's spirits a boost. "Yeah, I have a thing." She hated herself for being vague, and corrected course. "A doctor's appointment." She sighed. "I have, unfortunately, a doctor's appointment."

"Unfortunately?" Kate asked.

"Did I say that? Yeah, I guess I did." She dropped her focus to the ground and back up with an explanation. "They make me nervous. Not something I completely enjoy, not that it has to be a party, you know." She had no idea what made her confess these details to Kate, who seemed afraid of nothing. She must think Autumn was a total incompetent.

"You should take a friend with you," Kate offered gently.

"Yeah, maybe so, but people have lives, you know? Jobs, plans. I don't want to bother them. I got this."

"Then I'll go with you."

"What? No, no, no. That's silly. You don't have to do that. Above and beyond the scope of your friendship requirement."

"Right. But I'm going."

Autumn paused, touched by Kate's unflinching generosity but guilt-ridden for her part in this. "Why would you do that? Surely you have a million other options for your day than sitting in a boring, sterile doctor's office."

"Wouldn't matter. I'm doing it because I like you, and I don't want you to be there alone. C'mon, I'll drive."

And before Autumn could so much as utter a syllable, Kate turned and headed toward the parking lot of the complex, keys jingling from her fingertips.

"You kind of just do what you want, don't you?" Autumn called after her.

"Is that a problem?" Kate called back.

"Not at all," Autumn mumbled to herself, and followed Kate to her truck with a smile tugging. In a welcome turn of events, Autumn felt that tingly little sensation that hit when things were going well, when you're lighter and looking forward to something. She zeroed in on the appropriate word.

Happy.

That's exactly what it was.

Knowing that Kate would be there with her this afternoon had instantly calmed her worked-up nerves and made her feel supported and cared about, in turn, making her happy. She almost wanted to say the word out loud. *Happy*. How remarkable that something so small, so everyday as a friend going with her to a doctor's appointment, could bring about such a mood transformation.

Instead of dwelling, or reciting the word eight times like a lunatic, Autumn played navigator and directed Kate through the interconnecting highways of Los Angeles. Surprisingly, Kate maneuvered through LA traffic with ease and patience, way more patience than Autumn embodied in probably her entire life. "You're a remarkably calm driver," Autumn said in mystification, as a guy swerved to cut them off. Kate pressed the brake evenly. Autumn balked. She couldn't identify, but admired the quality.

"What's there to get worked up about?" Kate asked, and passed her a laid-back smile. Oh, Kate looked good behind that wheel. Autumn had never been a truck person but lately had a newfound appreciation for them. Solid. Sexy. In control. The metaphor was not lost on her.

"I just know that when I drive in afternoon traffic, I want to hurl my Big Gulp so it splashes fantastically across the windshield of whoever makes me mad. It's my number one driving fantasy."

"But then you'd have nothing to drink," Kate said simply.

Autumn shook her head. "Only you, Kate. Only you."

Kate laughed and turned up the volume on the radio as they drove the rest of the way, sans any sort of road rage whatsoever. Autumn could learn a little from Kate.

When they arrived at Dr. Arocha's office, Autumn walked in with a foreign confidence, with her friend by her side. They took a seat in the waiting room and Autumn held her head up high. It was stupid and trivial to let a small detail matter so much, but sitting there with another person, in a sea of coupled-up people, had her feeling like she belonged. She even smiled at the two women sitting across from them.

"Autumn?" the nurse asked from the doorway.

Kate stood when Autumn did, and they looked at each other. Oh, she was coming to the exam room as well? Kate didn't mess around. "You don't have to come back if you—"

"Stop saying that," Kate said. "I've never been to a place like this."

She grinned. "Then I will not get in the way of this unique experience for you."

"Thank you," Kate said, and they joined the nurse, a short, blond woman with a giant smile.

"You two make a striking couple," the nurse said, as they rounded the corner to Exam Room Two.

"Oh, we're not—"

"Thank you," Kate said, and shot Autumn an amused smile and shrug of her shoulders. Autumn met Kate's eyes and shook her head, chastising Kate silently. Secretly, she didn't mind playing house with Kate.

"Right through here," the woman said, and led them to a small exam room. "Change into this gown, and flip the switch on the wall to let Dr. Arocha know you're ready."

"Thank you," Kate said, and closed the door behind the nurse. They looked at each other.

"I can't believe you did that," Autumn said.

"She said we looked good. All I did was thank her." Kate gestured with her chin. "Aren't you supposed to put that on?"

Autumn glanced at the blue and white gown. "Right. I guess I should." Well, this was awkward and the opposite of sexy in every way. Kate had seen her without clothes on, but this was different, clinical and by the clear light of day.

Kate gestured behind her. "I'll just face the wall, so you can—"

"Awesome. Great. Yeah. Should just take a second and then—"

"No, take your time," Kate said, no longer sounding as calm and in control. Autumn happened to like seeing her feathers ruffled for a change. She slipped quickly into the gown, hopped up on the table, and turned to Kate.

"Decent. You can turn around again."

Kate smiled apprehensively and took a seat behind Autumn and the exam table. They sat in silence for a few moments before Kate slipped her hand into Autumn's. "Moral support," she said quietly and stared at the wall. Autumn gave Kate's hand a squeeze.

"For a firefighter, you're kind of a softy."

"Am not," Kate said. But when she returned her gaze to Autumn's, there was a twinkle in her eye. "Okay, maybe a little. Where certain people are concerned."

"Are you the type that rescues cats from trees?"

"Firefighters don't do that anymore," Kate told her matter-of-factly.

"I see."

A pause. "I do, though."

Autumn laughed. "See? Total softy."

They smiled at each other. "So, what's it like?" Kate asked, turning fully to face her. "Knowing you're on your way to being a mom?"

Autumn took a minute, as it was the first time anyone had asked her that question. "It's a little scary, if I'm being honest. A lot of exciting, mixed with a dash of hurry-up-and-happen-already."

"I can imagine. Know what I think?"

"What?"

"You're going to be the best kind of mom. Fun and vivacious like you are in the rest of your life. Any kid would love spending time with you."

Right there in that sterile exam room, a wonderful warmth hit Autumn squarely in the chest. "Thank you. I hope that's true. I think about all the things I want to be for him or her. A mentor, a source of comfort, a friend once they're all grown up. It's a lot to imagine." A pause. "And what about you? You have a lot to offer yourself. Kids one day?"

"I used to think no," Kate said. "Lately, that's shifted. Maybe."

"Can I ask what prompted the shift?"

"I made a couple of new friends back home."

"Kids?" Autumn was beginning to understand.

Kate nodded. "Good ones."

The door swung open. Dr. Arocha and his burst of energy filled the space, along with his smiley nurse. Autumn had come to understand that he had a lot of patients that kept him on the move throughout the day, and it always seemed as if he were attached to a motor. "Let's see how we're doing, shall we?" Kate held her hand during the exam, staying as close to the back wall as possible, and when it was all said and done, Autumn was cleared for take-off. "Lining looks great. With your donor all squared away, we'll get you started on a higher dose of the meds and see if we can schedule your insemination for next month."

"Wow," Autumn said, sitting up. "Just like that? We're doing it?"

Dr. Arocha shook her hand. "We are," he said, and sailed out of the room, on to his next appointment. Autumn turned to Kate, her eyes filling. "I'm going to be a mom."

"You're gonna be a mom." Kate, the softy, welled up, too. "This is so cool."

The cool part was being able to share that moment with someone like Kate, to know that she understood its importance to Autumn. It was, well, everything. While Autumn still didn't know a ton about what brought Kate to Venice, she was becoming more and more comfortable opening up her own life. Maybe with time, Kate would trust her and she could return the supportive friend favor.

Maybe…

For now, there was cause for celebration.

"How do you feel about a Big Gulp?" Kate asked, as they headed to the parking lot. "For some reason, I'm in the mood."

❖

Kate got on the road bright and early the next day, bound and determined in her quest. She carried with her the first name she'd managed to extract from DHS back home, and after a little detective work of her own, she had an address. She'd gassed up her truck and headed to Santa Barbara, hoping something she might say would make a difference to a woman she'd never met. As much as she wanted to, there was no way she could sit back and watch as Eva and Ren were sent off to separate foster homes, or worse, left in the hands of the state for who knows what kind of sterile upbringing. Not when there was something she could do about it.

Over the course of the two-hour drive, she thought back to Autumn's appointment the day before. She felt silly now for welling up, but there'd been so many dark clouds hanging over her head lately that the thought of a new little life, one that would clearly bring so much joy to Autumn, grabbed hold of her feelings and wouldn't let go.

The two of them had stopped for that Big Gulp on the way home from the appointment, and next to Randy, Kate decided that

Autumn was about the easiest person to talk to that she'd ever met. She wasn't sure how Autumn did it, got her to relax and open up, but she easily turned Kate into a talkative person—to her own shock.

She drove on, enjoying the unrelenting sunshine, humming along to the radio, and not thinking about how Autumn's day was going. Whether she'd tamed her curls or left them loose. What flavor she'd chosen as roast-of-the-day and why. Kate smiled and forced herself to focus on the task in front of her. Didn't mean Autumn didn't creep back in. Kate actually didn't mind.

An hour later, she pulled up to a modest one-story, tucked away in the suburbs of Santa Barbara. Kate checked the address to be sure. Yeah, this was the place. Not the best neighborhood she'd ever seen, but certainly not the worst. As she made her way up the cobblestone walk, she studied the small, yellow house with white shutters and took note of the tended garden in front. The sunflowers were evenly spaced and the lilacs had been given their own area to blossom and expand. Someone had given time and attention to that garden. They cared about it. That had to be a good sign for the woman who lived inside, right?

She took a deep breath and raised her fist to knock, pausing when the door opened before she could. A woman stood there, staring back at her. Thirties maybe. Dark hair pulled into a neat ponytail. She wore some sort of uniform, a green polo and khakis. She regarded Kate with curiosity. "Can I help you?" she asked politely.

"Kate Carpenter," she said, and extended her hand. "Are you Meredith Higgins?"

"Listen, I'm not interested and I'm late for work."

Kate held up a hand. "I'm not selling anything. I promise. Five minutes?"

"I'm sorry. I can't." Meredith maneuvered around Kate to the driveway, closing the door behind her, keys in her hand.

"It's about Eva and Ren."

That did it.

Meredith's head dropped and she froze. When she turned

around, everything about her had changed. Kate knew she'd struck a nerve.

Meredith walked back a few steps. "Kate Carpenter, you said? Who are you exactly?"

"I'm just a firefighter from Slumberton. No one to be worried about, and I'm not here to cause you any trouble. Just wanted to have a conversation. I pulled them from the fire."

She closed her eyes as if the words sliced through her. "God, thank you for that. But, listen, I haven't seen them in years."

"Three, to be exact. I don't know why that is, and I'm not here to judge you, but I do know that they're still your kids. That won't ever change, no matter how long it's been."

She shook her head. "Trust me when I say that I was a horrible mother. Whoever they end up with will be better than I was for them. I left them, and it's something I have to live with every day."

"You don't have to. It looks to me like you have a pretty decent life happening here. A house. A job." She studied the polo, realizing Meredith worked for a hotel. Better than anything they had with their father.

Meredith checked her watch and sighed. "Things are better now. But back then I was a mess. It took me years to get on track, and I can't risk screwing up for them again. Anyone else would be better. Look, I'm sure you're a very nice person, but I think I have to ask you to leave."

Kate handed her phone to Meredith.

"What is this?" she asked, glancing at the screen and back at Kate nervously, attempting to hand it back.

"That first one is a photo of Eva playing hopscotch. The next one is Ren in a tree. He climbs things a lot."

As if drawn to the photos by a force larger than herself, Meredith studied the screen. As she stared, she placed a hand over her mouth. "They've gotten so big," she said finally, shifting the hand to the top of her head. She was at a loss, Kate realized. She cared more than she was letting on.

Kate nodded, building momentum. "They're really smart, too,

and way more self-sufficient than any kids I've ever met. They're honestly not much trouble at all. It's a testament to them."

Meredith handed the phone back to Kate, her face now drawn and haunted. "I was sorry to hear about the fire. About their father. It's awful." There were tears in her eyes. "I'm so happy the kids are okay, but this is all too much for me. I'm sorry."

"Wait. I'm not asking for any kind of guarantee here. Just your compassion for two children who have lost everything."

"Which is exactly why they don't need me around," Meredith said sorrowfully, opening her car door. "You'll need to find someone else." She hopped into the vehicle and pulled out in a hurry, leaving Kate standing there, the photo of Eva visible on her phone. Her last hope had just gone up in smoke. What in the world was she supposed to do now?

❖

"When should we start shopping for baby clothes?" Hadley asked, bleary-eyed from her spot at their table. It was seven thirty in the morning, and the gang had stumbled in, dragging more than usual. "I'm ready now. Get in the car. Well, as soon as I wake up, that is."

Autumn placed a double chocolate mocha in front of her. "This should help. As for baby clothes, I think you're supposed to be pregnant first, and far enough along where it's PC to acknowledge it."

"Generally speaking, she's right," said the bonus member of their Breakfast Club that morning. Taylor Andrews, looking sharp in black pants, heels, and a blazer for work sat incredibly close to Isabel. The two continued to steal smoldering glances at each other, making Autumn wonder what kind of fun night they'd just come off. She swallowed the looming jealousy and chose to be happy for them.

"And anyway, how do you shop for clothes unless you know the sex of the baby?" Gia asked.

"I don't think you know who you're dealing with." Hadley brushed her hair off one shoulder, then the other, in a taunt.

Isabel sat up in her chair. "Give that kid an apron and put 'em to work. Dressed. Solved. Steve will thank me."

"Child labor laws come to mind," Autumn said thoughtfully. "And coffee is hot for a baby to be handling."

Isabel shrugged. "Don't get caught up in the details."

"So, if we, you and I, had a child one day, you'd have them writing for the show?" Taylor asked, with a raised eyebrow.

The deep shade of red that descended on Isabel's face was priceless. "I'd have to think about that." But it was clear she was touched by just the mention of a family with Taylor, who kissed the back of her hand, enjoying the blush.

"I'll keep your suggestion in mind, Iz," Autumn said.

"So, when do we get the ball rolling?" Hadley asked. "How long do I have to wait for babysitting duty? The calendar is long and arduous."

Isabel nodded. "The calendar is a total bitch. Don't they know Hadley is waiting?"

Autumn laughed. "Well, when we saw the doctor this week, he said I'm all set. I've been good about taking the meds and the ultrasounds look great, so we're a go for insemination next month, according to the schedule the fertility coach provided me."

"Who's we?" Gia asked, snagging another slice of banana bread.

"What do you mean?" Autumn asked.

Hadley jumped in. "You're the one who said it. You said *we* saw the doctor this week."

"Oh! Kate went with me."

Right then and there, four women exchanged glances that said things had just gotten good. Hadley straightened in her chair, the haze of morning snatched from her demeanor altogether. She was now wide awake, alert, and looking hungry for details. Typical Had. "Kate went with you, you say? Was the name *Kate*?"

"I distinctly heard the name Kate," Taylor tossed in.

"Not just me, then," Gia said.

"You guys are ridiculous." Autumn brushed off the questioning stares. "She came to keep me company. That's it. It's not what you think."

"And what do we think?" Hadley asked with a twinkle in her eyes. "Say the words."

"That there's a burgeoning romance. That we're falling for each other. We're not. We haven't known each other that long."

Isabel tapped her lips. "Well, over a month now. Heading into two."

"She's great, but we're not going to have a baby together."

Isabel turned her hand in a rewind circle. "Let's just focus on the great descriptor, sans baby issue."

Autumn tossed a towel onto her shoulder. "Fine. Kate *is* wonderful. I stand by the statement, but we're both unavailable, amid wildly weird times in our lives. A non-issue."

Hadley took it from there, resting her chin in her hand. "But if you *were* both available? Let's just play that game."

"We're not."

"Were, though," Hadley said more forcefully. "Were, were, were."

"This would be a very different conversation," Autumn said, unable to resist the smile that hit at the thought.

"You're glowing," Hadley said happily. She sat back in satisfaction. "Like Isabel, two minutes ago."

"I don't glow," Isabel deadpanned.

"Oh, but you do," Taylor said, stealing a kiss. "It's the best." She glanced at her watch. "Speaking of, we should glow our way to the office. There's an ex-assassin who needs words to say, and a network that demands schmoozing." She turned to the group. "Thanks for letting me crash your breakfast, everyone. The coffee was heaven-sent as usual, Autumn. Maybe even more so."

Autumn smiled, proud of the batch. "Roasted the beans a bit longer this time to enhance the caramelization."

"No idea what any of that means," Taylor said with a smile, "but it worked."

"That means you fucking rocked." Isabel smiled at her own translation.

"I can work with fucking rocked," Autumn said. "Thanks, Taylor!"

"Anytime."

Taylor and Isabel headed off to the studio, with Hadley, who was opening the store that morning, on their heels. That left her with Gia. Gia, who with just one look could understand everything that was going on in her head. While Hadley was Autumn's soft place to fall, and Isabel was her kindred spirit in the sarcasm department, Gia was the one she could talk to straight up. No holds barred. What was even better about Gia? She was a proverbial vault and came without judgment. She didn't get caught up in gossip or look for the exciting angle, she simply took each situation for what it was. Gia was no frills, and Autumn appreciated it.

"Saw the smile," Gia said. "You sure you're not getting caught up?"

Autumn dropped all pretense, knowing that she could. "Trying not to. It's not always easy, though."

"Call me protective, I just want to make sure you're doing what's right for you, whether that's Kate or no Kate."

Autumn decided to put it all out there. "When I'm around her, things seem easier and at the same time, more exciting. I don't know how to describe it, G, but when Kate's around, my life gets…better. A lot better."

"You slept with her," Gia said. Her intuition never failed to surprise Autumn.

"Yesss," she said, drawing the word out as she scrambled to figure out how to explain that particular detail. "But it's not going to happen again. We're both in agreement there."

"And things were…better there, too?"

Heat spread across her skin at the memory of that night. Her stomach dipped. "Like you wouldn't believe."

Gia took a moment and sent Autumn a look of hesitation. "I suck at advice. This is more Hadley's area."

"Don't sell yourself short. You happen to be the best listener I know." She stole a glance at Steve to make sure he had the counter under control, as Simon-the-Nodder had emailed that he was sick, apparently sticking to that vow of silence and avoiding a simple phone call. Satisfied all was well, she turned her full focus to Gia. "Lay it on me. For the good or bad. I don't care. What's your take?"

Gia rolled her shoulders. "Okay. I know you're set on having this baby right now, but I'd hate to see you miss out on what's right in front of you."

Autumn took a moment with the comment. "And you think that might be Kate?"

She shrugged. "I guess I'm just wondering if you think so and are just too far down the parent road to say so?"

"If you think what about Kate?" a familiar voice asked. Autumn turned to see Kate herself standing just a few feet from their table, which sent her into recovery mode. No. Scratch that. Overkill-recovery mode—the ridiculous behavior that strikes when one is trying to cover their stupid guilty tracks.

"I was just asking Gia here if she thought you'd be good, uh," her eyes scanned the room for help, "working behind the counter."

Gia, who was apparently better at storytelling, didn't miss a beat. "Told her you'd be great. How could you not be? You're great at everything."

"You want to hire me?" Kate asked.

"No. No!" Autumn said, now sounding really over the top with way too much animation in her voice. "That would be silly." She took a moment to laugh like a lunatic. "We just had an employee call in sick. Sorry, email in sick. And I thought, who could help out? Maybe Kate from next door could, but it was just a passing thought. I'm over it now. Over it!" She smiled and waved it off in a big, stupid gesture she hated herself for.

Kate glanced at the counter and back at Autumn. "I can help."

"You'll need an apron," Gia said and took a long, last swallow of coffee and headed for the door. "You two have fun."

Autumn stared after her, jealous of the escape.

Kate looked around. "Show me the way to the aprons, then."

"You know what?" Autumn shook her head. "I've changed my mind. We can handle it. You probably just want to grab a cup and get back to your book, or your sexy truck." Kate raised an eyebrow and Autumn continued to ramble. "I mean your *regular* truck, or whatever you have lined up today. Is the air heavy in here? I feel like I'm choking. I'll check the AC."

But Kate followed her. "I figure you'll pass the aprons sooner or later."

Autumn shifted her lips to the side as she pondered her options. They *were* short-handed. And she'd made a big deal about considering Kate. Maybe it would even be fun having her around for the morning, even if the whole thing was a big, fat sham. She adjusted the thermostat and gestured behind the counter. "Aprons are this way."

While Autumn handled the register, Kate outfitted herself in a blue Cat's Pajamas apron and returned looking rather proud of herself. "Reporting for duty. Where would you like me?"

Autumn took a moment, because she had definite thoughts on the topic. Kate pulled her hair into a ponytail and nervously smoothed the front of her apron as if trying to look her most professional. "Since you're not a trained barista, let's give you a try on register."

"Right. The register. Okay."

She was anxious and doing this for Autumn. Yet again showing her generosity of spirit. "Not a big deal. I'll give you a crash course. Honestly, most of the buttons do the job for you, and they're pretty clearly marked."

"Thank God."

Thirty minutes later, it was clear the button system had failed Kate. She'd struggled with most every order but was so nice to the customers they didn't seem to mind. She'd pushed aside her shy nature and truly rose to the occasion.

"I have no idea how to get you your change, because the drawer closed and locked on me," Kate told a local surfer chick. "I will figure it out, but while I do, please know that you're gonna kill it out there today on those waves."

"Thanks," the girl said, and smiled generously at Kate. "You can keep the change. How's that? Solved." And with a wink to Kate, she moved on.

Unbelievable. Apparently, Autumn wasn't the only one Kate affected.

"A red eye with an extra shot," Kate repeated back to the next customer, perusing the options on the keypad. "Hmm. A red eye with an extra shot. Okay. Where are you?" The older gentleman with a smile waited patiently. Another regular.

Autumn decided to step in. "You know what? On the house today, Stan."

"Why, thank you!" Stan said, beaming. "Best news I've had today." He nodded and moved down to pick up his drink from Steve.

"Hey, I'm really sorry about that," Kate said, but she was still smiling.

"How is it that you're enjoying yourself?"

"I have no idea. I suck at this."

"You do suck."

"But it's a lot of fun, too. I feel like the gatekeeper." Well, how was she supposed to argue with that? "I'll pay for the drink you just gave away. Your bank account shouldn't suffer because I'm awful on a register."

Autumn bumped Kate's shoulder. "No way. Comping stuff is one of the best parts of owning your own business."

Kate's hazel eyes met hers and held. "You're the expert," she said quietly, as the air around them thickened. You'd have thought they had the shop to themselves, hell, the planet.

As the morning progressed, Kate got better. But not a lot. They had a good time, though, Kate calling over drinks and she and Steve tag-teaming to turn them around quickly. Another interesting development was the number of neighborhood women who took an extra few moments, oh…deciding their order or batting their eyelashes as they made small talk with Kate. Autumn had their number and knew exactly what they were up to. Not that she blamed them. She'd stall for a little extra Kate time, too, if she were in their shoes. Luckily, she was blessed with a lot of Kate time that morning, and she was drinking in every minute of it.

"So, where'd you head off to the other day?" Autumn asked Kate. Steve had taken his break and the morning rush had tapered off, leaving them a moment on their own.

Kate turned and leaned against the counter, facing Autumn. "Oh, uh, Santa Barbara. There was a woman there I needed to see."

"Gotcha," Autumn said, ignoring the feeling she'd just been punched in the gut. Hard. And how stupid was that? She needed to get past that kind of overly sensitive reaction, and quick. She and Kate had been very mature about the nature of their relationship up to this point, and she was not about to go all jealous-girl on her now. "Cool."

"Not like that," Kate said, dipping her head to meet Autumn's averted eyes. She took a moment and seemed to make a decision. "I'd never met her before. She's the mother of a couple of kids from back home. They were in an accident and could really use her about now."

Autumn straightened. This was new information. "What kind of accident?"

Kate took a moment before answering. "A fire."

"The same one that brought you out here?"

Kate nodded, but it was as if a heaviness had descended on her. She stood ramrod straight, and her relaxed features were now guarded and weary. "They're okay now, but they lost their father. I couldn't get him out." She turned back to the cash register as if needing to study it, and right on cue, one of Autumn's least favorite customers and the owner of Seven Shores approached.

"Ms. Primm," Larry Herman said, nodding to her. He wore a brown corduroy blazer in May, but she decided to let that one go. If Isabel had been there, however, she'd have had a field day. Total missed opportunity.

"Hi, Larry," she said, wiping down the espresso machine.

"What can I get for you, Mr. Herman?" Kate asked. The professional diversion seemed to have snapped her out of the fog.

"Wait," he said squinting at her. He took off his 1980s plastic-framed glasses and put them back on his face. "You work here now? Ms. Carpenter, if you're here on a permanent basis, we'll need to revisit our rental agreement." The concept of any sort of change in Kate's plans seemed to have thrown Larry for a magnificent loop. He scowled as only Larry could, worked up over nothing. It must be exhausting to be him.

"Nothing's changed," Kate told him. "Just helping out a friend for the day." She made brief eye contact with Autumn, who relaxed marginally when met with that slight smile. She took a moment to enjoy the connection.

"If it does, I can draw up a lease. We should keep this as official as possible."

"It won't change," Kate said, matter-of-factly.

Autumn's enjoyment ended there, the door slamming shut. The reminder that Kate would soon pack up and be gone forever left her with a hollowness she felt all over. She focused on the room around her, checking her milk levels, scanning the dining area for tables that needed to be bussed. Anything to push past the sinking reminder of a day on the calendar.

"What can I get for you?" Kate asked Larry, all the while keeping an eye on Autumn. Of course, she'd sensed a shift in Autumn's demeanor.

"I'll take a triple macchiato, half sweet, non-fat with caramel drizzled like a lattice."

Kate stared at him. "No, but really."

"That's my order. The lattice is important to my routine. So, not a swirl, not a smiley face, but—"

"A lattice," Kate finished.

Autumn joined Kate at the register and rang him up. "Kate, welcome to Larry."

"Wow."

"Let me guess," Steve said, rounding the counter from his break and pointing at Larry. "Caramel lattice drizzle."

"Yes, my good man," Larry said. He moved to the pickup

station and looked back at Kate. "Since you're not staying, make sure you take care of that apartment, young lady."

"Will do." A pause. "Am I supposed to comment on your age and gender now, too?"

Autumn suppressed a laugh. "And with that, you have fulfilled your last duty to the Cat's Pajamas. Get out of here. Go enjoy your day."

Kate untied the apron. "When do you get off?"

Autumn felt the secret shiver. "Close to six."

"Cool."

That's when something awful happened. Olivia breezed in. "Hey, there," she said, practically to the room at large. She took a moment to look around. "Wow. Look at this place. Talk about a blast from the past. I haven't been in here in, what—three years now?"

"Just under two," Autumn said, her mouth tight. "What can I get for you, Olivia?"

Kate went still and leaned back against the counter, taking in the scene.

"I was just out and about, picking up an order for the gym at a print shop not far from here, and thought I'd pop in for a little caffeinated shot in the arm."

"An almond latte?" Autumn asked, hoping to speed this along.

Olivia winked. "You know me well." She dropped her voice and moved closer to Autumn. "About the whole faking-a-date to my wedding thing, I want you to know that it was so not a big deal. A girl's gotta do what a girl's gotta do."

"I didn't fake a date," Autumn said. "It was a misunderstanding."

"Hey," Olivia said, placing a hand over Autumn's on the counter. "You don't have to be strong with me. You're struggling. I get it. Listen, Betsy's offer to train you at the gym is still available."

Autumn saw Kate straighten in her periphery.

"The thing is, I want you to find someone who makes you as happy as Betsy makes me, and with just a little bit of fortitude," a cheerful smile grew on Olivia's face, "I'm confident you can."

"I don't mean to interrupt, but I gotta run. So, I'll pick you up at six?" Kate asked, pushing off the counter.

Autumn turned, her mind struggling to keep up with it all. Olivia had just bitch-slapped her, and Kate was referencing a conversation they'd never had, and the haze was all consuming. "Sure, yeah," she said, absently. Before she knew what hit her, Kate pulled her in and kissed her with the precision of a Renaissance painter, a classical composer, an American Ninja Warrior! Holy hell, was it a good kiss, and it still wasn't over. *Oh, keep going. Please keep going.* Distantly, she registered Kate's hand moving through her hair and behind her head, holding her in place. Distantly, because her body's instant reaction to the kiss occupied the forefront of her brain. Her toes tingled. Her shoulders went slack. The most delicious of tingles moved down her spine, leaving her in a partial shimmy-shake. Kate, at last, released her, leaving Autumn grappling for air and equilibrium and halfway to an orgasm.

"Perhaps I'm completely uninformed," Olivia said, looking between them, wildly embarrassed. She stuck out her hand to Kate. "Olivia. Autumn and I used to—"

"Date, right?" Kate said, squinting as if trying to recall. "I feel like maybe she mentioned you once."

Bless Kate. Bless her!

She turned back to Autumn. "Six, then? I can't wait."

Autumn nodded wordlessly and watched as Kate calmly walked the length of the shop and disappeared into the California afternoon. That's when she realized that Olivia was also watching after her in total and complete appreciation.

"I feel silly now," Olivia told her.

Autumn, returning to herself, raised a confident shoulder. "Don't. Pshh. There's no way you could have known about Kate."

"So, she *works* for you?"

"No, no. Kate's a firefighter. Fights actual fires with her bare hands. Was just helping out this morning."

"Gives them a little more time together," Steve said, leaning into the conversation and joining Autumn in her fantastical lie.

Olivia nodded slowly. "I would imagine so."

"About the gym, though," Autumn said. "I think I'm gonna pass. I have so much on my plate right now with the shop and Kate and, you know, I'm getting quite a workout already…in other ways."

"Plus, the baby," Steve supplied.

"What baby?" Olivia asked.

Autumn sent Steve a look and he guiltily busied himself at the counter. "Not a big deal. I'm working on getting pregnant."

"Whoa. A new relationship and a baby all at once. This little visit was more than I bargained for," Olivia said with a mystified grin. She held up the to-go cup that Steve had slid her way. "Really happy I stopped in here. Wow. A baby. And a firefighter."

Autumn nodded seriously. "It was a busy spring."

"Apparently. Take care, Autumn."

"Yep. You too. My love to Betsy," she called after her brightly.

The glass door closed behind Olivia, and Autumn and Steve turned to each other with holy-hell looks mirrored on their faces. Autumn couldn't hold back the triumphant smile if it killed her.

"That was amazing," Steve said, walking in a small circle, both hands shading his eyes. "I wish I had it on tape. I need a replay."

Autumn nodded. "Maybe one of the most satisfying moments of my adult life. I'm a no-good liar probably bound for hell for that, but I don't even care. Where's my handbasket? Sign me up."

"And what about Kate?" Steve said, pointing emphatically to the spot where she'd owned Autumn in broad daylight. "She didn't miss a beat. Who knew she was that good an actress?"

"Not me," Autumn said, inadvertently touching her still-sensitive lips. Was it possible to hold in a kiss? To keep it with you for a little while longer? She'd certainly like to try. And then Autumn realized that was the second time this week that Kate had gone out of her way to save her, to do something nice for her when she could really use it. She needed to acknowledge that, say thank you, even if it didn't seem like much. "You know what? I'll be right back," she told Steve, who nodded back knowingly.

Moments later, Kate was quick to answer the door and smiled uneasily when she saw Autumn. "Before you say anything, I get I was out of line. I just wasn't okay with the way your ex was—"

"Thank you," Autumn said, before she could even finish the sentence. She was beaming. That much she knew. "A million thank-yous for what you did back there."

"Oh." Kate took a moment with that one. "Really? In that case, you're welcome."

"But you're off the hook tonight. I'm certainly not expecting you to—"

"What if I don't want to be off the hook?"

Now it was her turn to say it. "Oh."

Kate stepped outside of the apartment. "It'd be nice to get out, if I'm telling the truth. Doesn't have to be a big production. Maybe we could take a walk on the beach?"

"We can, and I'll even do you one better. How about I bring dinner?"

"Dinner on the beach? Can't say I've ever done that before. That would be…great. Yeah, let's do it."

"Great."

"Great."

They'd turned into idiots. It had finally happened.

Autumn nodded several times, not at all sure what they were doing but excited by it at the same damn time. "Let's make it six thirty, just to be safe. I'll pick you up then."

"Looking forward to it. What can I bring?"

Your awesomely thick dark hair. Your kind heart. The lips I'd go to battle for. "Just you."

"I can do that."

Autumn headed off across the courtyard, keenly aware of her heated face.

"Hey, Autumn?" Kate called from behind her.

"Yep?"

"That kiss. Out of line or not, it was really…memorable."

She sighed dreamily in her head. "That it was, Kate."

Chapter Ten

What the hell was she supposed to wear to a picnic on the beach?

Kate stared in frustration at the neatly folded clothes in the dresser of her rental. It wasn't even so much that she didn't know what to wear that had her off-kilter, it was how much she cared. Fashion had never been on her radar, and what clothes she put on her body was generally an afterthought at most.

But here she sat, caring very much about her beach outfit and what Autumn would think of it. How annoying was that and who was she, exactly? She grumbled her way through the stupid selection of cutoff shorts and a white sleeveless top. Casual and beachy, she decided, glancing over her shoulder at the mirror. Right? Weren't cutoffs beachy? Did Google know?

She took a seat and waited for six thirty, watching the seconds crawl by and wondering about the shift in her vulnerability. When she'd first met Autumn, they'd clicked instantly. Everything was easy in the most refreshing sense. But as time went on, she noticed herself looking forward to each moment they got to spend together more and more. She resisted the urge to pop into Pajamas five times a day just to say hi, and now she was stressing about her *outfit*, of all things. There was only one answer.

The stakes had been raised.

Autumn was beginning to matter to Kate, and with that shift came things like wearing the right damn outfit for sitting in the sand and eating food. She sighed, wondering if she should cancel tonight before she got herself in any deeper or just steer into the skid at this point, knowing she was virtually powerless.

A few minutes later, when she stood face-to-face with Autumn in a blue and white sundress that fell just above the knee, she understood that the choice had been made for her. Kate smiled. "Let's go to the beach."

The early evening held tight to the warmth of the afternoon, sheltering them with a comfortable seventy-six degrees and a cool breeze off the Pacific. Autumn drove them down the beach to a spot she knew. The stretch of sand was quiet. Seagulls called overhead, and the soft sounds of the waves rolling in made for a serene soundtrack.

"It's nice out here," Kate said, shielding her eyes from the sun and looking down the beach. "Where is everybody?"

"About a mile that way," Autumn told her, pointing. "That's where all the action is. Only locals hang out here, and most have headed home after a day of surfing or are grabbing something to eat before heading back for the last few moments of daylight. Speaking of eating…" Autumn held the wicker picnic basket in the air.

"Let me do that," Kate said, taking the basket. She then fluffed the blanket she'd carried over from Autumn's car until they had a large square spot to sit. With the breeze gently rustling her hair, Autumn took a seat on the blanket and began unpacking their dinner. "Roasted chicken, smoked zucchini, new potatoes, and strawberry shortcake for dessert. The strawberries are fresh from this cute little town up the coast. I'll have to take you there one day."

"You made all this?" Kate asked in surprise.

"Not even close," Autumn said. "I worked all day. But I know all the best take-out spots. It's my superpower."

"Equally impressive," Kate said, accepting the plate Autumn assembled for her.

"I hope I get to make dinner for you myself someday, though. It's the least I can do after everything you've done for me."

"I haven't done anything," Kate said, moving the very attractive food around on her plate.

"You have, but I know you well enough that I expected you to say as much. You're a downplayer. If you won Wimbledon, you'd say it was an easy year."

Kate chuckled. "Trust me, if I won Wimbledon, it was an easy year. I've never picked up a racquet."

"See? Are you arrogant about anything? Is there one thing you know you're good at and will admit to freely?"

Kate inclined her head and met Autumn's gaze. "I have impressive taste in women."

Autumn opened her mouth and closed it, not sure what to say. "You're smooth."

Kate smiled lazily. "Been practicing that one." They ate for a few moments, all the while watching each other, the anticipation of the evening present like a third guest at dinner. So many unspoken thoughts, swirling in the sea air between them. What Kate wouldn't give to know what Autumn's were.

"I'm just going to go there. I like you more than I should," Autumn finally said, granting Kate's wish.

Kate took a moment, paying attention to the bolt of excitement she got from the declaration.

"And the problem is that I'm getting used to you. And yes, I think you're beautiful and kind and the chemistry hovers beyond the stratosphere, but that's not all."

"Then tell me," Kate said holding her gaze, reveling in their connection. "I want to know."

"You've become my friend. You're there for me, and I'm freaking myself the hell out because I don't want to get attached, but I'm—"

"Getting attached."

Autumn nodded solemnly and Kate took a moment, because they were entering the dicey waters they'd worked so hard to avoid. But honestly, was there really any way around them, other than staying the hell away from Autumn—a suggestion she knew was damn near impossible for her?

"Me too," Kate said, simply. It wasn't the most eloquent sentence, but Autumn was better with words. "So, what are we supposed to do with that?"

"I don't know," Autumn said. "Maybe we just eat dinner and enjoy the beach. If I had a magic solution, I'd offer it."

"I like the enjoying the beach idea."

"Then that's two of us."

They did just that, and Kate understood that when it came to take-out, Autumn Primm didn't mess around. The meal was phenomenal, as was the view. Neither matched the company. Talking or not talking, she enjoyed the serenity of being there with Autumn.

"Olivia was gobsmacked by your mere existence," Autumn mused, her fork making twirly circles as she lost herself in the memory. She was so cute when something excited her. "The look on her face when I said the word "firefighter" was worth every difficult moment she put me through." She squinted. "Well, almost."

"Were there a lot of those?" Kate sat up straight, not liking the thought. "Bad moments."

"Do nights spent on my own and the absence of any truly meaningful conversations count?"

"Yeah. Those count a lot."

"Then yes." Autumn stared off into the distance, thoughtful. "I guess I didn't realize how awful the relationship was until I was out of it, and then it was all about the heartbreak of being unceremoniously dumped for a woman with a third of my body fat."

"I don't like it when you say stuff like that. You're beautiful."

The comment seemed to have resonated with Autumn, and she placed a hand over her heart. "Man. You stun me silent, you know that? And I'm a chatty person. Known for it, far and wide, in fact." A pause. "I guess I haven't felt that way about myself in a while. Attractive. I have lately."

"Good. It's beyond me that you wouldn't. Do you think it has to do with the breakup?"

"Probably a portion of it."

"So, why'd it end?"

Autumn took a moment as if trying to answer a complicated question simply. "We'd been drifting apart for a while. Olivia had always been searching for something I couldn't quite put my finger on. Then one day she joined a gym, and I saw a shift. She spent more time in front of the mirror. Highlighted her hair and started counting every carb that went into her mouth. The owner of the gym, Betsy, took a special interest in her case, and from then on, it was, 'Betsy said we should be doing forty-five minutes of cardio every morning to start our day. Betsy thinks it would be better if we stopped going to restaurants. Betsy says no more popcorn at the movies.'"

Kate stared at her. "Betsy sounds like a buzz kill."

Autumn smiled sardonically. "In more ways than one. But it got worse. As Olivia fell deeper into it, the focus shifted to me, which was…hard. How I should come work out with her, and look into taming my hair, or work more on my tan when I had time off. I didn't realize it at the time, but I'd never felt more like a loser in my life. Well, until she left me for Betsy."

Kate was worked up and hating every detail she'd just heard. She sat up straight. "Thank God she did. Because that kind of life sounds awful. Getting away from Olivia might be the best thing that ever happened to you."

"Well, so far," Autumn said. They let the sentence linger. "What about you, though? Tell me about your history. When was the last time you were in love?"

The word was a tricky one for Kate. Love. She wasn't exactly sure what it meant, what comprised love in the romantic sense. "I don't know that I ever have been. Yet."

"Oh." That pulled Autumn up short. "But you date?"

"I date. Occasionally." Kate looped a strand of hair behind her ear. "Harder in a small town."

Autumn nodded, biting her lip. "I'd imagine so. Worst date you've ever been on? Go."

"You really want to go there?" Kate asked, smiling.

"I have to learn everything I can about the mysterious out-of-towner."

"Fair enough. Marissa Granson asked me to the sausage festival."

"Pause." Autumn held up a hand. "Clearly, I heard you wrong."

Kate chuckled. "You didn't. There's an annual sausage festival held every year just outside of Slumberton."

Autumn bathed in enjoyment, her eyes bright. "And it's somehow this sausage fest, a literal one, that seemed like the perfect place for Marissa to take her lesbian date? I'm not sure anything you say will top that. You can try. Won't work."

Now Kate was laughing. "The irony is not lost on me, as I hear it back now."

Autumn, trying to control her own laughter, waved them on. "Okay, okay, so you and Marissa, intent on a romantic lesbian one-on-one, are headed to the sausage festival. Got it. Given circumstances in place. Proceed."

Kate shook her head because it really did sound ridiculous. "Do you want me to be able to get through this?" Because the sheer act of trying *not to laugh* had tears filling her eyes.

"I desperately need you to get through it. Now, let's hear about your wild sausage adventure."

Kate took a long, deep breath, which helped bring her back to a semblance of control. "Well, to begin with, she brought her brother and her turtle."

That did it. Autumn erupted into silent laughter all over again, falling to her side on the blanket. She attempted to speak, failed, and then tried again. "Let me guess," she wheezed. "Turtles love a good sausage?"

"You'd think, but no. They're vegetarian. Marissa just happened to be very attached to LeRoy. That was his name. She took him most everywhere. Long story short, I wound up turtle-sitting most of the night while she stood in line for one sausage after another, and on top of it, I had to fight off advances from the stupid brother."

"Who probably had some sausage ambition of his own."

Kate covered her face. "You give it all new meaning."

"Well, someone has to. That sounds like a doozy of an evening, Kate."

She looked skyward. "It's not one I'm likely to forget."

"Okay, and now your *best* date," Autumn prompted. She tucked a strand of her curls behind her ear and rolled her lips inward in excited anticipation. "And if it tops the sausage fest in terms of storytelling, you've made my night."

"Okay, well here goes." Kate didn't even have to think on this one and answered automatically: "The observatory with a talkative redhead."

A pause. Autumn eyed her skeptically. Her smiled dimmed. "I can't decide if you're telling the truth."

"I am," Kate said. The laughter from earlier had her feeling light and playful. "You should have seen this woman. Her jaw dropped each time something along the way amazed her, and she indulged my space travel fixation. She was kind, and funny, and looked very, very pretty in a green dress I will never get out of my mind. Another night I will never forget for a whole separate reason. Nothing to do with turtles or sausages."

Autumn stared at her as if struck. "How do you do that with just, like, five sentences?"

"Do what?"

"Make me feel important."

Kate shrugged. "I just call 'em as I see 'em." They stared at each other for what seemed like an eternity. Kate felt the warmth move from the center of her back, up her neck, until her face felt hot. The rest of her body followed suit. But she didn't shy away from any of it. She held steady.

"Come over here," Autumn said quietly. Kate crawled over and nestled her body behind Autumn's, who sat cross-legged as they looked out over the water. "I've got a problem," Autumn said. "We've got this whole hands-off policy, yet when I'm around you, all I want is your hands…on."

Kate took a steadying breath at the declaration. She felt it in her stomach and most notably lower. The sound of the waves, the desolate stretch of beach, and the words Autumn had just confessed had her battling a gentle throbbing.

"I can help with that," she said quietly. She placed her hands on Autumn's knees, caressing upward to her lower thigh, exposing it beneath the sundress slightly with her movement, and back again. "Your skin is soft."

Autumn rested the back of her head on Kate's shoulder. "I'm the queen of methodical lotion application, required for a beach town."

Kate closed her eyes and enjoyed the sensation of the smooth skin beneath her fingertips. "It's really working for you."

"So, you like my skin."

"More than that. I like it all."

A pause. "What is it about me that you're attracted to?"

The question snagged Kate's attention because the tone in Autumn's voice indicated she was literally asking for clarification. She didn't get it. Ludicrous. "I like watching you talk, for one."

Autumn turned in her arms. "What does that mean? Watching."

"You hold your mouth in the most unique way, as if you're sometimes about to say something, but then change direction to something else. I really like that, watching it play out."

Autumn laughed. "Now that's one I've never been told before."

"You also have really great underwear." She let her fingertips brush the tops of Autumn's thighs this time, and back again. The constant motion had the throbbing moving into high gear and Kate's mind trotting off to…more intimate thoughts.

She heard Autumn suck in a breath. "Well, that *one night* I did."

"Are you kidding? More than that night. I might have stolen a glimpse here or there. The satin purple bra I spotted yesterday might be the winner."

"Wow."

"My thought at the time." Kate continued to trace patterns across Autumn's skin. Had her attention grown increasingly intimate? Yes. Had she briefly brushed the insides of Autumn's thighs with the lightest of touches? Possibly.

Autumn shook her head slightly. "What are you doing to me right now?"

Kate smiled into Autumn's shoulder. "I have no idea what you're talking about." Except she had so *many* ideas. All of them R-rated.

"You should know that I'm about to combust in your arms."

"Are you asking me to make that happen?" she whispered in

Autumn's ear. The nod was almost imperceptible. Kate pressed her hand boldly beneath Autumn's dress, to the patch of fabric between her legs, and pressed gently.

"Oh, my God," Autumn breathed.

"Let's try for more of that."

She pressed back against Kate's hand. "Fuck."

"That, too."

Kate surveyed the expanse of the beach, noting that they still had it all to themselves. The last soul they'd seen was a man walking his dog, but that was a good fifteen minutes ago. With one eye on the beach, she stroked Autumn softly, pressing into the fabric, moving across it. Over and back again, listening to sounds of the waves and Autumn's accelerated breathing. She nuzzled her face into Autumn's hair and traced circles now, inching slightly higher, so that—

"There," Autumn managed, grasping Kate's forearm for emphasis. Autumn nodded her endorsement and leaned back against Kate fully, adjusting to allow Kate more access. The circles Kate traced became smaller, quicker, and more focused until Autumn shuddered, stilled, and cried out quietly in Kate's arms.

Her breath still came in short gasps. "On the beach," she managed anyway. "Right here on the fucking beach you did that."

"We had it to ourselves," Kate said, grinning. "I couldn't help myself. You…inspire things in me."

"Yeah, well, you just inspired a soul-scorching orgasm in *me*." She nodded several more times. "This is definitely what I would classify as living life more fully."

"We need to go now," Kate said. Autumn turned in her arms and met her eyes questioningly. "Because I didn't get to fully touch you, and now you're saying words like 'orgasm' out loud, and I have more to offer on the topic."

Autumn's eyes went dark. "Dear Lord, help me."

Hours passed as they did decadent things together in Kate's apartment, yet it didn't feel like hours at all. When she was with Autumn, time flew, and because they were already familiar with each other, the night took on a different tone. They were bolder, more playful, and a lot more at home with each other. As the sun crept through the window in the early hours of the morning, a thought occurred to Kate. "Hey, are you supposed to be at work?"

Autumn, who lay naked and gorgeous and nestled into Kate's side, shook her head. "Not opening today. I give myself one or two days a week to sleep in, if only a couple of hours more. Why? You trying to get rid of me?"

"I'm trying to keep you," Kate said, and pressed a kiss onto her forehead. "I also don't want you to ever put your clothes on again."

"That might pull looks."

She laughed and pulled Autumn in closer. She let her eyes drift closed and felt the humming of her body, satisfied and heavy from Autumn's expert attention. She was a firecracker in every aspect of her life, and the bedroom was certainly included. "Hey, do you have names yet?" Kate rested the side of her head on her palm.

"As in baby names?"

"Yeah."

"That's something you would want to talk about?"

Kate softened. "Of course it is. You don't have to keep your actual life tucked away. You act like talking about what you have going on is a burden. Your doctor's visit, this conversation—all things I want to participate in, because they're connected to you. Do you get it now?"

Autumn sat up in bed, pulling the blanket with her. She smiled, and blinked back sleepily. "I get it now."

"So, what are the names?"

"I don't have any," she said simply.

"Come on," Kate said. "Everyone has thought about what they would name their children."

Autumn shook her head. "Not me. I think I'm afraid if I do that, I'll…"

"What?"

"Start to buy into something that would make me happy. But what if it doesn't happen? What if it doesn't belong to me? Names just seem too…assumptive. Big things don't tend to happen in my life. So I'm cautious."

Kate understood that Autumn was not the type who did

much for herself. She worked hard, looked out for other people—especially her friends—and expected the worst from pretty much every other aspect of life. Maybe that was Olivia's fault. Maybe her mother's. Regardless, it made Kate want happiness so badly for Autumn it hurt.

"Hey, look at me. It's okay to hope. And while I don't have any sort of guarantee, I know in my heart that this is going to happen for you, and I want you to start thinking that way, too."

A ghost of a smile passed Autumn's lips. "It's terrifying, but I can try."

"Try hard, because you're the most deserving person I know. And the most amazing, and not just when you're vertical."

Autumn grinned fully at the cheeky comment. "Okay, I'm gonna say something here. Are you ready?"

"Ready."

"Do you know what you do for me?"

Kate shook her head.

"Well, beyond the obvious"—Autumn bounced her eyebrows—"you give me confidence, and it's the strangest feeling."

"Nope. All I did was remind you."

She lay back down in bed with her cheek turned to Kate. "When can I see you again?"

"Are you free for a late lunch?"

"Today's my lucky day. I am."

She snuggled back into Kate, and they caught what little sleep they could before Autumn had to head over to Pajamas. Their date and the memorable night that followed felt like a breakthrough. She remembered the words she'd spoken to Autumn on the beach. She'd never been in love. That part was true, but Autumn was different from any other girl she'd ever been with. In her heart of hearts, she knew that much.

How did she get here? It had all started out so innocently. Okay, not entirely, as they'd had sex on the first date. The worry crept in, the fear that she was no longer in control. She'd be heading home soon, and these would all be just memories to pull out on occasion when she went one way and Autumn went another. As difficult as that pill was to swallow, she realized how important it was to remind herself of their reality. She'd continue to see Autumn, but she'd have to find a way to guard her heart.

It was the only way.

For now, she pulled Autumn closer and refused to watch the clock as their time together ticked away, one important moment at a time.

❖

Kate stood in the courtyard several days later, phone to her ear, shaking her head at what she was hearing. The bag of groceries she'd purchased sat abandoned on the pavement for the more important phone call. She'd been waiting on Jennifer from the DHS to get back to her, and at long last she had. The news wasn't good.

"We have a foster home lined up for both Ren and Eva for a month. It's temporary, yes, but it's the best I could do."

"They need a permanent situation," Kate said, agitated at the thought of the kids, suitcases in hand, moving from one home to another because the adults involved couldn't do any better for them. Unacceptable.

Jennifer sighed. "We're on the same page here, Lieutenant. It's just not easy, especially if we want to keep the siblings together."

"Well, we do. We definitely do. Anything new from their mother?" She decided not to mention her own unsuccessful field trip to Santa Barbara. She was pretty sure that wouldn't go over well.

"She's stopped taking my calls," Jennifer said. "I checked her out, and she's been on the straight and narrow for a while now. Honestly, I think she's overwhelmed by the prospect and running scared. I was hoping with time she'd come around, but that doesn't seem to be the case. The last time we talked she pretty much told me to go to hell."

Kate stared at the pavement, processing. "So, that makes the kids adoptable, right? If she's essentially giving up her rights?"

A pause. "Why? Are you offering?"

"No." Panic struck. "I didn't mean me. I just meant…someone."

"We can move to have her rights terminated. Once that happens, both children would be adoptable should the right person come along."

"Yeah, well, the sooner the better. And, hey, Jennifer? I appreciate you keeping me in the loop. I know this isn't exactly protocol. It's probably the opposite, but I appreciate the favor."

"As far as protocol goes, this isn't an average case."

"No, I guess not."

They wrapped up the call, leaving Kate feeling like they were no closer to any sort of resolution. The guilt settled heavy and uncomfortable on her heart.

"I didn't mean to eavesdrop," Isabel said, turning in her spot on the outdoor couch.

How had Kate missed her sitting there?

"Sounds like you're dealing with some pretty big stuff."

Kate nodded soberly and stared at her phone. "A couple of kids I know lost their father in a fire."

"One you worked?"

She looked up. Isabel's eyes held startling sympathy, but not in the pitiful way everyone had looked at her back home. Kate nodded, and for reasons beyond her, it all came tumbling out. "It's weighing on me like nothing I've ever experienced. It's like I can't get out from under that day. I think about it and play it back at all hours." She placed her hand across her chest, realizing that, even in that moment, she was finding it hard to breathe.

Isabel nodded. "Wanna sit down?"

Because Kate didn't know what else to do with herself, she did.

Isabel watched her and seemed to settle on a decision. "Here's the deal. I don't talk about this much, but I live with some pretty major anxiety. Panic attacks, whatever you want to call them. They can be crippling." She held out a hand. "And if you'd rather not talk about it, I understand. Just tell me to shut the fuck up."

"It's fine." Kate nodded. "I have trouble sleeping sometimes. The fire, all of it, replays in my head."

"Been there."

She decided to take advantage of this opportunity. "How do you get it to stop?"

Isabel raised her eyebrows and sighed. "Yeah, that part's harder. Talking about it helps. I see someone once a month. It took me a while to bite the bullet and just do it, but it was the right thing. My therapist seems to think I've made progress, and the attacks hit less and less."

Kate nodded. "My captain had the same recommendation. I don't think I'm up for talking to some doctor."

"Then maybe just someone you trust?"

"Yeah, maybe." Only one person's name came to mind. Everything lately seemed to bring her back to the same place. The same person. Autumn. The image of her smiling on their beach picnic flooded her with warmth, and something loosened. Maybe Isabel was onto something after all. "What are you working on?"

Isabel lifted the laptop next to her. "Second to last episode of the season is mine. Our ex-assassin has to figure out how to shuttle six second-graders to ballet, take down a serial killer before he can hurt anyone else, and figure out how to get the woman next door to notice her."

Kate raised her eyebrows. "My kind of show."

"Mine, too. I'm lucky to write for it," Isabel said. "Hey, can I ask one last question?"

"Shoot."

"I heard you mention adoption. Are you thinking you might take those kids?"

"No. It's not even something I would consider. I can't be someone's parent. I live alone and eat frozen pizza. So that would be outrageous. I mean, it would be, right?"

Isabel smiled and offered a one-shouldered shrug. "You tell me."

❖

Autumn's small house in West Hollywood wasn't much, but it had character. She'd taken her own flair for funky design and made the intimate space come alive. At least for her. She wondered now what someone more conservative like Kate would think of her bright purple and green curtains.

They'd made plans to see a movie at the indie theater down the street, and Kate was scheduled to arrive shortly. Would the vintage Italian movie posters throw her? Or the dark gray walls and restored wiry chandelier that hung over the recovered sectional? She ran her bare foot across the furry grape rug beneath the coffee table, which itself looked like several planks of wood, one rotating on top of the next. When she'd bought it, she knew the coffee table would be the cornerstone piece to her home. She hadn't been wrong. Friends commented on it constantly.

Still. Looking at it through new eyes—Kate's—had her aware of her own unique style.

Three short, sharp knocks on the door killed the thought. She glanced at the clock with Tweety Bird in the center pointing at the time and took note that Kate was early. This was no surprise. She was Kate, the epitome of precision and confidence. She was probably early everywhere she went and super calm about it. *No big deal. I'm just early and looking hot on your doorstep.* Autumn shook herself out of the daydream, swung open the door, and grinned that it had become her real life. "Welcome to my place."

"Hey," Kate said, smiling back at her. She produced a bottle from behind her back. "I brought you wine. I feel like it's what you do when you come to someone's house."

"Not necessary, but thank you. You're very thoughtful. Come in. I'll give you the tour while we have a glass before the movie." As Kate walked past her into her home, Autumn realized there was something different about her tonight. Her dark hair was pulled back, but only partially this time, leaving the sides to fall along her face, past her shoulders. It added a whole new softness that had Autumn off guard and, okay, let's be honest: salivating a little. Kate was just as beautiful as ever. Tough and soft at the same time.

"Look at this place," Kate said, as she took in the room.

"Is that a 'look how crazy this place is. What is Autumn thinking?' Or 'look how awesome—Autumn is a freakin' genius'? 'Cuz that could go a lot of ways."

"Look how *you* it is," Kate said, moving toward her. "I love it. My place back home has a few white walls, a couch, and a bed."

"I have a feeling you prevaricate."

"Can't prevaricate. Don't know what that is." But she smiled, and Autumn knew it was her own brand of humor.

Autumn handed Kate a glass of the Malbec she'd brought. "And how was your day?" They hadn't seen each other since the day before. Kate had stopped in for coffee earlier, but Autumn had been meeting with a vendor and they hadn't connected. "Different. I talked to the social worker back home."

"About the kids?"

Kate nodded. "Still no home for them. It was strange. For a minute, the social worker thought I was volunteering to adopt them."

"Huh," Autumn said, sipping from her glass. The look on Kate's face, the thoughtful eyes, the drawn-in brows had Autumn wondering if there was something to this. Kate, after all, had a big heart. The thought made her spirits dip, and she hated herself for how selfish that made her. "Is that something you're considering?"

Kate shook her head. "I'm the last person who should take them. I don't know anything about kids, plus my head's a mess."

Autumn nodded. "That's fair." She waited a moment before deciding to press further. As much as she didn't want to give Kate a reason to head home, she understood that she would be leaving. One day soon even, and maybe this was something Kate needed to talk through with someone. She could help with that. "Doesn't mean you couldn't learn, you know."

"Such a huge responsibility," Kate said, shaking her head emphatically. She walked toward a painting of a woman pulling on a pair of stockings and stared. With her back to Autumn, it was hard for her to tell what Kate was thinking, what she was feeling. She knew, regardless, that it must be a lot for her to bring the topic up to begin with. "I mean, there's school, and friends, and things like bath time."

Autumn walked to her. "You wouldn't have to do all those things at once. That'd be weird." *Please don't leave.*

That pulled a smile. "I just…I don't think it's the right move."

A portion of Autumn sighed in relief. "And no one faults you for that." But Kate seemed unsettled, and Autumn wondered if maybe their movie date should wait. "Would you rather just chill here tonight? Relax?"

Kate turned to her tentatively. "That would be okay with you? I know you wanted to see the film."

Autumn took her hand. "I'm about to divulge a secret here."

"Okay," Kate said, eying her.

"I really just wanted to spend time with you." By the end of that sentence, Kate's tightly knitted brow relaxed, and she seemed more at ease. "Plus, I'm kind of a homebody."

She lifted their hands and intertwined their fingers. "What should we do?" She looked around for options. "I don't suppose you have *Ms. Pac-Man*."

Autumn laughed. "I absolutely do not have *Ms. Pac-Man* and never will. She's banned from this house. But I'm a pretty formidable board game shark."

"I'd play a board game with you," Kate said, meeting her eyes.

How was she able to make everything seem earnest and sexy? "Great. Scrabble it is."

"Uh-oh. We've already established you're better with words. You use like eight times what I do in a day."

"Which is why we're playing," Autumn said, energized now, her competitive spirit kicked into gear. "It'll be fantastic. We'll drink beer, and listen to music, and I'll win. Best. Night. Ever."

But it didn't quite go that way. An hour later, Kate had her by eighty-three points. Not only that, but she was purposefully turning Scrabble into an R-rated exercise. After she'd laid down "passion," "pleasure," "breasts," and "grind." Autumn passed her a look, doing her best not to indicate that the succession of words had affected her in the slightest. Her temperature hadn't *at all* risen steadily as the night went on. She hadn't *once* fantasized about easing that black T-shirt over Kate's head and having her delicious way with her. She certainly hadn't adjusted in her chair due to any sort of discomfort when Kate had played the word "thrust." But enough was enough!

"Quickie?" Autumn asked, staring at the board, incredulous. "You're playing 'quickie' on a triple word?"

"I am," Kate said calmly, looking pleased with herself. "Q comes with ten points, apparently. Strategic, right?"

Autumn leaned forward. "I don't even think that's a real word."

"Quickies are real," Kate said, meeting her eyes in all seriousness. "Are you arguing that quickies aren't real? Or maybe it's that you think they're not important?" Kate sat back and folded her arms. "I'm surprised at you."

"No, they're important, it's just—I can't even believe I'm having this conversation! This is madness. You're hijacking this game."

"Am not. But I can play 'climax' if you'd rather. X's are eight points."

"Don't you dare," Autumn said, in a deadly tone, the pent-up energy almost too much to manage.

"I'm just kidding. I don't even have an X."

That did it. Autumn was up and around the table and straddling Kate's lap in a matter of seconds. Her lips landed eagerly on Kate's, who didn't hesitate to give back as good as she got. "Is this a quickie?" Kate asked.

"Shut up."

With Stevie Wonder playing softly in the background, Autumn fulfilled that most imminent desire and removed that T-shirt, happy to greet the black bra and tops of breasts beneath. Her mouth moved to them. Hungry now. She licked, kissed, and lost herself in a haze of overwhelming lust. Cupping Kate's face in her hands, she looked down at her.

"We're right back here again."

"Always." Kate nodded, breathless. "Bedroom?"

"Bedroom," Autumn said with zero hesitation.

Once there, Autumn took the reins. She marveled at how free she felt, how in control. When she and Kate were together, she wasn't worried about how she looked, or moved, or performed—the way she so often had with Olivia. With Kate, she could just…be. They didn't need the foreplay, the buildup, this go-round. After removing the necessary clothing, Autumn climbed on top and with a hand between them, slid inside Kate with one fluid motion, pulling a sharp moan. She did it again, and closed her eyes at the heat that enveloped her hand, the way Kate angled herself for more and moved her hips. Her breathing turned ragged, and Autumn felt a little drunk with arousal herself. She kissed her as Kate trembled, their connection unbroken. Kate said her name quietly as Autumn continued to move in and out slowly and then not so slowly until they'd reached the precipice, the release imminent. Shuddering in Autumn's arms, Kate tumbled spectacularly, clutching Autumn's shoulders and moving her hips against the pleasurable payoff.

Autumn's phone buzzed on the nightstand, but Kate had her total attention.

"Climax," Autumn said. "C. L. I. M. A. X. Climax."

Kate tossed an embarrassed arm over her eyes. "I deserved that. Not that I'm complaining." The phone buzzed again. "Is that real buzzing or just the fog I'm in?"

"Real, but—" The doorbell sounded. Autumn glanced behind her. "What the hell?" She grabbed her phone and checked the readout. "No, no, no."

"What's wrong?"

Autumn looked down at Kate, still beneath her. "It's Vicky. She's outside."

"Your mom?"

"My mom. And she's not the type to go away. Ever. She'll park herself on that doorstep until she gets whatever it is she came here for."

Kate's eyes went wide. "I'm about to meet your mother, seconds after you, her daughter, just…I don't even have the right word. Mind isn't working yet." She blinked several times. "How am I supposed to—"

Autumn leapt into action just as the doorbell sounded again. "Step one. Get dressed." Autumn started the process. "And meet me out there." She hopped into the living room on one leg, pulling on her jeans.

"Vicky, what in the world?" she asked upon answering the door. "It's after ten."

Her mother looked wide-eyed and hurt. "You're pregnant? My daughter is pregnant and she didn't even tell me?" Vicky didn't wait for an invitation and breezed into Autumn's living room, depositing her designer handbag on the couch.

Autumn squinted and turned. "Not pregnant. Who told you that?"

"That quirky counter boy at the coffee shop. I stopped in to see you because I needed a favor." She'd noticed several texts from Steve as she'd glanced at her phone. He'd probably been sending up warning flares.

"And he announced, inaccurately, that I was pregnant? Not really seeing how that happens on its own." She glanced toward the hallway and saw Kate standing there, looking hesitant.

"He mentioned you had a doctor's appointment and I pried it out of him. Do you have Chardonnay?" Vicky asked, taking a seat. Only she didn't seem too steady and had probably already had one of those.

"Vicky, I want to introduce you to Kate."

"What?" Vicky said, placing a hand over her chest. Her eyes scanned the room until they landed on Kate in the entryway. "You have late-night company. A booty call?"

Autumn cringed. "Not at all that."

"Nice to meet you, Ms. Primm," Kate said politely.

"Sweetheart, call me Vicky." She pointed at Kate. "Your shirt is on inside out."

Autumn watched Kate's face shift to the color of a ripe tomato.

Vicky waved it off. "Happens to the best of us. About that Chardonnay?"

"All out, I'm afraid." Autumn held up her palms apologetically—

anything to get her mother to go home and not say anything else too embarrassing.

"What about the pregnancy? My grandchild." Vicky leaned forward. "Is it Steve's?"

Autumn closed her eyes and pinched the bridge of her nose. "No. That would be impossible. But while we're on the topic," she glanced at Kate, who offered a supportive smile, "I am trying to get pregnant. That part is true."

Vicky pointed at Kate. "I don't really see her getting the job done."

Autumn wanted to die. "A donor, Vicky. I'm using a donor."

She sat back, brow in a knit. "Isn't that expensive?"

"I have a small savings, and this is an important step in my life."

"Seems like a waste of cash when you could just meet a nice man and spend a lovely afternoon together. Get that job done for free." She whistled and punched her fist in the air.

Autumn wasn't shocked that Vicky missed the main idea or that she once again couldn't understand how Autumn wouldn't want to hoodwink some poor guy into knocking her up. Par for the course, all of it. But couldn't she at least be happy for Autumn? For once?

"You know what? It's pretty late," Autumn said. "Can we talk about this another time?" Of course, Autumn knew the likelihood of hearing from Vicky anytime soon would depend wholly on what she needed from Autumn.

"I took a cab here," Vicky said. She picked up her bag and rooted around inside. "But I'm not sure that I—"

"Here," Autumn said, pulling forty dollars from her wallet. She wasn't an idiot. She knew what was up. "All yours."

That seemed to appease Vicky. She turned to Kate. "It was nice meeting you. What was your name?"

"Kate."

"Kate," she repeated, then laughed. "That shirt. Are you dating my daughter? Is this who you're dating, Autumn? She's pretty."

Kate opened her mouth, but Autumn beat her there. "We're friends."

"If you say so..."

Autumn waited on the porch with Vicky until the cab arrived, feeling like the evening had taken a definite hit. She made her way back inside and found Kate sitting on the side of her bed.

She glanced up as Autumn entered. "I'm sorry she wasn't more supportive."

"S'okay," Autumn said. "Nothing new. I'm sorry she interrupted our evening. I'm also sorry she wasn't nicer to you. If I had to guess, she'd already had a Chardonnay or two before arriving. Vicky loves a good white wine."

"Don't worry about me."

"But I do." They stared at each other until Kate finally nodded and kissed the back of Autumn's hand.

"Want to sleep over?" she asked, touching Kate's cheek. Maybe after everything, Kate would just want to get the hell out of there.

"I'd like that," Kate said, touching her chin. "And I like you."

"I like you, too," Autumn said. Her heart soared and she kissed Kate softly, then lingered just beyond her mouth before pulling away. "Even though you hustled me hardcore at Scrabble."

"Did not," Kate said, pulling Autumn into bed with her. "I just happen to be a quick study."

"Oh? So that's why, when I think sex with you can't get any better, it does?" Autumn asked. "That's a huge compliment, by the way."

"I try to pay attention." The little strip of moonlight that slashed across the bed allowed Autumn to see Kate's very telling blush, and she happened to love it.

They didn't name it, what was happening between them, but as the days passed, the bond between them only grew. Somehow applying a label felt too permanent, like naming the lost dog you knew would eventually go back to his owners. Instead, they soaked up the time together. Kate stopped by Pajamas once, sometimes twice a day, and Autumn popped over to Kate's during her down time. They chatted about their days, the things that weighed heavily on their minds. For Autumn, her fear that her child would one day grow up to feel that Autumn was a burden in her life, like Vicky. For Kate, the hovering concern that she'd somehow lost a part of herself the day of the fire. It was something she talked about openly now, which only brought them closer.

"I'm not reliving it as much, which is progress. But there's still this cloud that follows me, you know?" They were cozy on Kate's couch one afternoon, Autumn's legs across Kate's lap, Kate's arms wrapped around them.

"It's going to take time," Autumn said, stroking the back of Kate's neck. "But I already notice a change in you. You're less, I don't know, pent up. You talk about it now, and that has to act as some kind of release."

"Because you make it easy," Kate said, meeting her gaze and not letting go. "I've never talked to anyone the way I talk to you. You seem to just…get me."

Autumn sat up a little straighter, needing to deviate from the conversation briefly, because the way Kate was looking at her was everything. The way she *always* looked at her. "Where did you learn this type of eye contact, anyway?" Autumn asked. "It's like you see straight through me. It's…intense."

"What are you talking about?" Kate asked, her eyes widening playfully as she moved her face closer to Autumn.

"That's terrifying. Stop that," Autumn said, holding up a finger and backing away.

"Can't," she said, making them even wider.

"That's not dreamy, like usual. Bring back the dreamy stare! You're trying to scare me!" She scrambled from the couch and raced across the room, only Kate had shaped her hand into a hook, crossed her eyes, and wandered toward Autumn like a pirate zombie on a mission.

"What? I don't see the problem," Kate said, her voice nonchalant.

"I don't watch horror movies for a reason, Kate! Ahhh!" She shrieked and ran out of the apartment, laughing the whole time, Kate fast on her heels. Once she hit the middle of the courtyard,

Kate closed the distance, catching her by the waist, lifting her, and turning her in a circle.

"Captured for all time by the monster maniac eye-contact commandant."

"That's an awful name," Autumn said, locking her arms around Kate's neck as she was lowered to the ground. "Doesn't fall trippingly off the tongue at all."

"I'll work on it."

"But you're looking hot in the aftermath of the attack. That's something."

"Hot?" she smoldered purposefully. "So I should chase you out of the apartment more often?"

"I'm just saying the reunion is a perk."

Kate leaned down for a kiss and was greeted by the sound of applause. They turned to see Hadley and Gia hanging over the second-floor railing. "I give that a nine out of ten," Gia said, in her best commentator voice.

"And I'm going with an eight, Gia, just because her feet were flat on that lift."

"Good call," Gia said.

"Robbed," Kate said under her breath, pulling a chuckle from Autumn. "My feet were perfectly arched."

"Hey! Anyone want to go out for Mexican food?" Gia called down. "Had's already in."

"Hell, yes," Autumn said, and turned to Kate, who grinned.

"If you're there, I'm there."

With Kate around, time seemed to slow down for Autumn in the most wonderful way. Days no longer blurred into other days but held unique meaning. They laughed together, read books, or sat in the courtyard under the stars trying to figure out what the universe all meant.

"So, Gia and Izzy do this thing where they have to choose between two awful things. I think we should try it. Just maybe not the awful part." It was after closing, and they sat on the tailgate of Kate's truck sipping the chocolate milkshakes Kate had surprised

Autumn with. Never before had the end of a workday looked so good. It was really nice to be thought of.

"Like roses or lilies?" Kate asked, licking her spoon.

Autumn paused a moment to watch the potent display, a welcome shiver moving through her. "Or Star Trek or Star Wars?"

Kate eyed her. "Is there even a question? If you say yes, my heart will splinter."

Autumn gestured wildly with her cup. "Now, that is the most dramatic thing I've ever heard you say, so the answer must be Star Wars. You people are unreasonable about your franchise love."

Kate hopped off the tailgate and faced Autumn in outrage. "You people? You *people*? You don't know the sacred ground you're treading."

"The Force is strong with me as well. Calm down there, sweetheart."

Kate grinned. "Authoritative. My turn. Winning the lottery or hired for your dream job?"

"Dream job. No question. I'd be the best mermaid this town has ever seen."

Kate choked on her milkshake and placed a hand on her chest. "Only you."

A pause hit as their quiet laughter came to a lull. The night air brushed gently across Autumn's skin and she took a breath. "I postponed the insemination another month."

That seemed to throw Kate. "You did? Why?"

She searched for the words to explain that she was in the middle of something important already, and if it was fleeting, well, she wanted to be able to drink in every moment of it. Kate had become *that* important to her. "There will be time for that soon. Right now, I'm just enjoying…right now." And refusing to think too much about the day creeping up when it would all be just a distant memory, that one time when a wonderful woman showed up and made life meaningful for the first time.

Kate placed a hand on Autumn's leg. "Hey, you don't have to do that for me."

She ran her hand across Kate's. "I'm doing it for me. It's what I want."

Kate nodded. "If that's true, I can accept that."

"It is."

The summer crickets chirped, and Kate stared down at their hands. "We're constantly touching each other. Have you ever noticed that?"

"Yep. It's one of my favorite things about us."

"Us," Kate said, repeating the word. She looked uncomfortable.

"Don't freak out," Autumn said, gently. "It's a casual term. I'm a pretty astute girl, Kate."

"Do you believe in forever and ever?" Kate asked. "All of that?"

Autumn considered the question. "I'd like to. Hadley would immediately say yes. But yeah, I think that I do. What about you?"

Kate stared off into the night. "It's a nice idea. But maybe it's just that."

The sentiment hurt, whether Autumn wanted it to or not. She pushed off the truck and walked a few feet across the gravel.

"Does that upset you?" Kate asked. "That I don't buy into it. Fairy tales are fun, but they're fairy tales."

"I don't know," Autumn said, wrapping her arms around herself and wishing away the weakness. "Maybe."

She heard Kate sigh behind her, and the weight of their reality settled. They didn't say much after that, each alone with her own thoughts. Autumn wanted nothing more than to push them out of it and regain the lighthearted evening that had started with surprise milkshakes. The words to do so caught in her throat.

Instead, they sat there. Awkward. Uncomfortable. Tense.

Kate broke the silence. "I've been thinking about the kids a lot. About Ren and Eva."

"Oh yeah?"

"All this time, I've struggled with the fire. The pointlessness of all of it. But maybe there was a larger reason in the end. Maybe the fire was meant to bring me to those kids."

"I think it's a definite possibility, Kate."

"I think I want to adopt them, which means I need to go back."

Autumn turned, surprised by the declaration. "Wow. Okay." Another long pause as she tried to find the words. "I did not see that coming."

"No, I didn't either." Kate ran a hand through her hair.

"When did you decide this?"

Kate stared at her. "I think I've known for about a week."

Autumn shook her head hopelessly. The glow of what had been such a nice night subsided. "And you didn't say anything? Didn't clue me in? Believe it or not, I have some stake in what you decide to do, you know."

Kate took a moment. "I don't want to hurt you, Autumn."

"Yeah, well, I don't think there's any way around that, and I'm sorry for being *that girl*." She tried to keep an element of calm present in her voice, but lost that battle. The emotions she was juggling were too strong. "We laid out the rules, and now I'm trying to change them on you without notice and hold all this against you. That's not who I want to be, but it's like I'm too far in and can't help it."

"You're mad." Kate seemed to be working the puzzle. "I get that."

"How could I be mad? You're doing something noble and wonderful. But I guess, at the same time, I wondered if what we had was enough to make you want to stay. It was stupid, and foolish, and self-motivated, but that's what part of me hoped for. There. I said it."

Kate's gaze took on a removed, distant quality that she hadn't seen from her in a while. "I don't think I can be who you want me to be. I never intended for things to go this far."

"I know," Autumn nodded sadly, an uncomfortable lump in her throat. "Fairy tales aren't real. I remember."

CHAPTER ELEVEN

Something had shifted for Kate the moment the social worker had asked her if she was offering to adopt Ren and Eva. Never in a million years had she planned on jumping into a ready-made family, being someone's parent, after living a solitary existence for so many years. No way.

But the thought gnawed at her until the concept didn't seem like such a crazy one.

Kate hadn't planned on the little rugrats latching onto her heart the way they had over those many months, when they'd played on the sidewalk or taken long walks through the neighborhood together. Or that they would come to need someone so desperately. She couldn't have anticipated that, no, but she *could* be that person.

She couldn't do it out of guilt, though. It wouldn't be fair to them. If she stepped forward, it had to be because it was what she wanted. Them. She grabbed her phone and dialed, not allowing herself to think much further. At the very least, this was an avenue she had to explore. She owed everyone involved that much.

"Lieutenant. Good morning," Jennifer said upon answering.

"Good morning. Listen, I'm sorry to bother you again—"

"That's all right. Unfortunately, I'm afraid I don't have any updates." Jennifer had to be growing weary of Kate's frequent inquiries to DHS, but she needed her help on this one.

"I was actually calling for a separate reason. I was wondering if you could arrange a visit for me with the kids? I'd like to check in on them. Say hey. Spend some time with them. It's been a couple of months. And maybe, while I'm there, you and I could talk about their future."

A pause hit. "Of course. They'd love to see you. Will you be in the area?"

"I will be soon." Kate knew what she had to do, what her purpose was. All of this had happened for a reason, and that reason was slowly coming into focus. She just had one stop to make first. It wouldn't be an easy one.

"Hey, you," Autumn said, as Kate arrived at the shop. She wiped her hands on her apron and picked up a cup. "The usual?"

Kate nodded. Autumn seemed upbeat and her eyes shone brightly when they landed on Kate's. Beneath it all, she knew Autumn was just as torn up as she was about their impending good-bye. Regardless of how she was feeling, Autumn was able to project the kind of positivity that drew people in. It wasn't just her outward disposition either; that light radiated from within. Kate's heart clenched at the wash of feelings that came over her. Autumn was a good person, and Kate wanted the world for her. There was an uncomfortable tug at the knowledge that she wouldn't be there to help her get it. Yes, she'd known that from the start, but that didn't assuage the pain now.

"So, there's a street fair near my house this weekend. Will you still be in town?" Autumn asked, handing Kate her drink.

Kate hesitated and Autumn picked up on it right away.

"So that's a no. Got it," she said, her smile dimming. She focused all of her attention on the countertop and her mission to scrub it clean—a guise to hide any and all emotion.

"Do you have a minute?"

"Of course," Autumn said, untying her apron. She followed Kate outside and around the building, but she wasn't herself. Like a robust balloon that had all its air drained away, Autumn's demeanor hung heavy. "Back home?" she asked, once they were alone.

Kate nodded. "I have to. Those kids need someone, and there's no one else. Maybe I need them, too, you know?"

Autumn attempted a grin, but it was through tears. "I do know. I think you're a good person, Kate, and you're doing a good thing. Doesn't mean I won't miss you."

Kate pushed her hands into her pockets, feeling like a fish out of water. She wasn't the type to get emotionally attached, but the rules didn't apply where Autumn was concerned. She was different, and she'd wedged herself firmly in Kate's heart. There would never be another Autumn.

"This isn't good-bye," Kate said; anything to help them through this. Her head swam and her heart ached. "I'm here until morning."

"Feels like good-bye."

Kate knew what she meant. The safe little world they'd created for themselves had been stripped away, as if someone had flipped on a bright light, revealing that the magic hadn't been theirs to keep.

"Come here." She opened her arms and Autumn fell into them. They stood that way on the sidewalk for several moments. Kate did her best to memorize every sensation, the way it felt to touch Autumn, the soft smell of her shampoo, the way her curls tickled the side of Kate's cheek. "Come over tonight," Kate said in her ear. Autumn nodded and held her tighter. Even though Kate knew that this marked the beginning of something new in her life, she didn't want to let go of what she had right there in front of her.

"I think I've blown this," Autumn said.

Kate stepped back and cupped Autumn's face in her hand. "What do you mean?"

"I've gone and fallen for you."

The words made her ache all over. She brushed her thumb across Autumn's lips in a gentle gesture. "You haven't blown anything." The fact was, she'd fallen for Autumn, too. There had been no way around that. She didn't say the words. She couldn't.

Autumn wiped away the tears that had gathered under her eyes and took a step back. "I better get back to work."

"Okay," Kate said, wishing she could have given Autumn more, confessed all to her in that moment. She deserved to know what she meant to Kate, how she'd saved her from a very dark time in her life. Instead, Kate stood there, wordless. Stuck between two realities.

"I'll stop by after closing," Autumn said.

Kate nodded and watched her go, regret welling up thick and tight. She wasn't sure how you got over someone like Autumn. She'd infiltrated Kate's life and made her feel things she didn't think were possible. Who was she going to talk to well into the night, or tease relentlessly, or recount the latest Grisham book to? Autumn had become her person. How was she supposed to just let that go?

❖

Autumn knocked on Kate's door just before ten that night. The day had been a long one, made longer when her newest employee had been a no-show and she'd ended up covering his shift in addition to her own. Her neck pulled, her arms ached, and her feet felt like if she didn't get off them soon, she might just keel over. Yet nothing hurt nearly as much as her heart, no matter how hard she tried to brace herself against it.

When Kate finally opened the door, the apartment behind her was dark. "Hi," Autumn said. She peered inside. "Were you asleep?"

"Not even close," Kate said, and took her softly by the hand, leading her inside. Only once she did, she understood that the room wasn't dark, but dimly lit with tealight candles. One on the island in the kitchen. One on the end table, and two on the bookshelf.

"It's so pretty in here," Autumn said, trying to make her brain work after such a bitch of a day. Kate continued to lead her farther into the apartment. "Wait. We're not staying in here? It's so beautiful."

"Nope." They walked down the short hallway to Kate's bedroom, where there was another handful of candles interspersed, and on to the adjoining master bath, where Autumn's breath caught in her throat. The garden tub was full and she could feel the magnificent warmth wafting her way. There were candles at all four corners of the tub and rose petals drifting on top of the water. Gorgeous. "For you," Kate said. "You had a long day."

Autumn nodded and looked up at Kate. "No one has ever done anything like this for me."

"Well, now they have," she said simply. She pointed at Autumn's Pajamas T-shirt. "May I?"

Autumn nodded and raised her arms, as Kate lifted the blue T-shirt over her head. Kate carefully undressed her one piece of clothing at a time and held her hand as she stepped into the waiting bath. "Oh, man," Autumn said in exhale. "This is heaven." Heaven grew exponentially more wonderful when Kate handed her a glass of wine that was waiting on the counter.

"Get out of here." She sipped the wine and sighed. "This is crazy."

Kate smiled and, with a slight candle adjustment, sat on the edge of the tub. Autumn sucked in a breath as Kate soaped up a washcloth and softly washed her shoulders, her back, her breasts. Autumn exhaled languidly, relaxing for the first time that day.

"I could get used to this," she said, and then realized she couldn't. That part wasn't an option. A lump rose in her throat, painful and persistent.

Kate must have picked up on the realization. "Don't," she said. "Tonight, let's not think about it."

Autumn nodded at the lofty request. After a lengthy and wonderful soak, she allowed herself to be helped from the tub and into a waiting towel, fluffy and soft. Kate wrapped it around Autumn, but not before her eyes blazed a trail across Autumn's naked form, sending a shiver through her that rivaled the heat from the tub. Channeling the confidence she'd discovered most recently, Autumn opened the towel once more, welcoming that gaze, reveling beneath it. She heard the air as it escaped Kate's lungs, and the flash of desire in her eyes told Autumn that the invitation had not been lost on her. That gaze led to an erotic thought, which led to another, which led to another, until Autumn was all keyed up and bothered. She wanted Kate, but more than that, she needed her. Moments later, she found herself lifted easily and set on top of the counter just feet away, towel still open and around her shoulders. She smiled at the intense look in Kate's eyes, doing everything she could to encourage this mission. Her gaze hadn't left Kate's but she felt the pressure between her legs, Kate's hand. She pushed back against it slightly, and then more firmly. Kate's lips parted and her eyes fluttered.

"You could have left today," Autumn told her, holding her gaze.

"No, I couldn't have."

"And why not?" Autumn asked.

"You know," Kate said.

"Because of me?"

Kate nodded, pushing into Autumn fully. A ragged moan tore from Autumn's lips at the sensation and the sentiment.

"You," Kate said, and pressed her lips to Autumn's neck. "Of course you." Autumn clutched Kate's shoulders, encouraging the motion of her hand, and her own need climbed like a sure and steady staircase, higher and higher and higher. Kate knelt in front of her. She kissed her inner thigh and went to work with her tongue in—oh God, wondrous ways. Her hands held Autumn in place on the countertop, strong and gentle at the same time. Autumn held on to the marble as the orgasm ripped through her in only a matter of seconds, shattering any semblance of control. She was calling Kate's name, that much she was aware of, as she fell further and further into a blissful oblivion.

A rag doll.

That's all she was, spent and breathless, and sitting on a bathroom countertop, a fluffy towel pooled around her waist. Kate kissed her cheek tenderly. "Should I carry you, or would you like to walk to bed?" she whispered.

"I got this," Autumn whispered back with a smile. On wonderfully wobbly legs, she followed Kate to bed where the crisp sheet was pulled back for her. She wasn't quite ready to slip beneath it and would much rather wrap herself around Kate. "Why are you still dressed?" she asked Kate simply, and took extreme pleasure in watching Kate remedy the problem. Autumn's eyes moved across that olive skin and toned physique. There was no getting used to it, and every time she had the pleasure of staring at Kate's body, she counted herself lucky. As Kate slid into bed, Autumn went to work immediately, enjoying the romantic glow of the candles not far away, the way they flickered across Kate's skin. She traced the pattern of that flicker with her tongue, chasing it. She made love to Kate slowly, savoring each gasp, each connection.

Curled into each other, limbs tangled, they stayed like that, talking, stroking each other's hair, and staring into each other's eyes, knowing this would be the last time.

"It's not your fault, you know," Autumn said, quietly breaking the silence. "The fire. You didn't set it."

"I didn't set it," Kate repeated evenly.

"And you're not responsible for that man's death."

Kate went still and silent at the declaration. Autumn moved a strand of hair from Kate's forehead.

"Do you believe that?"

"Mostly I do." Kate sat up. "Still haunts me, though."

"Then say the words. Say that it wasn't your fault." She placed a hand on the soft skin of Kate's back.

"I don't think I want to. What would be the point of saying it out loud?"

"Just try," Autumn said gently.

There was a long pause. Autumn couldn't see Kate's face, but she knew how difficult a request this was. Finally, she turned back to Autumn, her hazel eyes filled with sadness. "It wasn't my fault." Once the words had been released into the universe, the sides of Kate's mouth turned down and her face crumpled. Autumn was up and with her arms around Kate instantly. She'd never been one to show vulnerability, but here she was, raw and on display.

"It wasn't," Autumn repeated. "You did everything you could, and nothing else would have changed the outcome."

"I couldn't get to him," Kate said, her voice sounding broken and small. "The beams broke. We fell to the first story and no one could go back in after that. The order was given."

"And you were hurt."

"I know, but I can't help but wonder. What if I'd been able to go back in there one more time? I can't stop thinking about it. Day and night. The 'what if?' factor."

Autumn shook her head. "No. Would you have let one of the other guys, one of your friends, go back in there? Would you?"

Kate shook her head. "It would have been reckless."

"Exactly. And if you'd gone back in, you wouldn't be sitting here right now. I would never have met you, and what a shame that would have been, because you've made the biggest difference in my life."

Kate nodded, and Autumn held her as she cried, stroking her back and listening to the quiet sobs that eventually faded into the night.

Autumn dried her tears and kissed her lips softly.

Kate rested her cheek back against the pillows, facing Autumn. "Can I tell you something?"

"Anything."

Kate gestured between them. "This is far more than I thought it would be."

Autumn already knew that. She'd known she was in the midst of something important from that first week. "I've been one to play by the rules. Get good grades, go to work, make everyone happy. Then you came along and made me want to do all sorts of things not on the required to-do list. It's been a fun jaunt, Kate. But also, so much more than that."

Kate smiled. "Whoever would have guessed?"

"I couldn't have dreamt you up if I'd tried."

They fell asleep wrapped up in each other, and when Autumn woke for work early that next morning, Kate walked her to the shop. Their good-bye was wordless; it had to be. Autumn was too choked up to speak. She wrapped her arms around Kate's neck and held on, savoring the last few seconds of connection they would have. When she released her, she saw the tears as they fell from Kate's cheeks. She cradled Autumn's face in her hand and just looked at her for a few moments. With a final earnest kiss, she disappeared down the dark sidewalk, taking Autumn's heart along with her.

When Autumn took a break midmorning, the blue pickup truck was gone.

❖

"A double expresso with marshmallows, please."

Autumn paused and stared at the man wearing suede pants in the summer. She could let the suede go, but that drink order was another story.

"I think you mean *espresso,* and did you ask for marshmallows? Are you thinking of cocoa?"

"No, just toss a couple of marshmallows in there." The guy glanced at his folded newspaper as if what he said was the most natural thing in the world—when, in fact, it was blasphemous and wrong on so many levels. Autumn of last week would have smiled, rolled her eyes internally, and handed over the creepy, ill-thought-out drink in the name of customer service. Autumn of this week, Autumn sans Kate, had no tolerance for coffee nonsense. Who the hell did this guy think he was, barging into her shop and asking for marshmallows in his coffee?

"I don't think we can do that," she said evenly. She felt Steve's gaze on her from down the counter.

"You don't have marshmallows?" Suede asked.

"It's the soul-crushing fortitude it would take to hand you that kind of drink that I don't have, sir."

Steve stepped to her side, his voice low. "I got this one, Autumn."

She looked up at him. "You sure you want it?"

"Yep."

Pulling the towel from her shoulder, she decided to take five. Out of the corner of her eye, she saw Hadley, who had been reading a crime novel at a table close by, put down the book and follow her out of the shop.

"How you doing?" Hadley asked gently, joining her on the sidewalk out front.

"How does it look like I'm doing?" Autumn asked back, feeling frustrated with the world and her lack of control over it. Her spirits had taken a hit, which carefully stripped her of her ability to cope with even the most mundane.

"Like you might lunge across the counter and choke that customer out."

She turned to Hadley, a small smile creeping onto her face. "Is that an option?"

"I vote no." A pause. Hadley placed her hands on the hips of her designer jeans. "You're missing Kate."

Autumn sighed. "It's been a little over a week, and everything just seems to…matter a lot less."

"Have you talked?"

Autumn shook her head. "We decided not to. Clean break is better, you know? Why drag it out?"

"Makes sense. The old 'ripping off the Band-Aid quickly' mentality. Wanna sit?"

Autumn nodded and followed Hadley to the curb, where they took a seat and watched the traffic whiz past, the sound extra offensive, which Autumn knew was just her projecting.

"Being bad sucks, I've decided," Autumn said, her gaze fixated on the horizon. There were people on the beach just a couple of blocks away, frolicking, having fun, living their lives. Meanwhile, hers had fizzled like a defective firecracker on the sad little sidewalk.

"Oh, I don't know about that. I think walking on the wild side has its perks. I also think that you experienced a few juicy ones."

Autumn smiled at the memory of said perks. "That part's true. Bad girls get perks."

"Bad girls get perks," Hadley repeated. "We should put that on T-shirts."

"We'd make a killing." A fist bump was obviously in order, and they both went for it at the same time.

"Aren't you glad it happened, though?" Hadley asked. "That an amazingly kind and hot and sensible woman came into town, swept you off your feet—"

"And changed me forever?" Autumn nodded, letting the question settle. "Depends on how long it's going to hurt like this.

When do I stop missing her? Wanting to pick up the phone and hear her voice, even though we said we wouldn't go there?" There were those pesky tears again, springing into her eyes without consulting her at all. She was the equivalent of an emotional blender lately, all tossed together and lost in the whirring shuffle of feelings.

"Hey, now," Hadley said, wrapping both arms around Autumn. "I didn't mean to upset you. You have so many exciting things to look forward to. Just think about that."

Autumn nodded, knowing that Hadley was right. She just had to focus on the positive, the future, her self-proclaimed new lease on life, right? Surely she'd find a way back to that newly found spunk and move herself out of the sadness that had settled at Kate's departure.

Hadley released Autumn and met her gaze. "So, where's your head as far as…the rest of your future plans?"

"Are you asking if I'm still having this baby?" She looked at Hadley, feeling a little bit of light drift back to her. "Yes. I most definitely still want to be a mom. Not even a question in my head."

"And the big insemination day is?"

"Back on track for this month. I gave them a call. Three days from now, which means no more alcohol after that point."

"No more alcohol? Say no more." Hadley smiled innocently. "I think we're going out tonight."

❖

"Are there more people here than a minute ago?" Autumn asked, scanning the bar as it approached midnight. Her vision blurred slightly, and she blinked to clear it. The music was loud in a really good way and the bass pulsed its way through her body.

"I think that's called seeing double," Gia said loudly, over the eighties cover band playing across the room. She grinned as the song shifted, tossing both arms into the air. "Madonna!" she exclaimed, and commenced her perfectly timed lip-sync to "Like a Virgin," something Gia would never in a million years do sober. Autumn, who was not a giggler, giggled. Life was happier with alcohol.

She should have more of it. All the time. The world exploded with fun, and seemed noticeably easy and interesting, and look at all the colors! She'd probably stay up all night just enjoying the lights, the people. Hadley was right. This had been a fantastic idea. She was never leaving.

"No, no," Autumn said to Gia with a grin, gesturing at the room in general. "Not seeing double. I see all the people and they're just…people. Pretty, pretty people out for a party."

"Bonus points for alliteration," Isabel said, and took a pull of her bourbon and Coke that looked so dapper with that fancy little cherry on a stick. Isabel seemed to be taking it slower than the rest of them, which was not as exciting.

Autumn leaned across the table. "C'mon, Baby-Izzy. Catch up. It'll be a blast. Join me in drunk Neverland."

"Less of a blast tomorrow," Isabel said. "But Baby-Izzy is a new one from you."

"I'm super creative tonight."

"Unfortunately for you, I'm seeing Taylor after this and do not plan to be sloppy drunk."

"Sounds like a booty call to me," Gia said, still performing all the Madonna choreography in perfect rhythm.

Isabel stared at her. "Do I look in any way, shape, or form like someone who has a problem with that? Have you met my girlfriend?"

Gia grinned. "Good point. Haul your booty over there."

"You guys," Drunk-Hadley said, rushing to their table from the dance floor, where she'd been bopping the night away. "There's a really swoon-worthy woman on the dance floor and I got to sway near her."

"Introduce yourself," Isabel said. "You always think everyone's out of your league, and you're one of the most attractive women in this damn bar. Act like it."

"Nah. Not in the mood," Hadley said, bouncing in place. "I'm too tipsy. I just want to dance."

Autumn narrowed her gaze, and then gave her head a little shake so Hadley would drift back into focus. She opened her mouth to offer her own advice, but had to pivot at the much more important distraction. "Your hair is so *blond.* Like, look at it." She reached out and stroked the air near Hadley's head. "It's like the blondest of blonds, and I want to brush it."

"Okay," Isabel said, sliding Autumn's drink across the table. "And with that, I think it's time to cut somebody off."

"Yep. Do it." Autumn nodded and looked around the room. "Who?"

"Not important," Gia said, and carried Autumn's drink to the bar.

"She's got our drinks confused. She took mine." Autumn pointed after Gia in confusion. "S'okay. I can share!" she yelled loudly across the room. She turned back to see Hadley heading to the small dance floor. "I'ma dance now."

"I'ma?" Isabel asked. "We're going with I'ma?"

Autumn kissed Isabel's cheek and headed off after Hadley, racing to her so as not to miss another moment of fun. Only the arms she fell into on the dance floor weren't Had's, but they were super toned. Whoa. She squeezed the arms and glanced up into dreamy eyes. Not hazel, though. Not even close, which was a damn shame.

"Hi," the woman said. "Sorry about that. You okay?"

Autumn nodded, intrigued by the stranger.

"I'm Cooper."

She saw Hadley leap into the air behind the woman and point at her excitedly.

"Like the car? They named you after the car?" Autumn asked, her alcohol-influenced brain trying to understand why anyone would do that.

"Not exactly."

Autumn blinked and caught another glimpse of Hadley's face rising behind Cooper's. She gave Autumn the thumbs-up sign, before her feet returned to the floor, causing her to disappear again like a human Whac-A-Mole. "You're a *hot* car, though, Cooper Cooperson. Wanna dance?"

"I was hoping you'd ask," Cooper purred in her ear. Autumn didn't care for the purring. Who did that? Made her ears tingle weirdly, and her shoulders scrunch. To distract herself, she commenced bobbing around next to Cooper, which was all she really felt like doing anyway, now that she was here.

"Can I get you a drink?" Cooper asked, two songs later.

"Nah, my friend has mine. She's watching out for it. I'm good." And before she knew it, the song changed to something bluesy and sultry, and they were dancing extra close. A pair of lips pressed to hers. Instinctually, she sank into the kiss, absorbing the contact at first, and then moving her own lips against Cooper's. Autumn grabbed the front of her shirt and pulled her in closer. Cooper's lips weren't very warm, though. Chilly, in fact, from the ice in her drink. It felt like kissing a wet fish, flopping around against her mouth, and she wanted it to stop. She pulled back and stared at the floor.

"You're a knockout, you know that?" Cooper asked, just millimeters from Autumn's face. Why was she so close? And why was kissing her such a monumental disappointment? And why did the lights resemble alien spaceships set to land on their heads? The colors no longer seemed as captivating. Cooper leaned in again, intent on another kiss, but Autumn dodged her, feeling sick to her stomach and needing air.

She held up a finger, feeling herself sway. "No more of that, Madame Automobile. Finding my friends now." She pointed at a random woman across the dance floor. "Go kiss her now. Or somebody else. You choose." Autumn had stopped drinking twenty minutes ago, but it seemed like the alcohol was still seeping into her system, making her drunker by the second. With a final pat on Cooper's shoulder, she stumbled back to their table, where Isabel offered her a hand.

"Have a seat," Isabel said and slid a tall glass toward her. "Drink some water. All of it. That's an order. And if you finish that, we'll get you another one. I have an Uber on its way."

"Hey, you okay?" Gia asked from the chair next to hers. "You look upset."

Autumn nodded, acknowledging the sadness that had zapped her like a lightning bolt out of nowhere. Happy one minute, desolate the next. And it was the weepy overwhelming kind of sadness, too, where it feels like the world is ending and there's no point in going on. "I don't know why I let myself get attached, you know?" she said to Gia and Isabel, who squinted, probably trying to keep up with her ever-shifting emotions.

"Which thing are we talking about?" Isabel asked.

"I knew from the beginning she wasn't here permanently. Just a short time."

"Kate. Gotcha now."

Tears flowed. Autumn gestured wildly. "And now I'll be alone forever because no one kisses like her. Not even Car-Woman over there."

"Car-Woman?" Gia asked, rubbing Autumn's back like a good friend.

"Doesn't matter now. I need to blow my nose." Gia handed her a napkin, and Autumn went to town, then handed it back to her. "Sorry."

"Oh. Okay," Gia said, looking around for a trash can.

"I lost my shoe," Hadley said happily, appearing at their table from another turn around the dance floor. "I'm like Cinderella."

"A drunk one," Isabel said, and sighed. "Come on. I'll help you find it. Gia, can you meet the Uber, and take this one with you." She pointed at Autumn.

Gia balked. "The crying one? I get the *crying* one?" But Isabel was already gone, tugged away by Drunk-Hadley.

"No, I'm the dancey one," Autumn corrected, standing and shaking her hips. She was beginning to feel better already. Emotions were flying in and out on a dime. "I want to stay right here."

"I don't think that's a good idea," Gia said. "You were bawling two seconds ago."

"I'm dancing now, Gia Pet." Autumn held up her hands in surrender. "I won't go anywhere. Promise. Just gonna dance right here and watch the ceiling turn."

"Fine. Right there," Gia said, and headed for the door.

Once she was alone, Autumn got the best idea, and knew exactly what she had to do. She took out her cell phone and dialed, because there were things that she had to say. Important things, and this was the best time to say them, when she had such clarity.

When the call rolled to voice mail, Autumn sank into the chair at the rich sound of Kate's voice telling her to leave a message. *Kate.* It felt like forever since she'd heard that voice. She'd have to call back five or six more times just to listen to it after she left her very pressing message. She waited patiently for the beep, closing her eyes and bracing herself against the spins. She gripped the table with one hand as she spoke.

"Kate. It's Autumn." Kate probably knew which Autumn, but just for good measure, she added, "Primm. Listen to me, okay? Don't say anything. You do not in any way kiss like a fish, and I needed you to know that. You kiss like a goddess. Like a Greek goddess skilled in the ways of, like, love and passion and Scrabble. Thank God you were not named after any machinery. I miss you. You don't have to call me back or anything. I just needed you to know all of these things. About the fish and car and the passion. Well, maybe you could call me back."

"Whoa. What are you doing?" Isabel asked, holding Hadley's wrist with one hand and reaching across the table for Autumn's phone with the other. "Are you drunk dialing right now? Freeze. Drop the phone."

As Isabel moved toward her, Autumn headed around the other side of the table, knocking into the tall chairs as she went. "Isabel's coming!" she yelled into the phone. "Help! Help me!"

"Give me the phone," Isabel said, advancing. "Hand it over, Primm. Friends do not let friends drunk dial." She raced around the table after Autumn, dragging Hadley with her.

Autumn screamed and continued her message, shouting and speaking as quickly as she could. "Kate, I just wish you'd never left and hope that you miss me and that you still drive that really sexy truck."

"Uber's here," Gia called from the front of the bar. When Autumn glanced in her direction, Isabel snatched the phone.

"Hey!" Autumn yelled. "I wasn't finished yet."

"Well, you are now," Isabel said in frustration, and clicked off the call. "Sober-Autumn will thank me tomorrow."

"That was a really sweet message," Hadley said, reaching

across the table and squeezing Autumn's hand. "You're really good at expressing your feelings."

"Oh, God." Isabel rolled her eyes. "Into the car. Both of you."

"This was a very fun night," Autumn said, grinning at no one in particular as she was escorted from the bar. The cool night air smacked her in the face as they climbed into the car. Sandwiched between Isabel and Hadley in the backseat as they drove, Autumn leaned her head back against the seat and let her mind drift to that night at the observatory. Her. Kate. The stars. She located them through the sunroof of the vehicle, bright and wonderful and steady, and wondered if maybe Kate was looking up at them, too.

She raised her head. "You guys, I think I might be sick."

"Hey, there," Kate said, laughing, stumbling backward. The kids had shot like rockets into her arms when she'd arrived at the home of Mrs. Henderson, their foster mother, a smiley woman in her late sixties. Kate remembered seeing her around town, always very friendly and the type to pull just about everyone she knew into a grandmotherly hug.

"You're back!" Eva said with a wide grin. "We missed you!"

Ren stared at her. "I thought you'd moved away."

"Not quite. Whoa. Did you two grow?" Kate asked, staring into two beaming faces.

Ren nodded confidently. "I definitely did."

"Not me," Eva said. "I think I shranked."

"Shrank," Ren corrected.

Eva still wore a compression bandage on her left leg and would have to for many months to come, Kate was told. However, her perky exuberance seemed intact. "Shrank," she replied reluctantly, looking annoyed at her brother's correction.

"Are you feeling better?" Ren asked. "I am."

"Me too," Eva said. "I don't have to be in the hospital anymore. I'm out."

"I can see that!" Kate made a point of looking really impressed. She turned to Ren. "I'm good as new. Thanks for asking, pal."

"Where did you go?" Eva asked, sliding onto the couch next to Kate.

"I took a trip to California for a little while. I needed to rest. But I came back because I missed you both."

Eva slipped her hand into Kate's. The simple gesture brought on a pang of sentimentality. She was such a softy lately. "I'm glad you're back. Want to see my new coloring book? I've already colored three pages."

"Definitely," Kate said, grinning.

With Jennifer's permission, they spent the next few days together, Kate picking them up from Mrs. Henderson's and taking them on little field trips. The bowling alley, the movies, the petting zoo on the outskirts of town. They were kids, who of course got grumpy, and bickered with each other along the way, but for the most part, the three of them got along impressively. Kate was actually really surprised by her own ability with them and began to imagine her life in charge of them both for good. The fire, as tragic and horrific as it was, seemed to have set her on the path she was meant to be on. She'd never been one to get caught up in the mysticism that was fate, but she was starting to believe in its existence. Something unseen was ushering her along. She could feel it as clearly as she could feel the sunshine on her skin.

"Do you know where we're going to live now?" Eva asked one afternoon, as they took a walk through the small neighborhood where they were staying. "Ms. Henderson said that we are only her kids for a little while. Then whose kids will we be? Do you know?"

Her big brown eyes carried fear, and Kate wanted nothing more than to reassure her, to offer up her own life and tell Eva that everything was going to be just fine very soon. But there was still a lot of red tape to sort out with Oregon's Human Services. While Jennifer had been thrilled to hear that Kate wanted to adopt them, especially since she would be willing to take both siblings together, it wasn't as simple as just signing a form. It would take time, and home visits, and a ruling from a judge, and agreement from the kids themselves. That part was important to Kate. In the meantime, it was best not to get the kids' hopes up until they were further along in the process. They'd lost their father, and it was obvious that they still struggled to fully realize the extent of that tragedy. Eva had nightmares, Kate had been told, where she woke up yelling for him. Ren didn't talk about him as much, but he'd grown quieter, they'd noticed. Stories from both had revealed their home life had been less than desirable and chock-full of neglect, but the loss of a parent was huge and would impact them forever.

It was when she was alone that her thoughts drifted back to Venice. To Autumn. She missed her more than she would have thought possible, and when all was quiet, she allowed herself to remember the soft skin of Autumn's neck, her firecracker personality, the smart-aleck remarks, or her incredibly impressive mind for business. She thought of everything that was Autumn and went to sleep each night wishing for a way back to her.

Tonight was no different. After a quick shower, she cracked the window and allowed the breeze to move through her bedroom, opting to sleep in just a T-shirt. As she slid into cool sheets, she caught sight of a notification on her phone. A voice mail.

Hearing Autumn's voice on the recording, she sat up in bed, a bolt of excited energy shooting through her. She smiled when she realized Autumn was flat drunk on the message.

She missed Kate. That one hit her right in the center of her chest.

She laughed when she heard Isabel chasing Autumn and Autumn shrieking in response. Most of the message had made zero sense, but there was a takeaway: Autumn was thinking about her, too, which somehow made her seem not that far away. She debated calling back, but if Autumn was as drunk as she sounded, then maybe it wasn't the best night for it. Her friends were fantastic and would take good care of Autumn. Didn't mean Kate wasn't wishing she was the one doing those kinds of things.

As the hours ticked on, the pull grew that much more insistent.

She needed to hear Autumn's voice again, live and in real time. In fact, she could think of little else.

The next day, she waited until midafternoon when she knew Autumn would take her break at Pajamas. It was sunny and warm there. She'd checked the weather so she could imagine it. Yes, they'd made the decision to keep the break clean, not wishing to make their parting any harder than it needed to be, but if Autumn could break the no-calling rule once, so could she. It was like a free pass.

It took several rings for Autumn to pick up. When she did, her voice sounded tentative, maybe even a little embarrassed, which was understandable.

"Hey," Autumn said softly.

"Hi," Kate answered, smiling. "I got your message last night."

A long silence hit, and if she knew Autumn, this was the moment she was beating herself the hell up while turning an impressive shade of crimson.

"Yeah, I was afraid of that. Kate, I'm so sorry. I'm not even entirely sure what I said, but I do remember the highlights. Kill me now."

Kate chuckled. "You don't have anything to apologize for. But I wanted to make sure that you're okay today."

"If, by okay, you mean have a pounding headache, lifeless limbs, and a churning stomach, then I'm doing fantastic."

"Uh-oh. I was worried you'd say that."

Another pause. Autumn's voice was gentler when she spoke again. "You're sweet to call."

"No, I'm not. I'm selfish as hell. I wanted to hear your voice." Her words came fast and with unexpected honesty. She couldn't see Autumn, but she tried to picture her, probably standing in the storage room at the back of the coffee shop, one hand in her hair, the other holding the phone. Had that last comment upset her or made her smile? It was hard to know. She wanted to.

"Kind of the same reason I called you last night. Again, so sorry about that crazy message. I'm so embarrassed."

"Don't be. I was happy to get it."

Autumn sighed. "We said we wouldn't do this."

Reality arrived like an unwelcome houseguest. "Just a minor misstep. I figured if you got one, so did I."

"I suppose that's fair." Now Autumn *was* smiling. Kate could hear it creep into her voice. "You take care of yourself, Kate. And make sure you get a little sun up north."

"California taught me well." She lingered a moment longer just because she wanted to. "'Bye, Autumn."

"'Bye."

She clicked off and held the phone against her chest, as if not ready to let go of the connection to Autumn just yet. She ruminated on the call, reliving each moment of their exchange, before shoving it to the side for the sake of self-preservation. How had she let it go this far? She knew how. Their commingled best intentions had flown right out the window when they were within ten feet of each other. But no, that wasn't true either, because here she was, hundreds of miles away, and still she craved Autumn with her mind, body, and soul.

She had to find a way to stop. It was time.

CHAPTER TWELVE

Tuesday morning came with thunderstorms and blinding rain. It wasn't exactly what Autumn had imagined for insemination day, but it was what the universe had dealt her. Her appointment was for nine that morning, and the prospect of being late due to rain had her extra anxious. She'd followed all the instructions she'd been provided by her fertility coach, injecting herself with the trigger shot for ovulation a day and a half prior. And now here she was, squinting through the rain on her way to the clinic where her IUI procedure would be performed. If all went according to plan, she'd be confirmed pregnant in a little over two weeks.

Pregnant. She closed her eyes briefly and held on to the one thought that managed to bring her joy. It had been Kate who had accompanied her on the last few ultrasound appointments, and with her unavailable, Autumn had made the decision to go to the clinic alone—a decision she second-guessed now, as the nerves crept in and the monumental details of the day came into focus.

Moving herself out of that "poor lonely me" mind-set, she sat taller in the driver's seat as she pulled her car into the parking lot in front of the clinic, three minutes early. See? Rain or not, everything was going *just* fine. No reason to freak the hell out. She made her way into the waiting room to sign in and noticed it once again filled with happy pairings…and Gia. Play that back. But she hadn't been wrong. Seeing Autumn enter the clinic, Gia stood and moved toward her self-consciously.

"What are you doing here?" Autumn asked quietly, but inside

she was overcome with joy, relief, and gratitude to see that her friend had shown up for her on such an important day in her life.

"Can't really surf in a storm," Gia said with a shrug, and then leaned in. "That's a lie. I'd have been here anyway. Too big a thing to let you go through alone, even if you said it's what you wanted." She looked sheepish, and maybe a little nervous to have crashed the party. "I hope it's okay. You can tell me to get lost and I will."

Autumn reached for Gia's hand and gave it a tight squeeze. "It's more than okay, and please don't go anywhere. Thank you."

Gia met her eyes briefly and then looked away. "Cool. I'll just follow you around."

If her doctor was surprised to see her with yet another plus-one, he didn't let on. "Ready to get pregnant?" he asked, with a twinkle in his eye.

"More than ready," Autumn said, and held firmly to Gia's hand.

The procedure took roughly six minutes from start to finish, which Autumn found surprising given its importance. "That's it?" she asked when the nurse offered her a hand in sitting back up.

"That's it," the nurse said. "Take it easy today, and think positive thoughts. We'll see you back in two and a half weeks."

She turned to Gia, who had tears in her eyes. "Sorry," she said, wiping them windshield-wiper fast. "Wasn't expecting to get choked up. Just really happy for you. Big day and all. Ignore me. I'm stupid."

Autumn reached up and touched her cheek. "You're a softy, Gia-Pet. You just hide it really well."

Her lips puckered and her eyes narrowed. "No one can know."

"Aww, and they won't. Breakfast?"

Gia grinned. "On me."

They sat among a mountain of pancakes, because it's what people did in the middle of a workweek when they went for breakfast with an athlete like Gia Malone. They feasted. Gia reached for a chocolate chip pancake, and Autumn stole one from the pecan stack. One thing she loved about Gia, she didn't mess around. She wasn't satisfied with three measly pancakes. She ordered three of every kind on the menu.

When Autumn's eyes had gone wide at the suggestion, Gia

shrugged. “I’m in training. Do you know how many calories I’m burning each day?”

“I don’t even want to,” Autumn said, bowing her head in reverence. “I’m just privileged to share the rewards.”

“We should do this more often,” Gia said, pointing at Autumn with her fork. “Just you and me.”

Autumn liked the suggestion. They had a fantastic circle of friends, but the one-on-one time was different. She looked forward to those moments with each of them. “Once a month. We’ll pick a day you’re for sure in town, and I’ll swap my early shift for the late one.”

“You’re on like Donkey Kong.”

“There you go with the video game references again. There’s so much more to life.”

Gia grinned, not at all sorry. “You think I’m immature.”

“I think you’re youthful.”

“You think no one will ever date me.”

“No, everyone will. You’re a celebrity, and it’s not fair.”

Gia nodded, her chocolaty pancake hovering just shy of her mouth as she stared contemplatively. “Then why am I still single?”

“Because you’re not attracted to the everyday girl. You never have been.”

She quirked an eyebrow as she chewed. “I’m not?”

“Nope. It’s the reason you don’t date much. You secretly lust after the ones you shouldn’t, or at least the ones you’d rather not lust after.”

Gia shook off the notion. “No. Not true.”

“Oh, really?” Autumn said, quickly pulling up Google on her phone. She turned it around to show Gia the photo. “This shot ring any bells?”

Gia gaped at the photo of Elle Britton, number one female surfer in the world, talking to a throng of reporters in her swimsuit. Off to the side of the frame stood Gia, who seemed to be staring blatantly at Elle’s, well, curves. The photo had garnered a lot of attention in the surf world and had evolved into the question Gia was asked most on the circuit: just what exactly had that photo been about? "I can't believe you're bringing that up," Gia said, shaking her head. "That photo is the worst thing that ever happened to me. I am not checking her out, no matter what it looks like."

Autumn turned the photo around and studied it. "It looks hot, is what it looks like. You two would sizzle."

Gia leaned forward, eyes blazing. "I'd have to kill her first. Do you understand that? She drives me insane. She's a bobblehead, a media princess probably manufactured in a Pixar lab. Can't stand her."

"Wow," Autumn said, nodding. "You have a lot of feelings on the topic."

Gia leaned forward, her eyes flashing the way they did right before a tournament. "The only thing I care about when it comes to Elle Britton is her ranking. It will be mine. Mark my words."

Autumn pushed a stack of blueberry pancakes in Gia's direction. "I have faith in you, champ. Fortify."

The day had been a memorable one made up of the insemination, breakfast with Gia, and a fun day at work in which she and Steve had staged a one-on-one foam art competition, which, of course, she'd won. When Autumn turned in for the night, she placed a hand low on her stomach and wondered what might be going on in there. It was difficult to sleep knowing that soon she might not be alone in her own body. She grinned, wanting to turn and share the thought with someone. Well, really, just one person. She switched off the lamp next to her bed, set her alarm for quarter to five in the morning, and fell asleep looking up at the stars that carried so much meaning, her hand still on her stomach, hoping, wishing, remembering.

❖

Slot machines pinged, cards shuffled, and guests milled about. It was Casino Night at Seven Shores, and Hadley had turned the island in her kitchen into her very own blackjack table where she played dealer in her mock tuxedo. A sound effects track played from her wireless speakers, filtering all the background noise one would hear at a typical casino.

In solidarity with Hadley's once-a-month theme parties, Autumn donned her fire-engine-red cocktail dress that she'd stowed away in her car at oh-dark-thirty that morning when she'd set out for work. She didn't relish the theme nights the way Hadley did, but the last thing in the world she wanted to do was let Had down. Her puppy-dog face inspired too much damn guilt. Plus, she generally always had fun once they were all together, in costume or not.

"Do we know anything yet? About the potential bambino?" Isabel asked from her spot at Hadley's kitchen table. She held a fake cigar and wore a queen of hearts T-shirt. She turned to Taylor for commiseration. "It feels like it's been forever already."

"I'm sure it feels longer for Autumn," Taylor said gently, and passed Autumn a sympathetic smile underscored by Tony Bennett's "Luck Be a Lady."

"Another week before I'm scheduled for the official blood test," Autumn said, twirling a poker chip and finding irony in the song. She had been counting the hours herself. Honestly, though, she was starting to have doubts that the pregnancy took, and that fear hung heavy, like a black cloud stalking her every move.

Shouldn't she feel something? A twinge? A tingling? A telegraphed message from within that said: *Hey, I'm in here!* Anything? Autumn didn't know the answer, but she most assuredly hadn't felt a damn thing, and she'd been paying close attention. She refused to give the doubt too much consideration, because underneath it all, she still carried hope. Regardless, she was going to be okay. No matter what happened. She was a strong, capable woman, and that would continue no matter what those test results revealed.

"Who's next?" Hadley asked. "Step right up! You, sir!" she said to Larry Herman, who entered the apartment wearing some sort of lavender zoot suit.

Isabel turned to them. "I think Had might be confusing Vegas dealer with carnival barker."

Autumn waved her off. "She is, but she has one night a month where the little theme world she's created in her head comes to life for all to see."

Taylor nodded. "Agreed. I would hesitate to take that from her by way of character notes." She squinted as if intrigued. "Though I don't think I've ever seen someone so happy to deal cards. She really enjoys life, doesn't she?"

"Does Hadley enjoy life? Hmm, let's see." Autumn widened her eyes. "Does sand crawl into your bathing suit and have a picnic?"

"Now, that's some imagery," Taylor said, turning to Isabel.

"Already taking it down," Isabel said, typing into her phone.

"I always forget the dangers of hanging out with screenwriters."

"That's for the best," Taylor told her. "Material's better that way."

"I just lost two hundred dollars," Gia grumbled, joining them at the table. She set her beer down extra hard.

"Wait," Autumn said, glancing over at Hadley. "She's playing with real money?"

Gia nodded emphatically. "Larry just threw down five hundred."

"We're all going to prison," Autumn said, covering her eyes. "I've stumbled into a gambling racket."

"Run by Elsa from *Frozen*," Isabel supplied dryly. "After everything, who knew this would be the way they'd take me down?"

"Relax," Taylor said, and slid her a hundred-dollar bill. "If you're lucky, you'll win first." They exchanged a glance, the kind that couples did. Autumn used to find it cute. Now she looked away, jaded and over it.

"Oh, hey, did you see we have a new tenant?" Gia asked. "Another of Larry's Airbnb folks."

Autumn's heart sank at the knowledge that someone else was living in what had been Kate's place. Life marched on, apparently, as cruel a sentiment as that sometimes was. "Who is it?"

Isabel turned to her. "Some guy with a guitar. You can hear him singing and strumming all the way out in the courtyard. It's not awful, but I miss Kate and her Grisham novels. Much more contained."

"I think I hate him," Autumn said, staring at the rather impressive Vegas-themed bar across the room, from which she could have nothing.

Isabel nodded emphatically. "We all hate him. Solidarity." She offered a purposeful fist bump and headed off to the blackjack table while Autumn played with swizzle sticks and wondered why time moved so slowly.

❖

Three days later, Autumn had to fire Simon-the-Nodder. She hated firing people, especially the college kids. Luckily, she'd gotten good at it based on the sheer volume of entry-level employees she'd dealt with over the years.

"I think you do a fantastic job, Simon." A lie, but why demoralize him completely? "But it really came down to your communication skills combined with the no-call no-shows." He only stared at her, so she pressed onward. "If there's any particular reason you don't speak to me and my staff, specifically, could you let me know?"

He stared at her harder and then shook his head and shrugged his shoulders.

"Perhaps you're nervous? Or it's part of a disability?"

He shook his head.

"Or an aspiring mime? These are things I can work with."

No response.

Right, well, there wasn't much she could do with that. "Anything you want to say?"

He smiled at the irony. She did, too.

"Well, I appreciate the hard work you've done and wish you nothing but the best, Simon."

He nodded, handed her his apron, offered a salute, and was out the door.

What an odd kid. Luckily, she'd seen this coming and had yet another new hire all lined up and ready. Surely this next one would pan out.

The afternoon was busy. The temperatures had warmed considerably and everyone clamored for iced coffee and frozen mochas, but Autumn was otherwise distracted. She'd promised herself she wouldn't do any at-home pregnancy tests before her official doctor's appointment. They were less than reliable this early, and why get her hopes up, or down, only to have it all reversed later?

But she'd bought one.

A total impulse decision made between procurement of a carton of milk and a package of Double Stuf Oreos. A decision she now paid for. The test, tucked away in her bag, taunted her. She could either bite the bullet and just take the damn thing or shut the hell up and wait the last handful of days until the blood test. She'd still yet to experience any potential symptoms. Maybe it would even be better to—

"Yeah, I'll take an Earl Grey. Grande."

She turned to regard the customer across the cash register. Tall, curly hair, a jean jacket, and a guitar strapped to his back. Her ire flared. It was *him*. The Airbnb replacement, and this was not the day for it. Not after she had to fire an employee and face off against Satan's Pee Stick!

"What's wrong with coffee?" she asked innocently, forcing herself to smile.

"I'm sorry?" His pretty blue eyes held confusion. Of course they were pretty. She hated him more.

"You ordered tea. Just wondered if there was some sort of coffee bias hiding out in there." She tried to laugh, to make it better. It sounded hollow and didn't work.

"No, ma'am." A light Southern accent. How lame.

"And I'm guessing you want a medium, because grande is Starbucks, and we certainly aren't them."

His smile faltered. "A medium, please."

"Coming right up."

"Thank you!" he called, as she turned away to pour his boring hot water.

She turned back. "Don't be charming. Just don't do it."

He nodded and commenced slinking his way down the counter. She couldn't blame the guy. He must think she was some kind of dragon lady. And she had been lately. Talk about mood swings. She froze mid–drink creation. *Mood swings.* Her eyes flew to her purse below the counter. "Hey, Steve," she called into the back, sliding the water and tea bag unceremoniously to Mr. Blue Eyed Country Singer.

"What's up?" he said, poking his head out of the storage room.

"Mind the counter? I need to take five."

"You got it."

She snatched her bag, locked herself in the employee restroom in the back, and took the test, going against everything she'd promised herself. But mood swings! That was a legitimate symptom, and with that little kernel of hope, she could construct a mountain of persuasion. There was no way to stop her from taking this test after a revelation like that. She waited the required four minutes, watching the seconds tick slowly by, before daring to approach the stick that held so much power. Two little lines was all she needed. Two. She prayed for two.

She walked to the waiting stick slowly, as if frightening the thing would make a difference. Peering down, she braced herself for whatever she might see, and then there it was. Emphasis on *it*. Her heart fell with a thud. One line. One very apparent, bold line that seemed to be laughing at her.

But then…wait.

There was one very apparent line, yes, but next to it was a second faint one. It definitely wasn't a fully formed line, but it wasn't not-a-line either. Did the faint one count? What were the line rules? Quick! She snatched the packaging from the trash can, but the instructions didn't get into how faint or vibrant the second line should be. Was this a fake-out second line? She placed her hand on her forehead and took a moment, letting the emotions swirl and settle, her stomach now off-kilter.

"Okay, okay. Not a big deal. We can figure this out." With her phone in hand, she set out for Google, where a hundred other women had asked the same question. Did the faint line count? She lifted her head victorious as a small smile crept onto her lips. The faint line most certainly counted. This was happening. It was real.

Autumn Primm was pregnant.

CHAPTER THIRTEEN

God, she'd bought a lot of stuff.

Kate surveyed the shopping bags lined up in her living room, and with a hand on her head took stock of her score. Several bags of toys—some educational, some just for fun. Bedding, a handful of outfits matched to both Ren and Eva's sizes as provided by DHS. Odds and ends like toiletries, toothbrushes, a footstool for the sink in the spare bathroom, new towels, a few children's books for Eva and chapter books for Ren. She ran a hand through her hair to figure out what she'd missed. There was so much to do to get ready for…them. She'd go grocery shopping later that week so she'd be stocked up on foods they liked when her first round of official overnight visitation hit. Ren was definitely the pickier of the two, but she could work with that. No fish and only select vegetables.

Kate was exhausted, nervous, but also really excited. In the end, this was going to be a good thing. For all of them. And once she'd settled things with the kids, maybe then she could think about going back to work. *Maybe*. The trickle of trepidation appeared right on time when she imagined fighting another fire. Didn't matter. She loved her job and would find a way to swallow that fear.

"What's with all the bags in the back room?" Ren asked a few days later, once the visit commenced.

"Just some stuff I picked up for when you guys are here," Kate told him.

"That's really cool of you." He stared at her as if trying to piece it all together. They hadn't talked about her plans just yet. They'd get there soon. "Can I play outside?"

"Yeah, go for it, dude. Dinner's in an hour. Burgers."

"Awesome," he said, and let himself into her backyard with the soccer ball she'd presented him.

Eva walked around the space for the third time. "This house is nice," she said.

Kate followed her. "Nothing special, but it's mine."

"It's on my same street."

"That's the reason I met you, remember? We were neighbors."

Eva nodded emphatically, realizing the connection. "You're right! I like this street."

"Good," Kate told her, and ruffled her hair. "Me too."

Eva looked up at her. There was a long pause as she tried to figure out what she wanted to say. "How come you're so nice to us?" she asked, finally.

The question squeezed Kate's heart. She knelt, understanding that not everyone in Eva's life had been. "Because you're the best little girl I know. My very favorite in the whole world."

Eva seemed awestruck by the comment. "Me?"

Kate nodded. "You."

Eva seemed shy, and she was never shy. "Oh." And then, "Thank you."

"Nothing to thank me for." Kate stood. "I'm gonna start dinner."

"I can help!"

Kate chuckled. "I was hoping you'd say that. Follow me to the fridge. Let's see what we can make happen."

"Okay. Guess what? I like princesses."

"Well, who doesn't?"

❖

Autumn hadn't told anyone about the pregnancy. She had, however, taken four more tests, and all had produced a faint second line. After celebrating on her own for the rest of the day, comping drinks for her favorite customers, humming a little tune as she worked, that joy had shifted pretty quickly to abject terror.

What the hell had she been thinking, venturing out to be a single mom? That had been a crazy idea, and now what was she supposed to do? There was no going back. The deed was done. She would devote the next eighteen to twenty-two years raising someone who would likely wind up dodging her calls and cursing her name. Oh, God! What if she turned into her mother? Vicky was awful, but what if somehow (and okay, she wasn't sure quite how) Autumn was even worse?

She didn't sleep the next couple of nights. Instead, she'd lain ramrod straight in bed, clutching her sheets, and envisioning all the ways she could screw this up.

Tonight, she'd given up on sleep altogether and sat at her kitchen table, reminding herself of all of the reasons she'd set off down this path, and of her long-standing desire to be a mother, to enrich her own life and someone else's. The rationalization had worked, and slowly but surely, she came to understand that her excitement still existed beneath the thick blanket of fear. She'd had a temporary freak-out about a major life change. That was all.

"So, what else is new?" she asked her kitchen, which she was apparently talking to now.

The takeaway floated to her like a feather in the breeze. She closed her eyes and smiled as serenity returned. She was going to be okay. In fact, she would be better than okay. She would be the happiest version of herself in just nine short months. The internal pep talk had done wonders, though the late nights had added up, leaving Autumn exhausted and bleary-eyed when she headed in for her official blood test that next morning. She was powering through the workday and fighting off the exhaustion when the call came that she wasn't pregnant.

The world came to a screeching halt.

"I don't understand," Autumn said to the nurse on the other end of the line. "Are you sure?"

"Unfortunately, yes."

She shook her head, trying to keep up. "I took an at-home test. Four of them. Two lines on all of them." There was no way this was happening.

"The reason we advise against testing prior to your official blood test is that often the trigger shot might still be in your system and can produce a false positive."

"The trigger shot," Autumn repeated blankly. She hadn't known it could do that. The stupid shot had supplied the extra line. All the excitement and celebration and fear and excitement all over again had been for nothing.

The world dimmed.

"I am so sorry." The nurse said the words as if they were the most delicate of objects, each one capable of breaking and shattering Autumn. And each one did. "Why don't you take some time and give us a call when you'd like to move forward."

Move forward? As in start all over at the beginning again? She tried to imagine that as everything in her mourned for what would not be. There was no baby. Just Autumn and her sad little life, once again. "Well, thank you for calling," she said, tears strangling her voice.

It was all she could manage.

❖

Two days later, as her friends trickled into the shop for breakfast, Autumn kept her head down and assembled their various drinks. Focusing on tasks, any kind of busywork, helped occupy her mind and keep her emotionally afloat. "Hey, Cody?" she asked her new employee, a surfer kid with shaggy blond hair and a tendency to drum on every surface he encountered.

"What's up, A-Dawg?" He glanced up from his solo on the nearby bar stool.

"Would you put four old fashioned donuts on a plate and take them to the table my friends are sitting at over there?"

He glanced over at the women and seemed caught off guard.

On alert now, he straightened and took a moment to smooth his eyebrows, then toss his hair. Oh, Cody. He had no idea of his uphill battle.

"Who's the new kid?" Isabel asked several minutes later, admiring the foam Autumn had shaped into a sun just for her. "He asked me for my digits. Who says 'digits'?"

"Cody does. He might write you a song composed entirely of drumbeats."

Isabel's jaw fell. "My lifelong dream."

Autumn tried to laugh, but it never quite manifested itself. She felt Gia's eyes on her. She and Hadley exchanged a look.

"Autumn, you doing okay? You're not yourself," Hadley said. "Nervous about the results?"

It was now or never. "I have the results. It turns out that I'm not pregnant. At least not this go-round." She tried to sound hopeful, strong, so they wouldn't know what a pitiful basket case she was. She was over her repetitive role as the sad, vulnerable friend. She reached for a donut as the table sat silent. "What?"

Her friends glanced around the table at each other. "I think that *fucking* sucks," Isabel said, setting her drink down. This time Autumn did smile. No one put things quite like Isabel.

"It does," Gia said. "Just wasn't the right time, I guess. Like you said. Next round."

"Definitely," Autumn said, nodding. Underneath it all, she didn't know if there would be a next round, if she was up for it.

Hadley had yet to say anything. She stared at Autumn, her eyes sad. Then something remarkable happened. She burst into tears. Not Autumn. Hadley. Her friend sat next to her sobbing.

Autumn leaned in. "Had? You okay?"

"I'm sorry," Hadley managed, finally pulling in a loud lungful of air. "I just know how badly you wanted this for yourself, and I wanted it so badly for you. You deserve some good news, Autumn, and this just feels so unfair."

Hadley of the Big Heart had showed herself yet again, this time in a touching display of empathy. Autumn placed a hand on Hadley's shoulder. "You're a good friend, Had."

"You are," Isabel choked out.

Wait, was she crying, too? "Iz?" Autumn asked. "Are you—"

"I'm not crying," Isabel spat out. "Had's crying. I don't ever cry. I'm a sarcastic hard-ass, okay? You're seeing things. Move along." But then her face crumpled and she covered her eyes. "Damnit," she whispered.

Unable to comprehend what was happening, Autumn's gaze flew to Gia, the tough athlete, unflappable in the face of cutthroat competition when all the world was watching. Remarkably, she, too, had tears pooling in her eyes. "Sorry," she mumbled, and shrugged. "Just love you is all."

Well, that did it. Autumn's carefully constructed walls came crashing down, and her own eyes filled, sad for herself and touched by her friends' compassion. An uncomfortable lump arrived in her throat right on time. *Bollocks.* "We can't all be crying," she whispered to the table.

Isabel pointed. "Hadley started it. She should find a way to make it stop."

Hadley balked as tears cascaded down her face. "Do you think I have control over this? Have you met me?"

"Here." Gia picked up a stack of napkins and passed them around the table. "Guys, wipe your eyes. People are looking."

"No one's looking," Isabel said, wiping her face like a maniac. "Drummer boy over there has them all captivated with his one-man performance from *Stomp*."

"I really like *Stomp*," Hadley said meekly.

"We all do, sweetie," Autumn said, and patted her hand.

So they sat there like four idiots, crying side by side in a coffeehouse. But those other three idiots belonged to Autumn, and she wouldn't trade them for anything. They weren't crying for her, they were crying *with* her, a testament to how much they cared. In what felt like a very dark time in her life, having lost Kate, having lost a pregnancy she never really had, Autumn felt surprisingly solid.

She wasn't alone.

These three, as different as they all were from one another, sat right there with her, holding her up, crying so she didn't have to anymore. The strength she drew from that small action was staggering.

With her friends by her side, maybe she would find a way to make it through all of this.

❖

Right on time, Kate registered a knock on her front door. She took a moment to smooth her clothes and check the mirror to make sure she looked warm, like someone you'd be fine sending kids off with. Jennifer had mentioned that the first home visit shouldn't take too long but that the social worker would have some questions to go over. She'd made a mental list of what those questions could possibly be so she'd seem prepared. She'd organized a tour of her house, as well, meticulously deciding the route.

It was now or never.

She took a deep inhale, smiled, and opened the door, surprised to see Jennifer herself standing there. "Hi," Kate said, glancing behind her for the social worker who had been assigned.

"Hey, there," Jennifer said. "Can I come in?"

"Oh." Kate glanced behind her. "Of course. I didn't realize you'd be doing the visit yourself."

"I asked if I could be the one to stop by."

"Great. Follow me. And before you ask, yes, it's true that Ren skinned his knee outside. But I applied some Bactine and got him bandaged up. He seemed okay."

"I'm sure you handled things just fine."

Kate slid her hands into her back pockets and glanced around. "Thanks. So…how does this work? Should I show you around? We can start with Eva's room."

"Can we sit down first?" Jennifer asked.

There was something in Jennifer's voice that snagged Kate's attention and had her on high alert. "Sure. What's going on?"

"Well, there's been a development."

Kate narrowed her eyes, her mind already racing as to what the development might be. "Okay. What kind of development?"

"Meredith Higgins showed up in my office yesterday."

Kate felt the blood begin to drain from her face but played it casual. Jennifer, however, seemed anything but. Her face pulled at the edges as if she were uncomfortable with this part of her job. "She's had a change of heart. Said a woman visited her and she couldn't get her words out of her head."

"I see." Kate's blood ran cold.

"She wants to begin steps to take the kids."

Kate swallowed. While it was good news, it was awful news. All Kate seemed capable of focusing on, however, was the awful. They weren't going to be a family. The kids weren't hers. The future was now wildly off-kilter. All her plans were melting away. Wasn't this the path she was supposed to be on? Weren't those kids placed in her life for some higher purpose?

"Oh."

"I'm guessing you were the one who paid Meredith a visit. I can't imagine who else."

Kate glanced up, nodded, and realized she couldn't sit still anymore. Not with the shape of everything changing all around her. She stood and ran a hand through the hair she'd only recently made sure was combed. How far away that moment felt now. "She wants to take them to Santa Barbara? For good."

Jennifer nodded. "She's guilt-ridden for having left them with their father and wants to make it right. Solid employment. A decent-sized house. There'll be some more vetting, of course, and monitoring of the situation, but it's looking like a very viable option for the kids."

Kate nodded. It made more sense. They'd be with their mother. How could she get in the way of that? She turned back to Jennifer. "I guess that's it, then?"

"I think the state would give preference to a parent who's come forward, provided she checks out, but that doesn't mean you have to withdraw yourself."

"Yes, it does," Kate said softly. "It's the right thing to do. They're a family. I'm just…someone from down the street."

Jennifer offered her an apologetic smile. "You're a good person, Kate. You've been there for those two every step of the way."

"Yeah, well, I was the one who got them into this, so…"

"Not from where I'm sitting, and I've worked this thing start to finish. You're the one who made sure they have a life ahead of them."

Jennifer's words helped, but they didn't take away the disappointment, the confusion. "When do they leave?"

"There's some state-to-state paperwork that would have to be in place for Meredith to be granted temporary custody. The permanent legalities would come later. So, maybe a few days?"

"A few days." Not only would the kids not be coming to live with her, but they were leaving Slumberton altogether. She might never see them again. "What did you think of her?"

"She seems like a good person who took the wrong path for a time in her life."

Kate nodded. "Glad to hear it. Thanks for coming over here personally."

"I wasn't going to let some stranger tell you." They smiled at each other, their common goal over the past few months uniting them as kindred spirits. She let Jennifer out and turned around to face a home that would remain empty. She could take all her recent purchases back to the store, but the thought hurt her heart more than she could tolerate.

There was nothing holding her there anymore.

She'd come back to Slumberton for Ren and Eva, and without them, what was left? In the face of shock and devastation, there was only one thing Kate wanted. Only one person whose shoulder she wanted to cry on, but she was so many miles away.

Chapter Fourteen

It had been ten days since the four-way crying party at the Cat's Pajamas. Since then, Autumn's tears had dried up, which was helpful. She'd donated way too much of her recent salary to the Kleenex industry. The fact of the matter was that her life was stable. She had a job she loved, friends who had her back, and maybe there'd be a family for her down the road someday. For that, she still carried hope.

The one thing she didn't have was Kate. She missed her more and more with each passing day. Would she find a way past that and learn to go back to who she once was? No, the experience had forever affected her, and as hard as it was to deal with the loss, she had no regrets as far as Kate was concerned. Zero.

After a long day of Cody calling Steve "dude" and Steve threatening to end Cody's life if he left the milk out just one more time, Autumn was grateful that the end of the day was upon her at last. She decided to take the long way to her car, which involved a lap around the Seven Shores courtyard to see who she might run into. She found Gia sitting alone outside, staring up at the stars. She'd been on the road the past few days, and it was good to see her home. "Hey, you," Gia said, as she saw Autumn approach.

"So, where are you back from this time?" Autumn asked.

"The Oi Rio Women's Pro in Brazil. I was there four days, and it kicked my ass."

"How'd you do?"

Gia grinned. "I kicked its ass right back, and improved my ranking."

"No kidding!" Autumn said. "No longer number six in the world?"

"You're looking at number five."

"Whoa." Autumn held up a hand between them. "I don't think I'm worthy enough to stand here with number five, which is further complicated by the fact that I'm so tired, I can't stand anyway."

"You want to sit or are you gonna get outta here?"

Autumn adjusted her bag on her shoulder, feeling the ache of the long day. "Headed home. Just wanted to see your lovely number five face." She ran a hand affectionately across the back of Gia's hair. "Congratulations, rock star."

Gia looked up and smiled. "Thanks, Autumn. Get some rest."

"On it."

Autumn headed to her car, proud of her friend and ready for a date with her bathtub. Bubbles might be called for, and maybe even some sort of robust red that would melt away the chaos of the busy day from her memory. If there was one of those bake-off shows on TV, she might just have hit the unwinding jackpot. There was a sound to her left. She turned, and blinked, struck still by what she saw. A blue truck, its tailgate down, and the most beautiful woman she'd ever seen sitting on the back. *Kate.* Her hair was down and partially covered one eye. When their gazes connected, she hopped down from the truck and gave her head a little gesture to the side, clearing her vision. The look on her face told Autumn very little. So she waited, afraid to breathe, afraid that Kate would disappear like a mirage on the shore.

"The ocean is just as peaceful as I remembered."

Autumn blew out a breath and placed her hands on her hips. It had been weeks since she'd seen Kate, and she wanted to talk about the ocean? "It's pretty reliable that way."

A long pause as they stared at one another. Kate grinned. Autumn inclined her head to the side, unable to hide her own smile regardless of the questions she had. Finally, Kate closed the distance between them, and Autumn wished she'd walk the hell faster so she could touch her, talk to her, kiss her. And then there she was, inches away from Autumn's hands, her lips. "What are you doing here?" she asked, resisting the urge to touch.

"You're here. So I needed to be."

"Really?" Autumn's entire being went warm as she took in those words. All this time, she'd wanted nothing more than to hear Kate say just that. "Do you mean it?"

Kate nodded. "The thing is, my world wasn't working without you."

Going up on her toes, she wrapped her arms around Kate's neck and drank in her scent, the welcome familiarity almost her undoing. Kate held her tightly, her face buried in Autumn's hair. The world could continue around them. Autumn wouldn't notice, because in this moment, she was home, safe, and holding on to the person who mattered most to her in the world. "Let's get out of here," Kate whispered. "Can we do that?"

"God, yes," Autumn breathed.

"I'll follow you."

She didn't even have a chance to properly unlock her front door before the kissing commenced. Kate started it, and once that tidal wave had been released, there was no stopping it. They'd been apart too long, and she'd daydreamed about Kate endlessly. The feel of her skin beneath Autumn's fingertips, the soft sounds she made when she was turned on, and the commanding, yet gentle, way she took Autumn. God, did she want to be *taken* right now.

And taken she was.

They were hurried and slow, careful and reckless, hard and soft, all at the same earth-shattering time. And when they'd ravished each other through and through, and Autumn's body hummed with spent pleasure, they lay together in her small bedroom, sheets to their waists as Kate traced a pattern across the palm of Autumn's hand. "I was away from this hand for too long," Kate said and placed a kiss right in the center.

Autumn nodded as she stared at the detail of Kate's face, her lips, her nose, her chin. Kate was back. Her Kate. "It missed you," Autumn said. "I missed you."

They hadn't talked about any of the details, and there was so much to say, to figure out. Kate didn't know about the false pregnancy, and she had so many questions of her own about the kids and Kate's path to adoption. But the long day and the rather athletic evening had Autumn's eyes drooping and her breathing slowing down. There would be time for all of that later, right? For now, they had each other, and Autumn couldn't imagine anything that could top that.

"Are you falling asleep on me?" Kate asked.

Autumn nodded groggily and smiled.

Kate wrapped her arms around her and placed a kiss on her temple. The warmth and security of her presence, of her arms holding her, ushered Autumn into the most restful night of sleep she'd had in months.

For the first time in a while, it felt like maybe things were going to be okay.

❖

The next morning, Autumn left for Pajamas before the sun came up. Kate enjoyed watching her get dressed and pack up as she lay bleary eyed in Autumn's bed, staying there at Autumn's firm instruction. It felt good to be back.

"You're really sexy right now," Autumn said, looking down at her with her bag slung over her shoulder. Her hair was extra wild and curly today, and Kate loved it. She wanted to slide her fingers through those curls right then and there.

"No," Kate said, shaking her head. "You're the sexy one in this duo. I'm just a person."

"Then you don't know yourself very well." Autumn placed a lingering kiss on Kate's lips that made her toes tingle. "I wish I could stay and kiss your just-a-person lips again."

"Me too." She propped herself up on her elbows. "But we have later, right?"

"Later," Autumn said, as if trying on the word and liking it. "You're right. We do have later. And we should talk. About things."

"We will."

When she woke a couple of hours later, Kate found a slice of coffee cake on the counter with a note for her to make herself at home, and that Autumn would cut the workday short if she could manage it. She smiled, ate the coffee cake, and walked the small house, taking in all of Autumn's unique touches.

After a quick shower, she pulled on jeans and a white V-neck and headed to Venice. The smile on Autumn's face when she arrived at the coffee shop told Kate that her idea to pop in had been a good one. She was obsessed with that smile and would do everything in her power to inspire it.

"I've been dreaming about this coffee," Kate said, accepting the house roast. Nothing back home had even come close. Autumn had apparently turned her into a connoisseur who looked down on anything that wasn't freshly roasted. But then again, Autumn had brought on a lot of changes in Kate. The first sip almost brought her to her knees.

Autumn laughed. "Good?"

Kate held up the cup. "It's like witchcraft what you guys do here."

"I'll take that endorsement." She came around the counter. "If you can hang out a few minutes, I can grab a break. We can walk down to the beach."

"You're on."

The sand felt warm beneath their toes as they walked along the shoreline. With spring having eased into summer, the warm weather was giving way to hot. Luckily, the slight breeze off the water hit their faces in pleasant greeting as they walked. "So, tell me where you're at," Kate said. "What have I missed?"

Autumn's face fell and she went on to tell Kate about the recent heartbreak, and all she'd been through since they'd last seen each other. The knowledge of how difficult it all must have been for Autumn, and the fact that she hadn't been there, jabbed at her. "I had no idea. How's your mind-set now? Are you okay?"

"I am." Autumn shrugged.

"I feel awful. I'm so sorry."

"You had no way of knowing. We had a deal, remember?"

Kate crossed her arms and held them against her body. "Screw the deal."

"Is that really how you feel? Is that why you're back?" Autumn's eyes searched hers.

"I'm back for you," Kate said. She didn't have words beyond those. She hadn't gotten that far yet. When the adoption and what she thought was to be her future was taken off the table, she knew exactly where she wanted to be. Where she'd always wanted to be. She didn't pause to analyze it, or to question herself about her intentions, or what it meant in the big scheme of things. She'd just driven.

"Yeah. You said that last night." Autumn watched her. "But what does that mean? There was a reason we said good-bye. What about those details? Our different trajectories."

"I don't know. I guess it just *means* that I'm glad to be standing here."

But that didn't seem to be enough for Autumn, who shook her head. "I get that part. The right now. But our lives, and all that's in them, are so very far apart. You live hours away and are on the verge of sharing your life with two children. We should talk about where I fit into those plans, if I even do."

Kate kept her focus straight ahead as they walked. "The adoption isn't happening. The kids are going to live with their mother. She's decided to step up."

"What?"

"Yeah. They were so excited when they heard the news. Ren especially. He said she used to sing to him and rub his head while he fell asleep." A moment passed. "I said good-bye to them yesterday."

Autumn paused their walk and turned to Kate. "Are you okay with that?"

"I'm hurting," she said, meeting Autumn's eyes briefly. "I feel like someone just flipped the board on me. But it's best for them, and that's the part I care most about."

"Kate. I'm so sorry that happened to you." She moved a strand of hair out of Kate's eyes. The breeze rustled past. "That you're hurting."

"It hurts less when I'm with you," Kate said, reaching for Autumn, who to her surprise took a forlorn step back as a look of understanding crossed her features.

She closed her eyes. "That's why you're here."

"What are you talking about?"

"I get it now. You've been dealt a blow, an awful one, and you're looking for a way to get air, to cope. It makes sense."

Kate nodded. "Maybe."

"That's my function," Autumn said, as much to herself as to Kate.

Kate felt her defenses flare. "No. That's not at all your function. You don't have a function. You're just Autumn to me."

"Yeah, but I'm not your real life. Think about it, Kate. I'm the girl you run to when you need to escape it. And I can't believe I'm saying this, but I don't know that I can be that anymore. It's become…too much." She placed a hand on her heart as if it hurt just too deeply.

"No." Kate felt a little sick. "Hey, look at me. Please?"

Autumn did.

"That's not true, you being some sort of escape for me."

"Unfortunately, it is," Autumn said. "The only reason you're standing here is because something went wrong. You're running again, Kate. It's what you do when you're hurting."

Kate didn't know what to say, because while there was validity in that statement, there was so much more to it, to her and Autumn. To hear Autumn minimize it was jarring and had her on her proverbial heels. This hadn't been what she'd expected at all. "So, what are you saying?"

The next part seemed to come hard for Autumn. "I think I'm saying that it's really good to see you." She touched Kate's cheek softly, and then withdrew her hand. "But I need to take care of me right now."

"We can take care of each other."

Autumn nodded. "Until you're feeling better and on your way again?"

"I don't know," Kate said honestly. "I'm focused on the present. What's so wrong with that?"

"Nothing. But if I've learned anything from all of this, it's that the long run matters. At least to me." She smiled sadly. "You take care of yourself, Lieutenant. Find your happiness. You deserve it."

And then to her shock, the most amazing girl in the world, the most amazing person, turned and walked in the opposite direction down the beach, and right out of her life.

❖

Autumn didn't cry over Kate.

She wanted to. Her heart felt like it had splintered in a hundred different directions, but it was the time in her life for strength, and she drew on those reserves now. She hadn't planned on it, but she'd gone out there and fallen in love. She'd been in love before, sure, but it hadn't been anything like this. With Olivia, their connection had been about the fun they'd had, the restaurants they went to, the friends they'd made. The sum of their life together.

With Kate, it was about that other person. It was about who they were to each other. She'd be perfectly content in a drab room alone for hours, talking or not talking, as long as Kate was there. They just fit in the most perfect way imaginable. But that wasn't enough. She needed Kate to want a future every bit as much as she did. She deserved that.

She'd put her heart on the line and it hadn't worked out.

Did she wish things could be different? More than anything. But she knew where they stood now, and unless she was a glutton for punishment, it was time to protect her heart. The battered thing was barely hanging in there.

She considered running to Hadley or Gia or Iz, but to what end? At some point, she had to depend on herself, and she would. From this moment on.

"There's my baby girl!" she heard, upon arriving back at

Pajamas. She turned. Oh, please, no. Not her mother. Not today. Vicky had her hand on Steve's shoulder, no doubt enjoying herself at the objectification of Autumn's assistant manager. "We were wondering where you'd snuck off to," Vicky said.

Steve passed her an apologetic glance.

"Steven was just filling me in on how to cool the beans after a roast. He's very smart. Cute, too." She winked at Steve, and Autumn cringed.

"Vicky, please don't flirt with Steve. He's younger than both of us."

"Steve doesn't worry about age, do you, Steve?" She rubbed his bicep.

He smiled politely. "Not when there's other things to worry about, like this afternoon's roast. I better get to it."

That's right, little man. Run, run far away from this barracuda of a woman. "So, what brings you by, Vicky?" She tossed a glance around the shop, and thank God, they were in the midst of a lull. Larry Herman sat in the corner nursing a cappuccino with lattice drizzle, but other than that the place was desolate.

"I wanted to hear if this little science experiment of yours worked. Are you pregnant? Am I going to be a Gigi?"

"No, you're not." *A Gigi?* Autumn let it go.

If anything, Vicky brightened, the sides of her mouth turning up ever so slightly, which made Autumn's stomach turn. She was gloating. "I'm sorry, sweetkins."

Autumn had had enough. "No, you're not," she said, her voice ice cold, much to her own surprise.

Her mother blinked several times in silence before responding, clearly offended by the insinuation. "Excuse me?"

"You're not *sorry*." Autumn stole a glance at Larry, who was looking in their direction with interest. She lowered her voice and moved toward her mother. "You would rather have my heart broken than face the fact that you're old enough to be a grandmother, which, by the way, you are. News flash. No matter whether you call yourself Gigi or Granny, which, God, is so my personal preference, you remain the same age, and it isn't twenty-two. Wake up!"

Vicky's heavily lipsticked mouth fell open and she adjusted the expensive new Prada bag that she could in no way afford. "Who raised you to speak to your mother that way?"

Autumn looked around. "I'm guessing you. Though you weren't really home that much."

"Well, look who's tossing stones now."

Autumn ignored the misuse of the phrase.

"A woman in her thirties with no husband, no family, and just a lonely little coffee place to make her feel important. You're the pathetic one, not me. Always have been."

"That's not a very nice thing to say, Vicky." They turned to see Hadley standing at the entrance, glass door propped open with her hand.

Vicky brightened as if the sun had just come up. Her gal pal was here! She'd always seen Autumn's friends as her contemporaries to Autumn's embarrassment. "Hadley, come give me a hug. I haven't seen you in months."

Hadley didn't budge. "Why would you say that to Autumn?" she asked, wide-eyed, but still very polite. "She is in no way pathetic. If anything, she's amazing. She's accomplished a ton."

"Not as much as you, sweetie, working on Rodeo Drive. I'm sure your mother is very proud of you."

"I have two dads."

Vicky faltered but only momentarily. "Well, I just want the chance to feel that proud of my daughter. I'd hate to see her live out her final years all alone." She turned back to Autumn. "Do you know I make up stories about you to tell my friends?"

"What a waste of time when the truth is so impressive." Hadley's eyes flashed in a way Autumn had never seen them. "And your daughter will never be alone. Do you know why? Because she is a kind, caring, and warm human being who people love to be around, which means she in no way takes after you."

"Yeah!" Larry Herman yelled, standing like a rabid fan at a hockey game.

"Wow," Autumn said, under her breath, loving every minute of this. She never thought she'd see the day when someone put Vicky in her place. She certainly never expected it to be Hadley.

"Well, fine," Vicky said, drawing out the word in dramatic fashion. "Why don't the two of you go be lesbians together? I can go where I'm more wanted. Where I'm appreciated."

"You say lesbians like it's a bad thing, when it's really the most awesome," Hadley said. "You should try it sometime."

"If you say so, sweetheart." Her voice was callous, condescending, and no longer dripping with pretense. She turned to Autumn. "Do you have a spare two hundred bucks? I don't have time to swing by the bank. Date tonight." And they were back to square one. Cold, hard cash.

Autumn counted out the money from the cash register and handed it to her mother. After years of falling in line, letting this woman push her around, Autumn found the courage to push back. She met Vicky's eyes and held her gaze solidly. "This is the end of the line, Vicky. The bank is officially closed. If you need money, try getting a job. You won't be getting it from me anymore. This is your final withdrawal."

She watched Vicky's face fall. "If this is about what I said earlier, I was just a little fired up."

Autumn closed the drawer. "I think it's time for you to go, and if you ever come back, I hope it's with a very different outlook. I'm not such an awful person to get to know."

"I do know you."

Autumn shook her head. "You haven't a clue who I am."

Vicky opened her mouth to argue.

"I'll walk you to your car," Hadley said, interceding, and looped her arm through Vicky's.

"Right behind you," Larry said, and shadowed the two of them.

Hadley glanced back over her shoulder with a wink to Autumn, who felt victorious for the first time in a long while.

She wasn't yet in control of her life and emotions, but she would get there.

One thing at a time.

CHAPTER FIFTEEN

Kate didn't know how long she'd been driving, but that wasn't the point. She followed the ocean for a while, watching the waves crest and greet the shoreline, stopping on the way for walks alongside it. The time on her own helped settle her restless head and wounded heart. But then she'd done it to herself, hadn't she? She was the one who'd blown into town without the wisp of an idea of what to do once she got there. If she was being honest, she still didn't know which way was up. She grabbed a rock and skipped it into the waves, knowing that she needed guidance, a sounding board. She knew exactly where she could find one.

"So, this woman, Autumn, kicked you to the curb?" her brother asked, as he stirred their coffee. Upon arriving back in Slumberton, her first stop had been The Plot Thickens. She needed an outside opinion, and Randy was generally a levelheaded guy. She'd looked up to him all these years for a reason.

Kate nodded. "She thinks she's my getaway card. That I use her to escape my problems."

Randy thought for a moment. "Well, don't you?"

"No, I have true and honest feelings for her, like nothing I've ever experienced, you know? And being away from her has only made them all the more clear." She'd never heard herself sound this emphatic. It felt jarring and satisfying in combination.

"Great." He licked the plastic spoon and dropped it in the trash. "So, you told her all that and she said what?"

"Well," she accepted the coffee, bracing herself for mediocre in the face of Autumn's brilliance, "I didn't say those exact words."

He sat down across the counter from her. "Katie."

She shook her head. From the moment she'd come on at the station as a probie, she'd looked forward to her job. Each call she went out on made her feel like she had a sense of purpose, and she knew right where she was supposed to be. The Higgins family and their tragedy changed all of that. Her whole world had been shaken up and she no longer felt like herself. Except when she was with Autumn. So why hadn't she said as much? She turned to her brother. "Maybe because I don't want to make promises I can't keep?"

He set down his cup. "And you think you'll get tired of her?"

"No. Never."

"Okay, so maybe you're not ready to move to California? Or convince her to move here?"

"I'm not against the idea of moving."

Randy squinted. "Do you see where I'm coming up short?" He ran his fingers through the curls on top of his head.

She nodded as a tight ball of emotion gathered in the center of her chest. She felt it rise and stared up at the ceiling to keep the stupid tears from falling. "Maybe because I don't deserve something as wonderful as she is in my life. People say I was a hero, but I let that man die because I wasn't fast enough." She shook her head. "And now I just get this gift handed to me? A whole new life?"

"So this is how you punish yourself." He stared at her hard. "Do you know how stupid that sounds?"

The word choice and his exasperated tone stopped Kate short.

Randy never spoke to her that way. "What is it that you always say? Everything happens for a reason."

"I used to believe that." Her voice grew louder to match his. Somehow the tension helped open her up, made her reflect honestly. There was nothing to lose. "I believed that the fire led me to those kids, that we were supposed to find each other. It wasn't the case."

"Yeah, well, it also led you to Autumn. Did you ever stop to consider that?"

She sat back in her chair with a thud. She hadn't. The realization struck like a lightning bolt. "I'm in love with her," she said. She looked up at Randy. "I've known that for a while, just wouldn't allow myself to go there."

"Yeah, well, maybe it's time."

She sighed. "Not sure it matters. She's upset with how I treated her. Plus, there's a lot going on in her life right now. *A lot.*"

Randy relaxed and sighed. "Yeah, well, what relationship isn't messy? Anything you can't handle?"

She shook her head. "I want to be there for it all. The hard parts and the easy parts. Doesn't mean she wants me to be."

"It's your handsome, bookish brother's opinion that you find out once and for all."

Kate stared at him. "I'm getting really good at road trips."

He grinned. "Think of it as the upside."

Kate nodded, understanding that this one might require some additional planning.

❖

"You guys need to see Thursday night's episode," Isabel said, as she pulled the wrapper off a warm apple spice muffin. It was just after seven thirty a.m., and they'd gathered for Breakfast Club that Friday to bring the workweek to a close. Well, that is, if any of them worked a normal schedule.

"Oh, yeah?" Hadley asked, sipping her Caramel Knockout, one of Autumn's newest menu items. She was rather proud of its recent success and had named it after the momentous afternoon she'd finally stood up to Vicky—not that Vicky needed to know that. Hadley ordered them regularly now.

"It's one Taylor wrote, and she fucking killed it. I could make out with her over it. It's that good." She glanced up from the muffin with a grin. "Oh, wait, I already did. Twice."

"Is that buttoned-up woman from the PTA on this week, the one who's the nemesis to our girl, Genevieve?" Autumn asked. She loved the show. Genevieve was an ex-CIA agent and, in her new life, played the role of doting parent by day and vigilante assassin by night.

Isabel's eyes glimmered. "That's exactly why I'm telling you to watch. That's all I'm going to say."

"Oh my God, if they take each other's clothes off I'm going to lose it," Hadley said. "My TV will likely combust." She turned to Autumn. "Speaking of, where did you get these muffins?"

"New vendor stopped by and I thought I'd give them a chance. Good, right?"

"Can we keep them?" Had asked around a mouthful.

"I also support the muffin," Isabel said, holding up what was left of hers.

"Hey, everyone. I don't mean to interrupt." Four faces turned in the direction of the voice. Kate stood a few feet in front of the door. Her three friends swiveled their gazes to Autumn, but her own eyes refused to leave Kate's. She was stunned to see her there and didn't know what to say. After that day on the beach, she didn't know if she'd ever see Kate again, and that thought had been too much to reckon with. So she'd set it aside, hoping there would come a day. Seeing her now sucked up all the air in the room.

She took a moment to drink her in, steadying herself against the always-present visceral reaction. Kate wore slim-fitting jeans and a dark blue T-shirt that looked like it was made deliberately for her form. No one looked as good in clothes as Kate did…or out of them. She had no idea what brought Kate there, but with her own heart beating out of her chest the way it was, she was ready to find out, if a little afraid of the answer.

"I don't want to get in the way of your breakfast," Kate told Autumn. Her gaze shifted to the counter, where Steve looked on with interest. "Or the morning rush."

"Get in the way," Hadley said automatically, and then covered her mouth. "Sorry."

Kate swallowed, looking nervous as hell. "I just need a minute or two."

Autumn turned to her friends. "Maybe you guys should give us a—"

"It's all right. They can stay," Kate said. She smiled at them and lifted a hand in greeting. "Hey, you guys." Gia and Hadley nodded and smiled back. Isabel waved. Kate turned her attention back to Autumn. "You weren't wrong on the beach." There was that unrelenting eye contact. Autumn felt their connection move through her, familiar and wonderful, but she refused to give it too much attention.

"About what?" she asked. This part mattered. What Kate did or didn't say would make a big difference in her own happiness. She dared to hope, but also knew what a risk it was. "Please tell me."

"I *have* been running, just not in the way you think." She glanced around at the occupants of the coffee shop, who seemed to have taken an interest in what she had to say. Kate didn't let them deter her. "I think fate stepped into my life and did me a favor. The stars, I guess. Through tragedy, I was led to you, and God, nothing was the same. Not the trees, not my outlook on life, not a damn cup of coffee, and, like a magnet, I couldn't stay away."

Autumn swallowed, feeling herself melt little by little.

"If it seemed like I was running, I apologize. Maybe I was. But if anything, I'll be running straight to you from now on. In fact, I think that's what I've been doing all along."

"Oh, that's nice," Hadley said to Isabel.

"Points," Isabel whispered back.

Gia shushed them. "I'm trying to listen."

Autumn ignored her friends and took a deep breath, doing what she could to keep a level head in the midst of a moment she'd dreamt of for a while now. She stood, and Kate moved to her, taking her hand. "I guess I'm wondering what it is you're saying?"

"That I'm here, and I won't be going anywhere ever again. I have what I need."

"And what do you need?" Autumn asked.

"It's been pretty simple for a while now. Only you."

Autumn blinked at the perfect words and the understanding that someone was saying them to *her*. Not just *someone*. The best person.

"I fell in love with you here, in Venice, so this seems like the perfect place to continue our lives together, but only if that's something you want, too. I'm here to find out."

Hold on. Rewind that first part. "You fell in love with me?"

"I did." Kate nodded.

"You've never said that before."

"Biggest mistake ever. I'm every bit in love, and standing here at seven thirty in the morning to make sure that you don't go another minute without knowing it."

Okay, on second thought, maybe *those* were the most perfect words.

Kate reached into her pocket and pulled out a small ring box.

Autumn closed her eyes briefly, wondering if she should grab ahold of something to steady herself, because inside sat the most exquisite band with a single sparkling diamond in the center. Oh, God. What was happening?

"I'm not rich, but what I have is yours. What I want more than anything is to walk through this world by your side, to start our own family together, whether it's tomorrow or next year or in five."

"What are you doing right now?" Autumn asked, shaking her head in mystification. She was smiling at the same time and trying not to wake up from this wonderful daydream.

Kate grinned, and her hazel eyes sparkled in a way Autumn wanted to memorize for always. "What I'm *trying* to do is move to Venice and marry you, but then there's that little detail of whether you'll have me."

Autumn didn't hesitate. "Kate, I love you."

Kate seemed to take a moment with the declaration, closing her eyes briefly. "So, what do you say, Autumn Primm? There's a question on the table. Will you marry me?"

She heard the intake of air from her friends. Her own heart hammered out of her chest as the seconds inched by. She wasn't confused or conflicted or wondering what it was she should say. Autumn knew her answer. She just wanted the moment to last forever. "I will," she said finally.

Lots of women would have gone for the ring first, anxious to get it on their finger, but Autumn reached for Kate, pulling her down by the face to kiss her senseless. Behind them she heard the applause, not just from her friends but from Steve and all her regular morning customers. That's when she realized that she'd just shared the happiest moment of her life with the people who meant the most to her. Autumn felt like she'd just stepped into a patch of warm sunlight.

"I love you," Kate said, cupping her face. The gesture made her throat tighten. Her lips were on Kate's again.

She smiled against them. "It's about time," she whispered.

❖

Kate loved the rain. She hadn't known that until she lay in bed with Autumn listening to it the next night. The chaos in her head, the regret, and the reliving of the fire seemed to have subsided substantially. The conversation with her brother had been a turning point, her realization about where she really belonged. Right where she was. With Autumn.

Home. That's what it felt like. She admired the word and the future that came attached to it. There had been ups and downs and bumps along her journey, which had been full of unexpected twists. But it had led her right here to this, what she and Autumn shared. The result had been worth the strife. She'd go through it all again if a life with Autumn was waiting at the end. The world had never felt more exciting, bursting with hope and possibility. Her once small existence felt big and full.

"When should we get married?" she asked lightheartedly, as she played with a strand of Autumn's curly hair. They lay facing each other on the pillow as the rain fell gently against the window, providing a cozy underscore.

"I'll need sufficient time to plan a wedding." Autumn pushed herself up onto her forearms and looked down at Kate. "We'll need caterers and a photographer and attendants and music. I can't even wrap my mind around all there is to do."

"I have no taste, but I can help. We can take our time."

"Great, because we skipped some steps, you know."

"No way," Kate said. She sat up, fully enjoying this conversation. "We did not."

"Well, most people date for a while longer before deciding to be together forever. A year, maybe two before settling down to become boring."

"That's silly. I don't need another year to decide that you're the best thing that's ever happened to me and probably the nicest person I'll ever meet. You're the one I want to be boring with. Plus," she said, pulling back the sheet and sliding on top, "nobody makes sexy noises in bed the way you do. The search is over."

Autumn laughed and Kate melted. "You mentioned us starting a family. You meant it?"

Kate nodded solemnly. "One hundred percent. At your pace." Whatever child they had would no longer just be Autumn's. It would be theirs. She smiled and marveled at how quickly life could change, how much better this felt than being the supportive force on the sidelines.

"Let's take a little time for us first," Autumn said. "We'll get there."

"We will." And since they were on a roll… "Where should we live? Here?" Kate glanced around Autumn's dimly lit bedroom. She liked her house a lot. Unique with a lot of character.

"We could live here," Autumn said, tracing the column of Kate's neck. "It's a pretty long drive from work, though. I've never loved that about it." She raised her eyebrows as a thought seemed to hit. "There's always Venice."

Kate turned her head to the side, her eyes wide. "You know how I feel about Venice."

Autumn laughed. "You love it."

"That's right, because it's the place I was very first introduced to…" She stole a kiss. "You." Another kiss. "And *Ms. Pac-Man*."

"Oh, no." Autumn said. "You did not just lump me in with that arcade game. I don't even own a bow."

"It's a compliment. And we could get you one."

Autumn gasped and flipped their positions easily. "Now you pay."

Kate didn't mind the payment at all. In fact, she savored it. When they were happy and wrapped up in each other, they slowly drifted off to peaceful slumber. Kate had a smile on her lips because with tomorrow came the promise of so many more tomorrows.

She was well on her way to her happily ever after, one she never saw coming.

Epilogue

Six Months Later

November temperatures had cooled the streets of Venice significantly. As Autumn walked with her hands shoved into the pockets of her fluffy purple jacket, she took a moment to watch the dry leaves dance, frisky and happy, as the wind bounced them along the stretch of sidewalk that led from the parking lot to Pajamas. She shrugged her shoulders to hold in a little bit of the electric energy that came with fall, the season she was named for.

"Well?" Gia said, the second Autumn pushed through the door. Hadley and Isabel stared at her expectantly. They were there well past their usual breakfast hour. She'd come in late that morning, taking a little extra time for herself, and a little extra for Kate, too. They'd had breakfast together before Kate headed in for her shift, the newest member of Station 63. She'd adjusted well to her new company and had made a lot of new friends on the job. Autumn wouldn't have expected anything less. She smiled at her own friends, realizing they were waiting there for her in anticipation.

"It turns out," Autumn said, drawing out the sentence, "that we are, in fact, pregnant."

Hadley looked like her face might explode. She shot to her feet, silent. Isabel made a dash for Autumn and crushed her in a bear hug. Gia seemed caught in the middle, unsure what to do with herself. "You guys are gonna be moms?" she asked, meekly.

Isabel released her. “It’s actually happening.”

“Yep.” Autumn eased a strand of hair behind her ear. “It looks that way.” She looked around Isabel and Gia to Hadley, who had sat back down in her chair. Her face was red, her hair pulled back in a ponytail, and a genuine smile lit her face. “You okay over there?” Autumn asked gently.

Hadley nodded. “I was hoping so hard.”

Autumn walked to her and kneeled down. “I know. It worked. But there’s more.”

“More?” Gia asked.

Autumn stood. “The blood test indicates that we’re working with two.”

Hadley stood immediately. “Twins? There are going to be two? No! That can’t be right.”

“Yes!” Autumn laughed. “It’s not what I had planned on, but I will quote my wife and say ‘the more the merrier.’”

Her wife. Autumn never got tired of that term. After gathering a million different brochures to plan the picture-perfect wedding, Autumn had come to realize that elaborate wasn’t what she wanted at all. It’s what Vicky would have wanted or Olivia or a million other women out there. There was nothing wrong with a big ceremony, but for Autumn, the most important part was the day after the wedding. And the days after that.

They’d stood before a justice of the peace two months prior and promised to love, honor, and cherish each other as their closest friends and family looked on. Vicky had been there and, lo and behold, behaved herself. Kate’s brother Randy and his wife had also attended, bringing extra added joy for Kate, who even received an unexpected call from Santa Barbara in which Eva and Ren had excitedly congratulated her. The group had all gone out for a fancy dinner afterward, and when it was all said and done, Autumn Primm was a married woman. With a family on the way.

She looked around the shop, the business she’d started from the ground up, and at the excited faces of her three best friends as they hugged and covered their mouths in happy disbelief. She took stock of how lucky she was that Kate had rented the very apartment that she had, and that they had fallen into each other's paths.

Maybe there was a plan for everything.

Maybe the stars watched over us all.

Autumn knew one thing for sure: she couldn't wait to see what they had in store next.

About the Author

Melissa Brayden (www.melissabrayden.com) is a multi-award-winning romance author, embracing the full-time writer's life in San Antonio, Texas, and enjoying every minute of it.

Melissa is married and working really hard at remembering to do the dishes. For personal enjoyment, she spends time with her Jack Russell terriers and checks out the NYC theater scene as often as possible. She considers herself a reluctant patron of spin class, but would much rather be sipping merlot and staring off into space. Coffee, wine, and donuts make her world go round.

Books Available From Bold Strokes Books

A Heart to Call Home by Jeannie Levig. When Jessie Weldon returns to her hometown after thirty years, can she and her childhood crush Dakota Scott heal the tragic past that links them? (978-1-63555-059-7)

Children of the Healer by Barbara Ann Wright. Life becomes desperate for ex-soldier Cordelia Ross when the indigenous aliens of her planet are drawn into a civil war and old enemies linger in the shadows. Book Three of the Godfall Series. (978-1-63555-031-3)

Hearts Like Hers by Melissa Brayden. Coffee shop owner Autumn Primm is ready to cut loose and live a little, but is the baggage that comes with out-of-towner Kate Carpenter too heavy for anything long term? (978-1-63555-014-6)

Love at Cooper's Creek by Missouri Vaun. Shaw Daily flees corporate life to find solace in the rural Blue Ridge Mountains, but escapism eludes her when her attentions are captured by small town beauty Kate Elkins. (978-1-62639-960-0)

Twice in a Lifetime by PJ Trebelhorn. Detective Callie Burke can't deny the growing attraction to her late friend's widow, Taylor Fletcher, who also happens to own the bar where Callie's sister works. (978-1-63555-033-7)

Undiscovered Affinity by Jane Hardee. Will a no-strings-attached affair be enough to break Olivia's control and convince Cardic that love does exist? (978-1-63555-061-0)

Between Sand and Stardust by Tina Michele. Are the lifelong bonds of love strong enough to conquer time, distance, and heartache when Haven Thorne and Willa Bennette are given another chance at forever? (978-1-62639-940-2)

Charming the Vicar by Jenny Frame. When magician and atheist Finn Kane seeks refuge in an English village after a spiritual crisis, can local vicar Bridget Claremont restore her faith in life and love? (978-1-63555-029-0)

Data Capture by Jesse J. Thoma. Lola Walker is undercover on the hunt for cybercriminals while trying not to notice the woman who might be perfectly wrong for her for all the right reasons. (978-1-62639-985-3)

Epicurean Delights by Renee Roman. Ariana Marks had no idea a leisure swim would lead to being rescued, in more ways than one, by the charismatic Hudson Frost. (978-1-63555-100-6)

Heart of the Devil by Ali Vali. We know most of Cain and Emma Casey's story, but Heart of the Devil will take you back to where it began one fateful night with a tray loaded with beer. (978-1-63555-045-0)

Known Threat by Kara A. McLeod. When Special Agent Ryan O'Connor reluctantly questions who protects the Secret Service, she learns courage truly is found in unlikely places. Agent O'Connor Series #3 (978-1-63555-132-7)

Seer and the Shield by D. Jackson Leigh. Time is running out for the Dragon Horse Army while two unlikely heroines struggle to put aside their attraction and find a way to stop a deadly cult. Dragon Horse War, Book 3 (978-1-63555-170-9)

The Universe Between Us by Jane C. Esther. Ana Mitchell must make the hardest choice of her life: the promise of new love Jolie Dann on Earth, or a humanity-saving mission to colonize Mars. (978-1-63555-106-8)

Touch by Kris Bryant. Can one touch heal a heart? (978-1-63555-084-9)

A More Perfect Union by Carsen Taite. Major Zoey Granger and DC fixer Rook Daniels risk their reputations for a chance at true love while dealing with a scandal that threatens to rock the military. (978-1-62639-754-5)

Arrival by Gun Brooke. The spaceship *Pathfinder* reaches its passengers' new homeworld where danger lurks in the shadows while Pamas Seclan disembarks and finds unexpected love in young science genius Darmiya Do Voy. (978-1-62639-859-7)

Captain's Choice by VK Powell. Architect Kerstin Anthony's life is going to plan until Bennett Carlyle, the first girl she ever kissed, is assigned to her latest and most important project, a police district substation. (978-1-62639-997-6)

Falling Into Her by Erin Zak. Pam Phillips, widow at the age of forty, meets Kathryn Hawthorne, local Chicago celebrity, and it changes her life forever—in ways she hadn't even considered possible. (978-1-63555-092-4)

Hookin' Up by MJ Williamz. Will Leah get what she needs from casual hookups or will she see the love she desires right in front of her? (978-1-63555-051-1)

King of Thieves by Shea Godfrey. When art thief Casey Marinos meets bounty hunter Finnegan Starkweather, the crimes of the past just might set the stage for a payoff worth more than she ever dreamed possible. (978-1-63555-007-8)

Lucy's Chance by Jackie D. As a serial killer haunts the streets, Lucy tries to stitch up old wounds with her first love in the wake of a small town's rapid descent into chaos. (978-1-63555-027-6)

Right Here, Right Now by Georgia Beers. When Alicia Wright moves into the office next door to Lacey Chamberlain's accounting firm, Lacey is about to find out that sometimes the last person you want is exactly the person you need. (978-1-63555-154-9)

Strictly Need to Know by MB Austin. Covert operator Maji Rios will do whatever she must to complete her mission, but saving a gorgeous stranger from Russian mobsters was not in her plans. (978-1-63555-114-3)

Tailor-Made by Yolanda Wallace. Tailor Grace Henderson doesn't date clients, but when she meets gender-bending model Dakota Lane, she's tempted to throw all the rules out the window. (978-1-63555-081-8)

Time Will Tell by M. Ullrich. With the ability to time travel, Eva Caldwell will have to decide between having it all and erasing it all. (978-1-63555-088-7)